# Hack

**By the same author**

Snap

**Non-fiction (with Peter Mason)**

Criminal Blunders

Trouble and Strife

John Burns

# Hack

PAN BOOKS

First published 1996 by Masquerade Publications

This edition first published 1998 by Pan Books
an imprint of Pan Macmillan Ltd
Pan Macmillan, 20 New Wharf Road, London N1 9RR
Basingstoke and Oxford
Associated companies throughout the world
www.panmacmillan.com

ISBN 0 330 35488 4



3 5 7 9 8 6 4

A CIP catalogue record for this book is available from
the British Library.

Typeset by Intype London Ltd
Printed and bound in Great Britain by
Mackays of Chatham plc, Chatham, Kent



The characters depicted within have no resemblance whatsoever
to anyone living or dead or yet to be born. Anyone who sees
himself/herself in these pages should lay off the drink for a while.
The events and characters are marginally less factual than the
*Sunday Sport*'s exclusive, 'World War II Bomber Found on Moon'.

*To Rita, whose idea*
*this all was*

# Chapter One

Only one public-spirited citizen bothered to phone in and report the body, though at least a dozen must have seen the thing. Thirteen if you count whoever put it there.

I was just around the corner in Magpie Court when the tip-off came. Good as gold, Inspector McIvor gave me a bleep. It read: 'Maxwell lookalike found bobbing – Mac.' I called him back. He was in Hampton's, no doubt already blowing his twenty quid tip-off fee on a doxy or two. 'Good evening, you ageing lounge lizard,' I said sweetly. Mac loves it when I talk dirty. 'You rang?'

He said, 'Might have one for you. The river police have a corpse floating around in St Katharine's Dock. Could be a tourist, pushed in by one of our local muggers. Who knows?'

I was not exactly enthusiastic. 'Who knows, indeed. Might be a drunk who tripped and fell, might be a suicide, might be a heart case, a headcase, whatever. Might even be a police officer doing the world a favour.'

Mac said, 'Oh well, thought you'd like to know.'

He rang off and returned to his fleurie and his floosies, for Mac is a man of simple needs.

I was in Ross Gavney's flat, pouring fat tumblers of twenty-year-old Scotch down my throat at an unprecedented rate of knots. Ross and I go all the way back to Holly Hill comprehensive but we keep up the old ties despite everything. He thinks there is something richly hilarious in my being a crime hack, nay, the chief crime correspondent for a national red top. Ross does complicated things with bonds and futures, thereby earning himself more money than is humanly decent.

I am happy for Ross, especially when he calls me up and invites me to empty his decanters. Generally we sit around and rubbish each other's football loyalties. He, God help him, is an Arsenal man.

In the old days Ross was a yuppy, one of Thatcher's favoured children. He still has all the trappings, city slicker suits, fluffed out hair, docklands flat.

We were in the aforesaid apartment, arguing the toss over England's chances against Poland when Mac bleeped. While I did my ace reporter bit, Ross poured me another half gallon of single malt.

'What next?' he asked, after I had finished with Mac.

'Next?' I was puzzled. 'Nothing. I wait till the police haul him out, dry him down and then pronounce him dead. They're sticklers for that sort of thing.'

He said, 'How do you know it's a man?'

I flopped a languid wrist. 'It's either one or the other.'

Ross sipped thoughtfully. He persisted: 'When do you know if it's a story? I mean, this could be another Calvi case. All you crime reporters got that one wrong.'

This was unkind but true, which in my experience is usually the same thing. Roberto Calvi, aka God's Banker, aka head of the Banco Ambrosiano, where the Pope lodges his pay cheque, was found swinging under Blackfriars Bridge in the eighties. Suicide, we all cried, conveniently ignoring every fact which screamed murder.

I sighed. It was a sigh custom-built to say, 'Listen, dear friend of my youth, I have in my left hand a glass of Glenfarclas, and in my right, a cigar worthy of my deepest appreciation. Why bother me with trifles?'

Ross is not a man who listens to sighs. He said, 'So, you boys wait until the police tell you what they've found and you just put it into English?'

This was a vile slur on my profession. I have never knowingly put anything into English. Tabloid-speak, yes, journalese if I'm pissed. But if ever a phrase in English pops up in my copy, we have trained sub-editors to throw it out.

I lowered my glass and looked Ross dead in the eye. I said, 'This is the picture. A body, male or female, is found floating in the dock. Today all over London, bodies have been found in bed – sometimes their own – under a bus, in hospital corridors, in Cardboard City, wherever. A few – only a tiny few – are tastefully decorated with bullets, needles or knives. The rest have been topped by the Great Serial Killer in the Sky. In short, no story.'

'What's the betting?'

'Eh?'

Ross said, 'I'll bet there's a story in it.'

'Balls.'

After this it developed into a sordid argument about the size of the bet (my fiver against a bottle of his whisky) and then I did the biz. Just to impress Ross, I even rang Scotland Yard's press bureau to see if they had anything on the story. I wasn't expecting anything from them. Usually they don't know what day it is.

'Good evening. It's Thursday,' I said helpfully.

'Oh, it's you. What do you want?' asked a young lady. Ruthie or Zeintab.

I said, 'You know perfectly well what I want but we've no time for that malarkey now. Just tell me if you have anything on a wet corpse in St Katharine's Dock.'

'Nope.'

'You have been ever so helpful. Thank you.'

As I switched off the mobile, I was alarmed to see Ross breeze into the room, a belted Burberry over the navy pinstripes. 'Ready?' he asked brightly.

I kissed my glass goodbye and donned my hack mac. Outside the May monsoon scythed in off the Thames, running through the gutters and putting halos around the street lamps.

'Let me make a few more phone calls,' I begged. But Ross strode off and I splashed away in his wake.

As I said, Magpie Court is hardly a kick in the pants off the dock, but by the time we got there I was drenched through. Under his golf umbrella Ross was dry and debonair.

We rounded a corner by a snotty wine bar and ran smack into the police tapes. Beyond them was a clutch of sodden coppers gazing into the dock for enlightenment. A police river launch was parked in the middle with its spotlight aimed at the pointy end of a white yacht. You couldn't make out its name. You couldn't see anything, what with all that rain between us and the action.

A beefy figure swam out of the waterfall. It was Pennycuik, my friend H, a detective inspector of the old school. He'd tell me all about it. 'Hello, Harry,' I said warmly.

'Piss off,' he responded.

'Good evening, officer,' said Ross from about a foot above my head.

Pennycuik wiped his eyes and looked up at him. Clearly this stranger was not one of your scumbag reporters. Too distinguished for that. I could hear Harry's brain cell charging around in perplexity.

I said smoothly, 'Inspector Pennycuik, I don't believe you have met the Right Honourable Lewis Trefoyle, the junior Home Office minister.'

Ross didn't blink. He put out a nice dry pink hand and gave H a nice dry pink smile.

Harry said, 'Oh,' and stuck out a hand like a drowned fish.

'And what have we here?' asked Ross. His voice was just the right blend of fruity pomposity and blind ignorance we have come to expect from our political masters.

Our heroic D.I. favoured him with a yellow smile. 'It's a body, sir,' he said, displaying the lightning intelligence of London's finest.

'Suspicious?' I asked him.

Harry pretended I was dead. He addressed Ross. 'We got a call, about eight thirty, from a punter, ah, one of the customers.' He pointed towards the snooty wine bar.

'I cannot see the body,' said Ross peevishly. 'How could he?'

Harry said, 'It was before the rain. This just came on. The call was passed on to the river police and they located the body.'

'Man or woman?' This was me again.

He spoke to Ross again. 'We believe it to be a male, but it is lying face down in the water so we cannot ascertain exactly.'

Ascertain! I love the way coppers talk when they are in the presence of their superiors, which is mostly all the time.

'They're taking their time hauling it ashore,' I observed.

Ross looked at his Longines. 'Yes, it's gone nine.'

Harry shook the rain from his brow. 'It snagged itself in the cable of that boat. It shouldn't be long now.'

At which point there came a distant sound, as of a waterlogged stiff being hauled into a rubber dinghy.

'There it is,' said H happily.

Ross looked down his nostrils at him. 'Is this, inspector, what one would term a suspicious death?'

Harry shifted his feet in a puddle. 'The caller said

he heard sounds of an altercation shortly prior to the incident and then there was a splash.'

'That would probably be the guy hitting the water,' I said sagely.

H glared at me but let it pass. On the dockside a quartet of young coppers were falling over each other to unload the late lamented, now gift-wrapped in rubber sheeting.

The corpse, a skinny specimen, was manhandled past us, still face down. He was wearing a Casablanca trenchcoat, its white newness marred by ugly black oil weals from the yacht's hawser. Behind us there was a waiting ambulance. As the bearers reached it, they turned their dripping burden over. And everyone did a double take. The stiff was not a he, or anything like one. These were the mortal remains of a beautiful and, guessing by the bumps in the rubber sheet, shapely young woman. Her dead white face was fringed with jet black hair and her huge dark eyes gazed back at us in dumb surprise. Her carmine lips were slightly open and her eyelashes were matted with rain.

And slap bang in the middle of her forehead was the neatest little bullet hole you ever did see.

'My God!' gasped Ross. 'It's Claudine!'

And so it was.

# Chapter Two

Claudine. Claudine Tournier. Not looking her freshly minted, rip-roaringly happy customary self.

The pert lovable face which grinned out on the Great British eating public from a billion freezer packs was for once unsmiling and a shade on the grey side. Never more would we see her pout provocatively from the nation's TV screens, urging all and sundry to sample her frozen haricots bearnais or apple chartreuse. Nor would we hear her husky promise: 'I could be so good for you.'

All that healthy eating hadn't done much for her. But it had been a slick show while it lasted. The fair Claudine blended the two vital ingredients of our age – sex and green living – to sell her wares to those who deem it wrong to eat bits of animals.

She even made a virtue of such bizarre beliefs. Every pack of Claudine's wares carries a little sticker, saying that 2p or 5p of the cost goes towards conservation issues – saving the blubber-mouthed whale, keeping the Opeydopey tribe in clean loin cloths, that sort of thing.

Very praiseworthy, and very lucrative by all accounts. But nobody was bitching about that, not with Claudine spending half her life scooting off to what us hacks call the world's killing fields to plant couscous or reap noodles.

Naturally these endeavours made her something of a saint, marginally behind the Queen Mum and Mother Teresa in Britain's league of the great and good.

All these thoughts went clippety clop through my brain as I grabbed the mobile from my pocket and punched in the office number.

'News Desk,' announced a sad and bitter voice. Vic.

'Vic. It's Max. Ring the bells on Back Bench, we've got a belter here. Claudine Tournier's been murdered. Nobody else has it, so tag it exclusive.'

'What?'

Even Vic sounded interested. He probably ate her stuff.

I said, 'Yep. Shot in the head. Tell the monkey bench to get out her snaps and put me through to Copy.'

Vic said, 'When was she killed?'

'About forty minutes ago. I'm going to dictate straight on, but you'd better get someone there to dig out her cuttings and fill in the biog.'

'Wait a minute.' Vic put the phone to one side and I pictured him trundling across to Back Bench and dolefully breaking the news to the night editor and his bunch of ne'er-do-wells. I effed and blinded to myself in impatience.

Vic returned. 'Give us all you've got.'

This is honestly the way people on News Desk

talk. They think you would leave out all the good bits unless they reminded you.

He switched me through to Copy. It was Deaf Daphne in the final throes of terminal boredom.

'Hi Daff. It's Max Chard. This one's for News Desk.'

'Catchline?' I told her to call the story GONER and began dictating off the top of my head at about 500 words per min.

*Green queen Claudine Tournier was gunned down last night and her body tossed in the Thames after a secret date with a mystery man.*

'How are you spelling Claudine?'

A stifled scream from my end. I told her how, and spelt out Tournier too. By some great good fortune she knew how to spell Thames. Anyway, after a fifteen minute spelling bee, I got the story through. It ran on like this:

*The sexy chef who put the ooh-la-la into instant meals was shot between the eyes from point blank range after a blazing row.*

*French-born Claudine* (insert age) *was dumped into St Katharine's Dock in the shadow of London's Tower Bridge – a well known meeting place for lovers.*

*Claudine was married to top City money man Sir James Tomlin. Police were last night seeking him to break the tragic news.*

*Her young killer, who used a revolver fitted with a silencer, fled as drinkers in the trendy wine bar Port O' Call raised the alarm.*

*One man said, 'I heard a couple arguing furiously just outside and I thought it was a lover's tiff.*

*'Then there was a splash. It is horrifying to think I had just heard a murder.'*

*Claudine's body drifted under a luxury yacht moored in the upmarket marina and it took police 30 minutes to free it.*

*The chic chef was still in her trademark designer suit and dressed for a night on the town.*

*Detectives are baffled by the ruthless killing. A senior officer said, 'Miss Tournier was a very beautiful and much admired young woman.*

*'We cannot confirm whether her attacker was a boyfriend. She was not sexually assaulted and we cannot tell if she was robbed.'*

*Police are also investigating whether the killing was an underworld hit. One officer admitted the shooting had the signature of a professional hit man.*

*Claudine was slain by a single shot from a small calibre hand gun. She was dead before her body hit the water.*

*Police frogmen will scour the yacht basin for the murder weapon from first light today.*

*The smouldering French beauty used provocative TV ads to build an international empire with her Claudine's Cuisine range of freezer foods.*

*She ploughed hundreds of thousands of pounds back into helping the world's poor and saving animals facing extinction.*

*Her tireless work earned her the MBE in the Queen's birthday honours and . . .*

And blah blah and yet more blah. Not exactly deathless prose but sufficient for the IQ of our readers. I expect by now you're wondering where all that stuff came from. The hand gun and so on. Elementary. If it had been a Uzi submachinegun or a Kalashnikov, the guy in the bar would have heard it.

Small calibre? Well, it was a neat little hole. The quotes? That's what Harry and the drinker would have told me if they'd been feeling chatty. The line that her killer was a young man? He legged it before the alarm was raised. You don't do that if you're knocking on sixty.

OK, so when last seen she was wearing a rubber sheet, but underneath, you can bet your boots, she was not togged up in a shell suit. Hence my dressed to kill description. And that bit hinting the gunman was her secret lover? – well, you've got to make the reader sit up and go 'Cor!', haven't you?

Daphne put me back on to Vic. He was whingeing. 'You didn't tell me exactly where this happened. Pictures want to send a man.'

I said, 'No percentage. All they'll get is a grainy snap of the dock. The police have whisked her off.'

'You could have told us earlier,' he accused.

This again is how desk people think. If you found Lord Lucan holed up in Wagga Wagga they'd complain that he wasn't riding Shergar.

I just said, 'All right, if it makes them any happier, tell them to send a monkey to the wine bar. It's on the starboard corner of the dock, coming from the Tower Hotel. I'll be inside asking if anyone's got any nice shots of Claudine getting her head blown off.'

We parted on terms of mutual hatred. I switched off and turned to Ross who was a strangely silent man.

'Drink?' I suggested, pointing to the tastefully

frosted door of the bar. He tagged along. We plunged in and ordered a bottle that said it came all the way from Jacob's Creek. I shrugged off my mac and pretended the Austin Reed check two-piece was meant to cling moistly to my slender frame. The Law was much in evidence, asking decent drunks what they had heard/seen/suspected about tonight's merriment. I eavesdropped.

'Not a thing,' proclaimed a city gent jovially. Why are people always so damn happy to tell us they know nothing? The ones who do know are generally miserable.

I espied a secretary type who was sitting alone and looking as if she had just found a dead platypus in her ration of Jacob's Creek. I flashed the press pass. Her fuzzy blue eyes ignored it. I gabbled some gibberish about Claudine's little contretemps and asked what she knew. She was silent for so long I felt like introducing her to Ross.

After a slurp or two she finally said, 'I was supposed to meet Miss Tournier here.'

I patted myself on the back. 'You're her secretary?'

She shook her head no.

'You work for her?'

Another shake.

This could go on all night. Who was she to Claudine? Her next-door neighbour, her kid sister, her colonic irrigationist?

My voice was as soft as a pigeon's coo. 'So what do you do?'

'I work for Sir James.'

'Ahh.' This wasn't helping.

She clammed up and looked set to stay that way unless I did something. Here is where your trained hack suddenly appears to lose all interest in his hard-nosed probing. He changes the game. The trick is to get your quarry totally distracted from your evil aims.

So, with studied deliberation, I laid my packet of Bensons flat down in the middle of our little round table. I pulled out a single cigarette and placed it on top of the pack. She wasn't looking, but she would. Next, I pulled back my sleeves, thus exposing my manly wrists. I fetched a penknife from my jacket pocket, pulled out the blade and studied it earnestly. Now she was looking. My every fibre seemed absorbed with the strange ceremony of the penknife and the cigarette. I ignored her eyes. I took the knife and in slow motion I bisected the cigarette dead centre. Then I picked up the non-filter stub and carelessly tossed it on the floor. She goggled. I folded the penknife, replaced it, put the dwarf cigarette in my mouth and lit it.

I looked at her po-faced. I said, 'I'm trying to cut down.'

She blinked and gave a little giggle. But the show wasn't over yet, folks. I raised my glass, held it towards the light, and spoke almost to myself. 'You know, I was in Jacob's Creek last year . . .' Pause. ' . . . and it wasn't this bloody colour.'

Another giggle, this time deeper in her throat. We're almost there. I aimed a finger at her glass. I said, 'You don't seem to be enjoying it either. Can I get you something different?'

She glanced down, hesitated, then came: 'Just a mineral water, please.'

I detected an ever so slight thank you smile. Two minutes later the secretary bird was a new woman. I must try water some day.

Her name was Shirley. No second name. She dressed like a TV weather girl, all buttons and lapels. She came from Loughton. She worked in Freleng-Bourke, where Sir James earned his crust. She knew the late lamented who apparently was a frequent visitor to the offices. Shirley's baby eyes took on something of a glow when she spoke of Sir Jas. But it was hard to tell whether she loved or hated the man.

'So you had a message from him to Claudine?' I prompted.

Shirley went all dumb again.

'Not exactly,' she whispered at last.

I ran my finger round the rim of the glass, lit a cigarette, leered at a blonde, counted my fingers and waited. I had just embarked on a filthy limerick about a young lady called Shirley, who liked to be rogered most rarely, when she broke surface again.

'It was a message from me,' she said, nostrils flaring.

These kids watch too many soap operas.

'From you?'

A half nod. 'Yes. I had to tell her about Sir James.'

'And what about Sir James?'

She took a deep breath and looked at me with misery flooding her eyes.

'He's run off with his secretary,' she said.

# Chapter Three

News Desk woke me sometime gone three. 'Got a pen handy?' Vic demanded.

Sure Vic. I always go to bed with a biro stuck up my nostril. I rummaged round a bit, swearing and grunting just to make him feel bad. He probably felt better.

'Okay, Vic. Shoot.'

'You're on the 7.30 to Geneva. BA flight 401. The tickets are at the information desk. You pick them up thirty minutes before the flight. Pictures are sending Frank Frost. All right?'

I said, 'Would you care to tell me which sodding airport?'

'Oh. Heathrow. Terminal One.'

I said, 'That helps. You got a hotel booked? Is the hire car fixed? You got some money for me?'

'There's five hundred with your tickets.'

Five hundred quid! That might just buy me a cheese fondue. And he hadn't fixed the car, or the hotel. Thank you Shirley for tipping me off that Sir James was in Geneva. I growled myself back to sleep.

Four hours and forty-five minutes later I was in a window seat of an Airbus ripping holes through the clouds. On my right was Mad Frankie Frost who is roughly seventeen foot tall and not the best of travelling companions. He was saying: 'Then on the way back from Tokyo I got upgraded to First and there was plenty of room to stretch out in, but when we were chasing Fergie in Bali we were on an old Boeing and you couldn't . . .'

I was too tired to listen, what with the hurly-burly of the night before. I could still hear Shirley grassing on her boss. Great stuff altogether, but it meant I had to file a whole new update for the final. And after that, of course, I needed a largish gin or seven and things went downhill from there. Hence the present headache and feeling of impending death. Actually, a gin would come in handy right now. I flagged down a passing stewardess and outlined my requirements. She screwed up her freckled face and intoned, 'The drinks trolley will be circulating soon.'

Meanwhile Frankie was still rabbiting on about leg-space on long-haul. I had half a mind to fetch out my penknife and saw him off around the knees.

Freckles returned with a plastic tray containing objects heavily bandaged in clingfilm. 'Breakfast,' she announced.

I looked at the tray. 'Do you have any food instead?' I asked.

She frowned and wafted off in considerable dudgeon.

By the time we hit Geneva I had breakfasted off three gins. I only wanted one, maybe two. I ordered the third just to see Freckles wrinkle her nose up at me again.

Frankie went to the Hertz desk and got us a Volvo. Yes, a Volvo. I told him, 'You should have got a BMW or a Merc. This thing's a bloody tank.'

'Yes,' said he, 'but it's got more leg room.'

We took the Lausanne Road with Lake Geneva looking sullen on our right. A bullyboy wind was kicking the heads off the waves. Shirley, God bless her, had all the details. The lovebirds were roosting in a village called Morges. Rather apt, considering Claudine's present whereabouts.

My chauffeur had us there coming up lunchtime. We drove down a narrow street where everyone had the same taste in windowboxes. Red geraniums bloomed from every orifice. Maybe they get a subsidy for growing them.

We fetched up outside a bijou villa. Very romantic. Frankie whistled. 'This must have cost him a packet.'

Monkeys always want to know how much things cost. It is strange because monkeys do not like spending money.

I lit a cigarette and hung around while Frankie dressed himself from head to toe in motor drives, zoom lenses, filters, sureshots, flash units and all his other toys.

I walked up the front drive past a Peugeot the size of a shoebox. Frankie clattered and clanked behind me like Robocop. Just as I reached the front door it opened. A happy moment. There is nothing so stultifyingly boring as doorstepping a house where the inmates refuse to open up.

A young woman appeared. She was pretty, but not stunning. Good grey blue eyes, auburn hair, small mouth. She seemed surprised to see us, but that might just have been because Frankie was darting hither and thither, banging off pix.

Her mouth opened and she blinked in time with the motordrive. There was no sign of her paramour.

'Miss Pearson?' I said brightly. 'Good morning. I have just come from London to see you.'

She pondered this for a moment. 'Me?' she asked nervously, her gaze fixed on Frankie.

'It's all right,' I reassured. 'He's more frightened of you than vice versa.'

Her lips pursed up. 'Who are you?'

A trace of hostility there. Time for appeasement. I turned on Frankie and said snottily, 'Stop that right now. You're upsetting Miss Pearson.'

Frankie got the idea. He let his cameras dangle. I turned back on Emma Pearson and smiled. 'Now that's better, isn't it?'

Her stiffness eased a fraction. 'Who are you?' she persisted. Still no sign of Sunny Jim.

'I'm Max. Max Chard. And this is my friend Frankie Frost.'

'You're newspaper reporters,' she accused.

It is something I have never understood, but hacks always get pissed off when someone says: 'You're a reporter.' I wonder do double glazing salesmen, Ku Klux Klan pinheads and Arsenal fans get similarly narked when people suss them out. Maybe we're just more sensitive.

I looked hurt. I asked, 'May we come in?'

'Why?' Hands on hips.

She wasn't quite sure whether to display icy

disdain or blazing anger, so she came across sort of tepid. I gave Sir James's little rascal a long look, taking in the dove grey blouse, slim, short navy skirt, high heels. Chic on the outside, not so fantastic when unwrapped, I guessed. Maybe she was a nymphomaniac. I have heard there are such things.

I said carefully, 'I have something very important to say to you and I cannot really say it in the street.'

This is a useful hack trick because the reaction affords you a glimpse of your victim's nature. If their eyes glitter, it's because they think it might have something to do with the National Lottery; if they invite you in, they're bored and desirous of boring you; if they say nothing, they're as guilty as hell.

She said nothing.

I smiled a sharp sardonic smile. Or it might have been ironic. I couldn't see it. I said, 'You may think you know why we're here, but you're way off target.'

She gave a sort of 'Oh yeah?' snort.

Behind me I could hear Frankie getting restless. Any minute now he'd whip out the Canon and blow the whole thing. I had to do something drastic.

'You think my office has gone to all the expense of sending us here just to expose your affair with Sir James. Frankly, we don't give a damn,' I lied.

Emma Pearson made a sound somewhere between a gulp and an argggh. She reeled back in the doorway. I said 'thank you' and breezed past her into the villa.

I was three yards down the hall and still breezing before she twigged it. By then Frankie was halfway through the door and it was too late. She followed me dumbly into the lounge, a sort of Laura Ashley meets World of Leather affair. If the roguish James was around, he wasn't showing it.

I sat down. 'Mind if we sit?' I asked.

She hung around standing for a while then plonked herself on a distant sofa, straightening her skirt. She had nice legs. Her back was towards the open doorway leading from the hall.

Her voice was controlled and even. 'I have no idea why you are harassing us.'

Us. So the Great Lover was still in the neighbourhood. I spoke softly and lovingly. 'Perhaps you have not heard the news, Miss Pearson. Claudine Tournier has been murdered.'

Not a blink. Not a scream. Not even a joyful whoop.

'Murdered?'

'Murdered.'

She went through the who/what/where/when/why rigmarole and I told her everything but the who and why. I even pointed to the middle of my forehead to show where the bullet went in. Still no reaction.

'Is Sir James at home?' I asked gesturing around.

She said he wasn't but didn't feel like expanding on the subject.

'Naturally I would like to speak to him.'

'Well you can't.'

'It's all right dear,' said a disembodied voice. The hair on the back of my neck stood up. It took me a moment to spot the owner. A scale model human being, standing behind a shrub in a tub which in turn was behind the sofa. Sir James Tomlin in the flesh, all five foot nothing of him. He must have slipped in while I was eyeballing his beloved. He came forward and stared at me through darkened lenses. I stared back. He was fitted out in a double-breasted blazer. A tragic sartorial mistake.

There was silence, but for Frankie panting in the corner.

Sir James demanded, 'How did you find us?' Nothing about Claudine, please note.

I said, 'We took the Lausanne road out of Geneva and turned left at the signpost.'

He said, 'You know what I mean.'

Why do small men bark? I lit a cigarette without asking him kindly and puffed a lazy puff before answering.

'We know you and Miss Pearson have been having an affair for three months,' I began crisply.

'We know you took her on holiday to Antigua in March, while Claudine was off doing good turns. In April you occupied a suite together at the Sherry Netherlands in New York. This month it's Switzerland.

'We know you often overnight at 32C Drummond Lane, Maida Vale, which is Miss Pearson's flat. We know the lot.'

He balled his little fists. 'Who told you?'

I said, 'I can't remember. Anyways, it doesn't matter. My interest is why your wife was murdered last night.'

Tomlin said, 'You are accusing me? How dare you impugn my integrity.'

I turned to Frankie. 'Did I impugn?' Frankie said

he didn't think so and made a mental note to ask me later what impugn meant.

Sir James glowered. 'Emma – Miss Pearson and I arrived here yesterday morning. I could not have killed my wife.'

'You'd have to be one hell of a shot,' I conceded.

I wasn't bothered about upsetting him in his first day of widowerhood: he couldn't have cared much for Claudine if he was playing house with La Pearson. Just then a telephone rang in the hallway. Sir James the Lover reverted to Sir James the Captain of Industry. 'Answer that please, Miss Pearson.'

She went off. Her boyfriend sat down on a chair facing me and began breathing heavily. Both of us were trying hard to hear what was being said.

It went along these lines. She said, 'We know.' A long silence, then: 'No. Sir James wants it cancelled. It cannot go ahead now.'

From my seat I could just see her back. She was as stiff as a stick insect with hypertension.

More silence. Our Emma was not the chattiest of girls. After a while I heard: 'The complete package is off. Sir James doesn't care how many . . .'

Then her voice shot up an octave. 'Candy!' she exclaimed. 'Oh no! Candy must be stopped . . . yes, instantly.'

Opposite me Sir James went all rigid and porridge faced. He was the same size sitting down as standing up.

Out in the hall Emma was going ballistic. 'Candy must be stopped,' she repeated. 'I don't care how.'

Sir James popped up out of the cushions. He

bellowed, and that is really the only way to describe it: 'Emma! Not now! We'll call back.'

Her voice wound down to its usual alto pitch. She mumbled a sentence or two and put down the phone. As she returned to the lounge her boyfriend gave her the sort of glare he had previously reserved for me. She looked shaken and stirred.

I said, 'Interesting times we live in, eh?'

Sir James said tightly, 'Get out. Get out this very minute or I'll call the police.'

I rose languidly and made for the door, taking care not to get between the merry couple and Frankie who was going zap-zap-zap. Sir James chivvied him down the hall like a pygmy in hot pursuit of a giraffe.

The door slammed behind us and we were back on the street of a thousand geraniums.

'Strong drink is called for,' I said, and Frankie happily concurred, knowing I'd be buying.

So who the hell was Candy? And what mischief was she up to? And why was it so important to stop her?

These pretty puzzles occupied me while Frankie found us a bar. We sat outside in the fitful sunshine, drinking pissy beer that cost as much as the down payment on a studio flat.

'I am a bewildered man,' I told my monkey. My monkey furrowed his brow in sympathy.

'If we broke the sad tidings,' I continued, 'neither of them seemed the slightest surprised. They were more concerned with how we found out about their legover situation.'

'She's a bit of a dog,' Frankie said, conveniently forgetting the old slappers he hangs around with.

'And why is Candy in trouble?' I asked.

'Candy?'

'Yes. Emma Pearson said Candy has to be stopped.'

'I didn't hear her. Let's eat.'

Monkeys are the most primitive form of human life. Give them free drink, a meal on expenses and a bauble for their camera and they are happy little souls. We call them monkeys because they scamper about, chattering all the while. They call us blunts. This has nothing to do with our blunt pens. It has a lot to do with cockney rhyming slang. And there you have it in one single syllable word – the collected wit and wisdom of monkeys.

I abandoned the Candy conundrum and started thinking instead of what on earth I would write for the day's story. After an omelette which had more in common with a Michelin tyre than a Michelin star, I got through on the freephone to the Mother Inferior, to wit, Angela Whipple. Angela is News Editor. She was once a reporter and the battle-hardened veteran of a dozen Naomi Campbell picture captions, therefore she is uniquely equipped to tell us rough tough reporters our job.

'Ah, there you are,' she sang out, as if she'd spent a lifetime tracking me down.

I could not lie. 'Yes, here I am.'

I told her of the day's events. She asked me what the story was so I outlined something like: *Exclusive: I break news of Claudine's murder to runaway husband in Alpine love nest*.

'Great,' she enthused. 'Now go back and ask Tomlin if he's planning to marry his secretary, and who does he think killed his wife.'

Yes, you know and I know that Sir James was in no mood to unburden himself to me, but news editors lead sheltered lives. I said that was a terrific idea and I was on my way.

Angela added, 'And we need copy early. There's a colour spread on our bingo millionaire so all copy must be off stone by six.'

One of these days World War Three will break out and we won't have the story because we're running an eight-page sex survey showing that four out of three people bonk on their heads.

I rooted out Frankie who was charming the grizzled waiter into writing out false receipts for lunch. We returned to the scene of our crime. The Peugeot had gone from the driveway and no-one answered our knock. I sauntered round to the back garden and peered through the window. Nothing moved. Frankie fired off another hundred shots and back we went to the bar.

My story was on the thin side though there were some interesting and extremely questionable quotes from Sir James and his young lady. I didn't mention Candy.

Back to Angela. 'They fled while I was filing,' I said. 'Looks like they're flying back to London tonight.'

This was her cue to say, 'Hop on the next plane.' Instead she asked, 'You got a car?'

I checked over my shoulder. 'No. We've got a Volvo.'

'What? Anyway, I want you to see Claudine's mother. Maybe she knows something.'

I had a small query. 'Isn't her mum somewhere in France?'

Angela said, 'Yes. It's a place called Quimper.' She pronounced it Quimper.

She turned from the phone and shouted to our esteemed Foreign Editor. I could hear him thumbing through his Ottoman Empire atlas. Eventually Angela said, 'Yes, France.'

'Angie,' I reminded her, 'we are in Switzerland.'

'Well, Switzerland's next door to France.'

I gently pointed out that Quimper is a damn sight closer to London than we were to Quimper. Angela was not to be swayed. She knows that all these foreign places are in Europe, and that's where I was.

I said, 'We'll not get there until very late tonight. Maybe tomorrow.'

She tried to cheer me up. 'It doesn't matter. There's a great story breaking about a *Blind Date* guest accused of rape.'

In short, Claudine's murder was yesterday's news. You could wrap your chips in it. I'd be lucky if my story made a top on page nine.

I broke it to Frankie who was so upset he bought a round. We hired a room so he could wire his pix and then set off into the tail end of the afternoon.

I had maligned our hackmobile. It sang lustily all the way through to Macon, then over to Orleans and up to Rouen where we pulled in for the night at a place which looked cheap and cheerful but lied on both counts.

It was gone midnight and we were bordering on collapse. A bottle of wine apiece restored our sang-froid. We regaled each other with harrowing yarns of incompetent news/picture editors and Frankie, the shameless old tart, spoke of his many sexual conquests.

He was in rib-tickling form and I laughed 'til my nose ran. Frankie is a boon companion at times like these, not that I would ever tell him that.

Come the dawn, we breakfasted off croissants and bits of clammy ham and set forth again. Quimper, when we eventually got there, was wet and grey. We stopped and had a monster meal, picked up a couple of blank receipts and drove the final stretch to the humble abode of Madame Tournier. And pretty humble it was too. Picture a low grey stone farmhouse with puddles round the door and a bunch of bolshy-looking cows peering over the hedge, and there you have it.

The door was answered by a young wolf. Well, he didn't open the door, he just started ripping it to pieces when he heard our footsteps. The actual opener was a woman in her sixties with round healthy cheeks and big brown eyes. She was a fine looking woman for her age and would have looked even finer if she'd dried her tears.

I asked her if she spoke English and she did, which was a blessing as my French is fit to be taken out and shot. She said, 'You are journalists?' and I wasn't the slightest offended.

I went through the sorry-to-upset-you-at-such-a-distressing-time palaver and she summoned a brave smile and invited us into her maison. Frankie peeked around apprehensively. I think he expected to see English lambs ablaze on the table.

Madame Tournier asked if we'd like coffee and we said you bet and off she went to the kitchen while I took in the room. I can never figure out how the French are renowned for their style yet they live surrounded by all that is naff and hideous. The Tournier family seat was typical of the species. A good garage sale would have done it a power of good. Huge dark wooden dressers, tables built by Swan Hunter, knick-knacks, bric-à-brac, gimcrack whatnots adorning everything stationary. No doubt if the homicidal dog were not constantly on the prowl they would have stuck a carriage clock on his bonce.

There were pictures galore. Claudine at four, with a little girl half her age, squinting into the sun. They were obviously sisters. The whole family (Papa had a moustache) gathered proudly around a car. Some elderly French buffers cradling the infants. Claudine and the mini-Claudine with calves down on the farm. A wedding with the girls, now teenagers, in pink. Claudine in university gear. The other one in a bikini. A rather fanciable one that. Then shot after shot of Claudine up the Niger, down the Ganges, over the hills and far away. The biggest by far was of Claudine in power business suit, displaying her MBE. Not a single solitary shot of Sir James.

Madame Tournier returned just as the brutish dog began taking an unhealthy interest in the delicate area of my trousers. 'Sophie!' she admonished.

And the dirty bitch slunk off.

We sat down in big overstuffed chairs while Madame Tournier fetched out her hankie and blew a concealed trumpet into it.

She said in garlic-flavoured English, 'You know Claudine?'

I shook my head. Madame Tournier sighed and looked around the mugs' gallery on the dresser. She was a million miles off, somewhere I hope I never get to.

I said quietly, 'I saw Sir James yesterday.'

As conversation openers go, it was a real bummer. Madame Tournier flicked a contemptuous eyelid but said nothing. I gathered her son-in-law was not Mr Popular hereabouts. 'He's in Switzerland,' I said, just to start a fire going.

'He can stay there.' Through gritted teeth.

Half a dozen clocks tick-tocked to each other in French. Otherwise a heavy air of silence enveloped the proceedings. I let it hang there, knowing she would break first. She looked at me full face.

'Claudine told me such things about him . . . did you know she was planning to leave him?'

I arched my eyebrows obligingly.

'She had taken enough, enough of his . . .' Madame Tournier tailed off and peered into her coffee cup.

I oozed sympathy. 'Yes, I had heard about his . . .' I said, not having the faintest idea what she was talking about.

Madame Tournier fired me a fierce look. 'Maybe it will come out now?' she asked.

I tried a Gallic shrug. 'Maybe. But we need proof.'

'Proof! If you know, you just write and put it in your newspaper.'

It's amazing how little the French know of our libel laws. I looked away and said, 'I have just written a story about him and his girlfriend.'

A bitter laugh from her corner. 'That means nothing. Perhaps the English journals are too frightened to tell the real story.'

So it was something naughtier than Sir James's hanky-panky. What then?

Madame Tournier was inside her own head. 'I talked to Claudine on Tuesday and she was so looking forward to tomorrow.'

'Tomorrow?'

'Yes, she loves Asia so much.'

I guessed that meant Claudine was off on her travels again, or would have been if someone hadn't stopped her dead in her tracks.

I said, 'Where was she going?'

'She told me India, Sri Lanka, Cambodia and Laos. Her first time in Laos. She had so many plans. She adored her children.'

'Your daughter did not have any of her own,' I said.

This was a roundabout way of asking why the union of Tomlin and Claudine was not blessed with progeny.

Madame Tournier regarded me like I was some sort of dotard.

'Of course not.' She said it in French.

I was none the wiser. I said, 'No one in England can understand why Claudine was killed.'

Another acid laugh. 'Ask James Tomlin.'

I said, 'He denied having anything to do with it.'

Madame Tournier sniffed and said he would. So what was the point of me asking him then? I switched direction.

'You have lots of photographs,' I said stupidly. Claudine's mum took a dekko at the dresser and started off crying. Frankie and I exchanged glances and waited.

She dried up after a couple of minutes. I would have said sorry but that might have set her going again. Instead I pointed at one happy snap and said, 'You have another daughter?'

God knows where my brain was today. That was like saying to a man who has just lost his right leg that you see his left one is still hanging on in there. Madame Tournier just nodded.

She sipped on her coffee and said, 'Natalie is coming back from England with Claudine.'

Frankie eyed the pic of Natalie in her bikini. 'She's a real belter,' he said. Thank you, Frankie.

Madame said, 'She is just like Claudine. They are very close. Like twins almost.' She still spoke of her ex-daughter in the present tense.

I returned to the chase. 'Why should anyone want to kill her?'

She wandered around the question, inspecting it from here and there before answering.

'Maybe it was to do with the Foundation.'

The WorldCare Foundation was Claudine's baby. It administered her pet projects through a board of directors which included MPs, showbiz stars and sundry undesirables.

'You think it was someone in the Foundation?' I asked in a fairly desperate bid to get a story out of the interview.

Madame Tournier hesitated. 'Yes.'

God Bless you ma'am. 'Why?'

More dithering. 'Last month Claudine was here and she said there was a scandal. I do not know what scandal but my daughter was very upset.'

'Money?' I probed.

'No. I do not think so. It was something bigger.'

Bigger than money? Let's be realistic here.

'She was very angry. She said it would look bad. There were important people, Claudine said.'

Zip-a-dee-dooh-dah. I had a story. Readers might consider my reaction a mite cold-blooded. Sadly, this is the way we are. I remember once being in Ulster during the heady days of sectarian assassination when a Catholic teenager vanished. We all trawled round to see his granny. What do you think has happened? we asked her. She said, 'I'm dreading that my wee Tommy's lying shot down in a gutter somewhere with his dear life blood running out of him.' To which one of my colleagues responded, 'Great!' The idiot hack was only saying what everyone was thinking: what a great quote. But it fairly made granny blink.

Back to the present. 'What else could the scandal be?'

'I do not know,' she repeated. 'But Claudine said it would shock many people.'

'And destroy their reputations?' I asked, teasing quotes out of her. Madame Tournier looked vague but said that was about it.

For my own curiosity I asked, 'Did Claudine ever mention anyone called Candy?'

'Candy?' A quick flip through the memory banks. 'No, I have not heard of Candy. Who is she?'

I admitted my knowledge of Candy was on a par with hers, then I sat back to savour my lukewarm chicory while Frankie got on with his panchromatic artistry.

She showed us to the door. As I said goodbye I looked into a face that was fashioned for smiling but now was creased from crying. I felt sorry someone had popped Claudine. Or I felt sorry for her mum anyway.

Back in the Volvo I said to Frankie, 'Drink?'

'Yup.'

The story wrote itself:

*SULTRY murder victim Claudine Tournier was gunned down to stop her exposing a high society scandal, her mother revealed last night.*

Lovers of the English language might argue that Claudine was not the victim of a sultry murder. Fortunately my dear news editor Angela Whipple is not a lover of the English language.

'Nice one, Max,' she said when I rang through. 'Now what are you doing?'

I told her I was teaching French girls to English kiss.

She said, 'All right, as long as you're back tonight. You have a lot to follow up this end.'

I asked her what had happened to the Blind Date rapist. She sounded glum.

'They dropped the charge,' she said.

That's how it goes in newspapers. The Lord giveth, the Lord taketh away.

# Chapter Four

Home to Rosie.

Every girl I've ever met called Rose is sweet and placid, plain and simple. Every Rosemary is much the same, maybe with aspirations as A Thinker. You picture them reading the boring bits in the Sunday heavies just for the hell of it. Why is it then that every girl called Rosie is a stark raving nutter? Such is mine. She once stabbed me with a corkscrew for nothing. Something to do with another girl, I think.

She has what the poofs in our features department like to call a pre-Raphaelite face. What, incidentally, is a post-Raphaelite face?

No matter. Back to Rosie Bannister. She's got long gypsy ringlets, smoky eyes, a dirty voice, a shape that disturbs a man and a very nice flat in Battersea. Thence I sallied with a bottle of Oscar de la Renta and a litre of duty-free Gordons.

She was pleased to see me. She shut the door in my face.

'Rosie,' I begged the door. ''Tis I! Your darlin' Max.'

She said something rude. I looked through the letterbox at her legs. By God, they go on a bit. I wasn't worried. It was Saturday night so she was probably out of drink. I clinked the bottles together for encouragement. The door opened a sliver.

'What do you want?' a corner of her mouth asked. They come up with some dumb questions.

I said I wanted to soothe her fretful brow and bring laughter to her lips.

'Ha!'

'You see, it's working already.'

Rosie let me in. I wrapped her in my arms and nuzzled her neck. She examined the ceiling. It was a lovely neck. It really suited her. At length we parted and got down to the preliminaries.

'You didn't phone,' she accused, fetching ice, tonic and glasses. She was out of lemon.

'I couldn't. I was up to my ears chasing Claudine Tournier's old man and her family across half Europe.'

Her lips formed a gorgeous pout. They entreated: come and kiss me. So I did. Rosie said, 'Stop that. I'm cross with you.'

It took a couple of stiffish gins before she ran through her catechism of complaint. I looked repentant and we were friends again. We got on to her day. She had flogged some of her lizard designs to a fashion house and was feeling chipper. Rosie is artistic. She draws things, usually lizards, and makes fearsome iguanas to stick on your coffee table. I often think Rosie eyes me as base clay from which she will fashion something fabulous. One of these days I'm going to wake up covered in scales with my tongue poking out.

She was curled in one corner of the white settee, draped in a woolly smock thing, the colour of overripe strawberries, with leggings a touch lighter and bluer than charcoal. Every now and then she flicked away a rogue curl with an unvarnished hand. You could call her beautiful, but that wouldn't be doing her justice. Women mesmerise me. They just walk across a room, or flick the hair out of their eyes and I am in thrall. They don't even know they're doing it. Rosie has a million such tricks. The only thing is you get so enchanted by them that you forget everything else that's going on.

Rosie was saying, 'So, do you fancy going?'

I kick started my brain. 'Sorry, love. I was just thinking about the Tournier story. What were you saying?'

She clicked her teeth in annoyance. They're great teeth. She said, 'Kim and Dan are having a party tonight; shall we go?'

Kim and Dan Young were originally my friends but, like so much else in my life, have been shanghaied by Rosie. Dan is a lobby reporter and Kim a lady monkey, so it was a mixed marriage and no one gave it a chance. But after a year together they're still lovey-dovey which just goes to show something or other. When I introduced Rosie to the happy couple she giggled. Later I asked her why. She said, 'Kim and Dan Young. They sound like a Vietnam war atrocity.'

I roared too. Then we went on to invent suitable imaginary kids for them. We came up with Sam, Ben, Hugh. Oh how we laughed. I suppose you had to be there.

Returning to Rosie's question, my first instinct

was to say bugger Kim and Dan, let's stay home with the TV off, but I said, 'It's your call.'

Rosie looked sour. 'Why can't you make up your mind?' she asked, ignoring the fact she couldn't make a decision either.

We batted it back and forth for a gin or two and then we voted to go, which was what she wanted all along.

It was very much a hacks' party, though some desk people had slunk in when no one was looking. My fond news editor whooped with joy when she saw me, kissed me smudgily and said sweet things about my Tournier exclusive. She never can hold her drink.

By her side was her ever-loving Arfur. Arfur is a down table sports sub on the *Mail* so by rights we should have slung him out on his ear, but we are a bunch of big softies, us hacks.

Someone clapped her hands over my eyes and breathed throatily in my left ear: 'Guess who?' It was Dania, my favourite typographical error. Dania and I were hot stuff together not so very long ago. Come to think of it, it was because of Dania that I now have a corkscrew scar on my shoulder. She has since surrendered herself to Jonathon (sic) Elwood, though what she sees in the lout is beyond me. Jonathon waved a cheery glass in my direction and yelled, 'Great story!' which I took to mean: you're a God-awful writer but the story was good. I smiled between my teeth.

Of Rosie there was never a sign. Whenever we grace these thrashes she invariably goes off to talk to strange men, leaving me in the most dubious of company, like that of my mate Tommy from the

*Express* who had just discovered a new dive in Belgravia where the drink is cheap and the women cheaper still.

Next I fell among thieves, various riff-raff from the News of the Screws. The Wildebeest was there, one arm wrapped around a bottle, the other clutching a brace of hackettes. The Wildebeest is an appalling man whose company is shunned by every right-thinking member of society. We are bosom buddies. We fell in love during the hunt for the Biggleswade Bigamist when the Wildebeest bailed me out of a Danish nick after a sad misunderstanding at a strip club. He was regaling us with his latest atrocity, involving his paper's Prize Pets contest, where he ran over the winner, formerly a handsome tabby cat. And so the idle hours rolled by until Rosie appeared by my side. It was her sweet way of saying: 'They're down to the white wine. Any second now they'll open the aftershave. Let's get the hell out of here.' And get the hell we did.

Back in Battersea I rang my own flat to see if my answerphone had missed me. It had. There was one message, from a Miss Ham. It took me a moment to remember Miss Ham was our Shirley, the girl who blew the gaff on Sir James Tomlin. She wanted me to ring her at her Essex domicile. I promised the answer-phone I would, but not right now, for Rosie had just drifted into vision minus her smock and leggings. That's another one of her tricks.

*

The Sundays carried run of the mill stories on Claudine's killing. Nothing new there, though the Indy hinted at financial headaches at Freleng-Bourke, Sir James's firm.

Rosie and I went down to Richmond and drank gin and ginger beer with lime and ice whilst enjoying the sunshine outside a ye olde riverfront pub frequented by king-size American tourists. Gazing at Old Father Thames rolling muddily along I remembered I was supposed to ring Shirley.

For the first time I talked about the story to Rosie who was fresh and minty in green and white stripes. She reckoned it was Sir James what done it. Furthermore, she indicated that any man who is unfaithful to his woman should be chopped into small pieces. I took this as a coded warning.

I left my call to Shirley until the evening, reasoning she would be out on such a glorious May afternoon, spotting Ford Capris or whatever it is Essex people get up to in their off hours.

The phone answered after one ring. 'Yes?' said a plaintive voice. Shirley herself.

I lied a bit about having just got back from French France and asked her what's new. Sir James, she said, was in London, had scrubbed his schedule and was spending a lot of time with cronies behind closed doors.

Well, hold the front page girls, I thought. She wanted to know when she would see the grand I promised her for all the inside stuff on Sir James's love life. I told her soon. She didn't appear to have much to say for herself. I diagnosed newsitis. This is a distressing psychological ailment afflicting those who want to prolong their fifteen minutes of fame. You get their story, run it, and move on to the next one. But some people are not content with a one-off splash and colour spread. So they pester you for months, even years afterwards with every trivial event in their grey day in the fond hope you'll bung them another wad of tenners and make them a media star again.

I said I had a busy time at the Old Bailey next week and I would get back to her after it. She said okay, but didn't sound too happy.

I asked her if she knew a girl called Candy. She sucked on it for a moment and said, 'I don't know. It sort of rings a bell.'

So does my local innkeeper, but I don't write a story about it. Shirley said she would ask around. I made her promise. Then she said, 'Do you pay for other stories?'

I was wary. 'It depends if they make the paper and what sort of show they get.'

'It's not about the murder.'

What was it then? A crash on the Southend arterial? A three-in-a-bed in Theydon Bois?

I said, 'Shirley, I just do crime stuff. But if it's any good, I'll put you on to our News Desk.' Which is shorthand for I'm having a rare day off, so why don't you go and bother somebody else?

I could hear her chewing her lip as she mulled it over. She said, 'Maybe you could tell me if it's worth anything?'

I gave in. 'What is it?'

She said, 'You know Leon Knapp?'

'Leon Knapp? Oh, the pop singer.'

She said, 'He's vanished.'

I pictured the wrinkly rocker vanishing from the chat show circuit forever. It was a happy prospect.

I said, 'What do you mean, vanished?'

She said, 'Everyone's tearing their hair out looking for him. They're all worried frantic.'

'Who they?'

'His manager. His PR man. Sir James.'

I said, 'Sir James? Sir James! What's his connection with Leon Knapp?'

She said, 'Leon was going to be on the Asian tour with Claudine – well part of it. But they can't find him to tell him it's off.'

'I still don't get it,' I said trying to imagine Leon Knapp taking time off from his ego trip to give the Third World a helping hand. No, not the Leon we know and loathe.

'And,' said Shirley, 'he's one of the Foundation's trustees.'

'Aaaah!' A much more believable image popped up. Leon, his pockets stuffed with stolen Foundation money, topping up his plastic tan on some tropical island with a sugar bowl of cocaine for company. Rumour has it he's funny that way.

'Is it any good?' asked Shirley, meaning was the story worth a few bob.

I told her it might be. We'd have to check it out. He might just be chewing the wallpaper in some funny farm. Or plotting another comeback.

She was disappointed but she said she'd trust me, which almost qualified her for a story of her own.

We said bye bye to each other and I put the phone down. I looked in the mirror. There were deep lines of thought etched across my brow. I shook my head and they went away.

Monday. Off to the Old Bailey for the winding up of the Silence of the Crams murder. By rights it should have been a straight up and downer. Everyone knew the unspeakable Crams had done in their Kurdish au pair and grilled her on the barbecue. But the couple were on legal aid and their brief was determined to give us a run for our money. This morning, with the jury out, he was arguing that a drunken orgy pic of the Crams in the *Star* showed his clients in a bad light and was prejudicial and so forth. He looked like he had lots more nonsense where this came from. We fell into a dreamless slumber while he took his time to get to the point, namely that the pre-trial publicity meant his clients were denied a fair hearing, therefore the two loonies should be let loose forthwith. Mr Justice Seamley tittered and said he'd adjourn and think about it over a bottle of port, though he didn't mention the port out loud. He billowed out scratching his curls. We took his exit as a heaven-sent sign to head for the bar.

Nobody was feeling very talkative so with nothing better to do I glanced through our final edition. I had passed on Shirley's tip about the vanishing Leon Knapp to our showbiz man with his finger on the pulse of pop. He had furnished his usual glittering prose:

*Mystery last night surrounded the whereabouts of legendary rock idol Leon Knapp . . .'* it began. I read no further. If ever you see a newspaper story which begins: 'Mystery surrounded . . .' it means the reporter hasn't the faintest idea what's happening so there's no point reading on. I was also unimpressed with the word 'whereabouts'. This is far too long for our readers. By the time they get to the end of it they've forgotten how it started.

I cast our great organ aside and rang News Desk. I got Nigel. He's the guy with the friendly smile who sits beside Angela sharpening a stiletto and waiting for her to turn her back. He sounded really glad to hear from me. He was less chummy when I warned him there might be no show from the Crams today.

'Oh,' he said. I knew what he was thinking. News Desk people the land over are convinced that every morning the bigwigs of British justice and all the raggedy-arsed reporters get together to conspire against them.

Nige said, 'Leave it to Agency and come back.'

I said I needed more background stuff on Marjorie Cram and I was meeting contacts. He gave a grudging okay, knowing what I was really up to but unable to prove it.

Half an hour later we were still guzzling away when Big Ben, the hacks' friend, reeled in. Ben Ashbee is a detective super and a super detective. That is to say he talks to us hacks and tells us things. Well, he talks to me anyway. I asked him why he was hanging around the Bailey and he said he was just watching a bunch of druggies getting sent down.

Nothing to write home about there. I asked what else was doing. He said he was fronting the Claudine Tournier investigation which was nice for me.

'Any moves?' I asked, buying him drink and luring him to a secluded cloister of the bar.

He said the betting was Sir James was the guilty party; that it looked like a contract hit as Sir James had a most convenient alibi. The murder weapon a .32. Motive? Probably money. All very trite and tiresome.

'Can you pin it on him?' I asked. Ben, a melancholy man at the best of times, turned his mouth down, which I took to mean not a hope in hell.

We talked about the WorldCare Foundation and the singular absence of Knapp. He put the last item down to dissolute living. I asked whether a girl called Candy figured anywhere in the investigation. He said no and looked so forlorn I bought him a bag of smoky bacon crisps.

Tired out by all the excitement, I eddied back to the office. Things were even quieter there. I got out my black book and started ringing people so they could share my boredom. I caught Mac McIvor, my deep throat police inspector, just before he sneaked off to the pub. He said, 'My tip about Claudine's body must be a nice little earner,' signalling that he expected £500 at least.

I pointed out that he had not tipped me off about Claudine: all he had said was there was a corpse littering St Katharine's Dock. But I didn't really argue the point. It wasn't my money.

Mac said Sir James had been interviewed a couple

of times, with a smarty pants lawyer holding his hand. The Serious Fraud Office were taking a quiet interest in Freleng-Bourke. Otherwise Claudine's death was just like Leon Knapp's vanishing trick. Mystery surrounded it.

On a sudden whim I rang Freleng-Bourke and got through to Sir James Tomlin's private office. A male voice answered. Someone younger and doubtless taller than the passionate pygmy.

No, Sir James was not available, and who was calling please? He was polite but guarded.

I said, 'May I speak to Candy?'

A sharp intake of breath. 'Who is calling please?'

I came clean: 'This is Max Chard.'

'Oh!' followed by silence.

'I am the chief crime correspondent of—'

'I know who you are, Mister Chard,' he cut in. He was still guarded but had forgotten to be polite.

Chief crime correspondents accept this as their lot in life. I lit a Bensons and waited for him to tell me to eff off. Instead he said, 'Candy? Would you care to tell me what this is about?'

I said I would prefer to speak to Candy. He hesitated and said, 'One moment.'

I waited five moments. He came back on. 'I am afraid there is no one here who can help you.' He was lying but I didn't know what he was lying about.

'Is Miss Pearson there?' I tried.

He didn't bother looking. 'No.'

'And I suppose she won't be there all day?'

'That is correct.' He switched to patronising public

school twerp mode. 'I suggest if you have any queries about Freleng-Bourke you call our press office and—'

'And will they tell me about Candy?' I snapped.

Splutter of outrage and the phone went down.

It had been fun while it lasted, not that it told me anything. I returned to my Bensons and my little black book. I got all the way through to the Rs before I found anyone else worth annoying. Ross Gavney.

'I owe you a fiver,' I said by way of introduction.

'What? Oh, yes.' Ross sounded preoccupied.

'Are you preoccupied?' I asked.

'No. Not really. Well, actually, yes, just, yes, a little.'

Ross does not normally stick a comma after every word. I thought about it and said, 'You want me to go away?'

'Well, yes. Sorry, Max, but things are rather . . .'

I said that's okay, I'd catch him again, and if he cared to invite me round to slaughter his whisky, I'd gladly pay up on the bet. Ross said right, terrific, fine. And that was that. I replaced the phone and pondered on my old chum. The sunshine was somehow gone from his voice. Probably some awful mid-life crisis, like should he swop the Saab turbo for an XJS. I felt deeply perplexed and concerned. Maybe I was thirsty.

After lunch I got down to the serious business of the day. Expenses. If you've ever wondered why newspapers are singularly devoid of any imaginative spark, it's because the poor hacks devote every last ounce of creativity to doing their exes. As works of fiction they rival Dickens, the crime statistics and the *Sunday Sport* at their best.

I had returned from France with £350 in traveller's cheques, what was left of my £500 advance. There is a holy commandment in newspapers that you must never, never, never, *ever* return a single penny the office has advanced you: that you must show you spent it all in the pursuit of the story. My task for the afternoon was to launder the loose £350. My exes duly reflected that I paid forty quid for an interpreter in Switzerland, fifty for one in France. I bought route maps, newspapers, a bottle of champagne for Sir James, and a few outrageously expensive meals for myself. I also got the worst exchange rate in francs known to man. Grand total: £527, not counting hotel and car.

I was gazing on my handiwork with admiration when the phone rang. Shirley Ham on the other end. She bubbled and babbled incomprehensibly. There was a horrendous racket going on in the background. She was either calling from a Cairo street market or a British Rail station. I told her to calm down and start again. After a few breaths she got it together. She said, 'You remember you asked me to find out about Candy?'

I said I did. She said, 'I've got lots of news for you; you're going to be really surprised.'

I said that was nice, and what was the news?

She went all coy. 'Not on the phone,' she said, as if I were asking her to confess her sexual fantasies.

'Where then?' I asked.

'Are you free tonight?'

Steady on, Shirl. I'm not that sort of man. I

admitted I was free and happy to meet her anywhere, as long as it wasn't in Essex.

She thought about it and came up with a pub, the Scimitar on Mile End Road, which was a fair compromise as it was in no man's land, between the City and the wilderness.

I said seven o'clock. She said eight. She wanted to see someone first, she explained. She was about to ring off when she dropped me a teaser. 'You've got it all wrong about Candy.'

'What have I got wrong?'

A giggle. 'You'll find out tonight.'

Be still my beating heart. But I managed to survive the intervening hours without tearing my hair out. A black cab dropped me outside the Scimitar ten minutes off eight. I ordered a Gordons and took in the scenery.

In the old days this was a watering hole for the Krays and their hired help. Every Friday night the twins used to muscle in, put the frighteners on everybody, relieve the landlord of fifty quid, and muscle out again, pausing only to duff up stray drinkers. Since then the place had gone to hell. Now it was a theme pub and the theme was crooks. But not the local real life rootin' tootin' shootin' bad boys: the sepia prints on the walls featured Al Capone, Bugsy Siegel and Legs Diamond. Or maybe it was John Dillinger. I never can tell those two apart. For my money, the biggest crook on view was the barman, running a nice extortion racket with his prices. He was wearing a butcher-style apron, a clip on moustache, and he had his slicked-back hair parted dead centre. He did not seem embarrassed.

The wallpaper was doing its best to pretend it was bricks, bricks punctuated here and there with ragged edged bullet holes, designed to make you feel you were enjoying your pint of London bitter at the scene of the St Valentine's Day Massacre. Just the sort of place for a romantic date. Off the bar there were little wooden alcoves. I inspected the contents. No Shirley. The clientele were youngish, moneyed and not visibly gifted with taste. The men favoured shiny double-breasteds with ties as muted as Hiroshima. Their treble-voiced partners were blondes with Grand Canyon cleavages and Tenerife tans.

Back to the bar area where the barman was doing something awful to a shot of good gin with blue curacao and creme de menthe. I averted my eyes. The piano rag music came courtesy of Scott Joplin. I settled into another Gordons and pretended I didn't mind. When The Entertainer popped up for the third time, I was getting restless. Where was Shirley in this my hour of need? I started playing the fruit machine, a sure sign of desperation. I was down a fiver before I gave up and asked the barman for his phone. I didn't want to use my own mobile because all the poseurs in the place were flashing theirs. I got through to a grumpy old geezer who told me Shirley wasn't home; that she'd gone out to see a man called Mike or something.

'Max?' I suggested.

'Yer, that's it,' he graciously conceded.

I fed the phone another 50p while Shirl's dad took

his time about finding a pen and writing down my bleep number. I made him repeat it just as the money ran out. By now it was coming up 9.30 and if Shirley had walked in the door I would have been a shade tetchy with her. But she didn't. I gave the barman a message just in case she called in. I licked my glass dry and wandered out on to Mile End Road to hunt a taxi. They were all heading the wrong way, back to Ongar or Bow or wherever it is cabbies go to rest their mouths. I walked a good half mile, passing at least three pubs, before a cab rescued me. My bleep went off as I clambered aboard. It said, 'Call call call – Mac Mac Mac'.

I took this to mean McIvor wanted me to call him urgently, or three times, or possibly both.

'Where to, mate?' asked my driver.

'To London,' said I, pointing west.

# Chapter Five

I suppose it's about time I gave you the SP on Mac. His full name is Terence something McIvor and he's Irish, or Ulsterish, to be precise. He talks funny. In his youth, a year or so back, he was a rising star in the Royal Ulster Constabulary, a fine body of men who decided they could do without him after all. Mac prefers to draw a veil over exactly how and why he and the RUC parted company. But I gather a certain detective inspector and his missus are no longer calling each other snookyookums.

Mac came to England and naturally gravitated to the Met, who welcome all the riff-raff they can clap their hands on. It's a bit like the Foreign Legion only less picky. In the Met's ranks Mac looked like a choirboy with the brains of Einstein's smarter brother. They made him up to inspector but stuck him in internal investigations, the police department which turns over naughty plods and reports back to itself. One of these days someone will refer it to the Monopolies Commission. Mac didn't like the job, not through any moral scruple or sense of decency. Good God, no. He just found it boring. So he looked around for some amusing sideline to while away the tedious hours.

He was still looking when we first met, in the aftermath of the Milky Bar Killer storm. There was a school of thought in softy papers like the *Guardian* that the police were a mite over-zealous in shooting dead the young thug when he was (a) out of his tree on crack, (b) unarmed, and (c) asleep. Scotland Yard's heroic defence was: 'Our officers fired, believing they were about to be fired upon.' Though quite how they came to believe they were in danger from a snoring zonked out tearaway was never quite explained. In all the brouhaha over the killings it was sometimes overlooked that the Milky Bar Kid, a pasty-faced, four-eyed little runt, had already murdered a building society clerk. Our thoughtful leader writer redressed the balance. He inclined to the view that the Law had done us all a favour in putting Milky down. And seeing he was shot while he was sleeping, he didn't feel a thing. A sort of mercy killing, our Voice of Sanity argued. But the Grauniad and a posse of headline hunting MPs started fulminating about Gun Law, shoot-to-kill policies, that sort of tosh. Nobody said anything about stupidity.

Mac was on the squad set up to investigate the antics of the armed desperadoes from the Met's firearms unit. We bumped into each other in a bar down Richmond way, fell to talking about the Rugby World Cup, the price of drink, the shape of the barmaid and so on. I wasn't cultivating him: we just hit it off naturally. I suppose it was a case of opposites attract.

Somewhere in the course of our yattering Mac let slip that one of the Yard's gunslingers had a spot of previous. He was involved in the shooting of another unarmed villain when he was with Avon and Somerset. It gave me an exclusive splash with picture by-line and all. And that, I thought, was that.

But next morning, bright and early, I got a call from Mac, suggesting it might be a nice gesture on my part to bung him some readies. I got him £300 and he was my friend for life. Also he had found his true vocation, assisting us gentlemen of the Fourth Estate in our tireless pursuit of truth and justice. Since then he's built himself a network of like-minded coppers who tip him off when something's doing. He gives them 25 per cent of what we pay him and trousers the rest. I reckon he lifts forty grand a year, and that's not counting his police pay. We launder our payments through some addresses in Belfast and Donegal so the Met can't trace leaks back to him.

Mac is sallow and skeletal, has a long foxy face and wide foxy eyes. Women tell me he's attractive, but I can't see it. He likes dark suits, dark shirts and bold monochrome ties. Picture a jazz musician with an unhealthy interest in white powders and you have a photofit of Mac. He has never learned to tie anything other than a Windsor knot. His hair is mousy brown, lank, and flops over one eye. When he's not at his desk digging up stuff to sell, he hangs around Hampton's, a wine bar of dubious taste. I have never looked more than twice at a pretty woman there, because the odds are she's already been the victim of a Mac Attack. I would guess Hampton's pick up about five grand of the money Mac makes from us, for he is an alarmingly generous man.

Back to where we were: I called Hampton's from the cab. Yes, Mac was there, said Louise, just a minute, she'd get him. I listened to the background shrieks and guffaws that pass for civilised conversation in the dive. Mac came on.

'How's about ye?' he said in that quaint Frank Carson-ish way of his.

I told him I was in the jacuzzi with Michelle Pfeiffer and went Gluggle-bubble-giggle to prove it.

Up front the taxi driver said, 'You all right, guv?'

I ignored him. 'What've you got for me?'

Mac said, 'You're not going to believe this.'

I promised I wouldn't but said he could tell me anyway.

He licked his lips and said, 'They've found another body, another woman, in St Katharine's Dock . . .'

I said, 'Stone me!' Or something similar.

' . . . and at the exact same spot where Claudine Tournier was dumped. What about that, hey?'

He didn't know anything else, whether the latest victim had jumped or was pushed, what her name was and all the rest. I told him to line up a bottle for me and I'd be there within the hour, after I dropped by the dock.

'Just as long as you don't drop into it,' he cackled and was gone.

I told Big Ears, the cabbie, 'Change of plan. Take me to St Katharine's Dock.'

He had earwigged enough of the conversation to grasp there was another body in the Thames. He said, 'Are you a reporter, squire?'

I said no: that I worked for the Port of London Authority, and it was my sad duty in life to chart floating women who posed a danger to shipping. He said, 'Wot?' and gave me a funny look in his rear view mirror.

We trundled on through the gloom grey canyons of E1 until we found London's favourite bathing spot for fashionable young ladies. It was deja vu all over again. Daisy chains of police blue and white cordon tapes ringed the dock approach. On the quayside a motley gang of fourteen-year-old Plods were saying useful things like: 'Move along there' and 'There's nothing to see.'

For once they were telling the truth. The ambulance had been and gone. A fleet of yachts paddled in the ebb tide and all was serene, apart from the forensic civvies snapping souvenir shots and scribbling in their big blue folders in joined up writing.

I disembarked from my cab and was instantly confronted by my old mate, Harry, the defective inspector last seen hanging about these parts on the night of Claudine's splashdown. He was not a happy bobby.

'How did you know there was something going on here?' he demanded belligerently.

'I think it's a gift, Harry,' I said.

He stuck his finger in my chest. 'I've got a crow to pick with you,' he said in an interesting use of English.

I told him to pick away. He ordered me to think back to our last meeting. I thought.

'You introduced me to a bloke you said was Lewis Trefoyle from the Home Office.'

'Junior Minister at the Home Office,' I said, ever a stickler for accuracy.

H said, 'Well, I was watching *Newsnight* last night and Lewis Trefoyle was on and it wasn't him at all. He's about ten years older than your pal, bald as an egg and fat.'

My pupils dilated in shock, horror, outrage. 'Not him! But he told me he was Trefoyle and I believed him. I even bought him drink.'

Harry snorted and sneered.

I said, 'There is another alternative you might consider, Harry. Maybe the bloke who was on *Newsnight* was only pretending to be Lewis Trefoyle, and the one with me was the genuine article. The Beeb can get things wrong, you know.'

He stomped off a few yards and stomped back a few yards, muttering to himself. I lit a cigarette and offered the packet. For a moment he looked as if he might throw it, and me, into the dock. There was a long fraught silence.

I broke it, saying I was sorry about my phoney Trefoyle; that I was under the cosh to get the story in time for the edition, hence my shameful subterfuge; that I owed him a large scotch; that I felt bad about my trickery, grovel, grovel, grovel, lick, lick, lick. Harry peered at me intently and he could see I was sincere.

He said, 'Don't ever try anything like that again, Chard.'

I swore blind I wouldn't and moved briskly on to this evening's cabaret. Who was the victim?

Harry looked sly. He said, 'You can call her Unlucky.'

I said I could call her downright unfortunate. But what was her name?

'Unlucky,' Harry said. He had a silly grin slicked across his mug.

I narrowed my eyes and looked cross. Harry said happily, 'That's what Thames Division call her.' He nodded at a couple of bods from the river police.

I exhaled a long controlled jet of smoke. I said, 'And why do they call her Unlucky, H?'

He was practically in hysterics. 'Because they've got her listed as DB 13.'

'DB 13?'

'DB 13,' said Harry. 'Every time they find a body in the Thames they give it a number. DB stands for dead body. This is DB 13 – their thirteenth dead body this year. Unlucky 13. What would you call her?'

I let him have his little laugh. I said, 'What else?'

He said, 'All I can say is there's a connection.'

'With Claudine Tournier's murder?'

'That's what I said.'

I said, 'A copycat job? Shot in the head?'

Harry dithered over how much he would tell me. 'No, this one was strangled.'

I blinked. Our murderer shoots one woman and strangles another. I said, 'I don't get it. What's the connection?'

'Who the victim is, that's the connection.' He was enjoying himself.

'And you won't tell me that?'

'That's right.'

For a moment I thought I might chuck him in the dock. My steely self-resolve held. I said, 'Obviously Victim Number Two was dead before she hit the water, that's why you say she was strangled. She couldn't have told you who she was, or how she was linked with Claudine. So she must have had something on her that gave you the lead.'

Harry said, 'That's all you get.'

And he would have been right but for the sudden appearance of a pimply youth dressed up as a copper. He addressed his boss. 'The rest of Miss Ham's things have been sent to the incident room, sir.'

Miss Ham!

'Christ!' I said out loud. 'It's Shirley.'

Harry goggled and bulged. 'What do you know about her?' he yelped.

I flicked my cigarette into the dock. I bestowed a seraphic smile on H and said, 'She's called Shirley Ham. And that's all you get.'

It is never pleasant watching a middle aged nitwit go bananas. I closed my eyes and blocked my ears. Harry ranted through his repertoire of swear words, made up a couple more, vowed to rip up my Scotland Yard press pass, recklessly accused me of inventing quotes, and threatened to report me to the Press Association. I think he meant the Press Complaints Commission.

After a while he ran out of puff so he just stood there sweating and steaming.

I said in tones of sweet reason, 'Can we make a deal?'

'A deal!' More rude words.

I said, 'Just listen to me.' He grumbled but went quiet. I said, 'Let me buy you a drink and then I'll show you mine if you show me yours.'

I led him unprotesting to the Port O' Call, where I first clapped eyes on Shirley. He grunted that okay, he'd listen. And he'd have a glass of red. He didn't say please.

I parked him at the very same table where Shirley and I had sat and elbowed my way through the suits at the bar. A fluffy Kiwi barmaid gave me a welcoming wink and I winked right back. I can be ever so bold when Rosie's not around. I ordered a cheeky little sauvignon from the sunny side of the Andes and returned to Harry who didn't look as if he'd missed me.

We each had a hearty slurp and I got down to it. I filled him in on my supposed meet with Shirley, her job at Freleng-Bourke, her gossip about Sir James.

Harry nodded at each point but he wasn't impressed. I took a deep breath, hesitated, then told him about the mysterious Candy and how Shirley had called to say she had the info but was topped before she could tell me.

That made Harry's little pink ears stick out. He even dragged out a notebook and scribbled in it.

I said, 'That's the whole deal, H. Everything I know. Now, what made you link Shirley with Claudine?'

He waffled something about the papers she was

carrying but shut up. I topped up the glass to ease his lockjaw.

He guzzled a mouthful before he unbent. He said, 'Her handbag was lying on the dockside. She had credit cards, cheque book, a tube season ticket with her picture on it. That's how I know who she was.'

I said, 'Yes, but where's the Claudine connection?'

Harry patted his pocket. 'Papers,' he said.

It took a third glass of sauvignon before he allowed me a peek. The only interesting stuff was bumf on the WorldCare Foundation, a copy of a letter to the trustees, outlining Claudine's planned schlep around Asia. It listed all those to whom copies had been sent. I spotted Leon Knapp's name, and Proudhoe Veizey, the silver-locked thespian. The itinerary was longer than the Great Wall of China – Calcutta, Bombay, Dacca, Madras, Colombo, Kandy, Bangkok, Chiang Mai, Vientiane, Phnom Penh, and back to Blighty. There was a list of dates and functions, opening birth control clinics, meeting people with five syllable names, and so on.

I said, 'Shirley didn't work for the Foundation. Why does she have this letter?'

Harry said, 'No idea. But you can see there's a connection.'

I handed the letter back to him and we lapsed into silence. There was something tugging away at the back of my brain. Something about the letter.

I said, 'Let's see it again, H.'

I started reading from the very top and got halfway down the second page before it hit me – the bit where it said '. . . Madras, Colombo, Kandy, Bangkok . . .'

There it was, in letters a hundred foot high. Kandy! That was Shirley's big surprise for me. There never had been a mystery woman called Candy. But there was something funny going on in Kandy. I smiled to myself.

But of course I never said a word to Harry.

Nothing ever gets done in newspapers until after morning conference. In the meantime, news editors like to pretend they call the shots by despatching reporters to doorsteps and shouting into telephones and running around with bits of paper. This goes on for a couple of lunatic hours before conference begins in the Editor's office and a companionable hush falls upon the newsroom. Reporters lounge around telling lies and trading hooky meal receipts.

Meanwhile, behind the mock mahogany doors of the Editor's suite, the big boys and girls are getting down to the things that really matter. The Editor reveals he spent the previous evening watching a re-run of *Hancock's Half Hour* and everyone agrees it was a hoot, though not a single one of them saw it. He tells the Features Editor to do a piece on the Beeb's treasure trove of comedy, which we've already done twice this year. The Features Editor says: 'Good thinking' into his beard. The Regional Editor, an ageing harridan who thinks she's a sixteen-year-old sexpot, agrees it's a knock-'em-dead idea and goes on to waffle about how footballers' legs give her a kick. The Sports

Editor guffaws heartily because he and the Regional Editor are currently enjoying a secret affair, a secret known only to the entire office. The City Editor, a woman of some intellect, says she doesn't think footballers are the slightest bit sexy, but hasn't the England fly half got a terrific bum? The Features Editor glares at her and intimates that only a frustrated old boot could find anything sexy in a rugby player. The Leader Writer, still thinking about *Hancock's Half Hour,* recalls a particularly hilarious episode. Nobody laughs because the Leader Writer is universally and justly loathed. The Foreign Editor regales the company by telling him how he almost cut his toes off with the lawnmower yesterday. That reminds the Editor of the time he closed the Mercedes door on his thumb. Everyone coos in sympathy. The Pictures Editor, fresh back from a freebie to Acapulco, informs the gathering of the right way to drink tequila. The Executive Editor says that personally he's never liked tequila, but seeing he has never professed to liking anything, no one is at all surprised. The Diary Editor fondles his tie and lets slip a totally fabricated indiscretion about a minor royal and a rent boy. The News Editor says the *Mirror* buy-up of the polo groupie hooker ('How I Made A Mint From Polo!') was a waste of sixty grand. The entire company gives her a dirty look; she has just reminded them they're supposed to be talking about newspapers. The Editor sighs and says: 'Okay, what have we got today?' One by one his lieutenants produce their menus and argue about why such and such is a great story. The Editor, who is not fit to edit the *Beano*, wibbles and wobbles and makes his ruling. No one argues, for the Editor's indecision is final, and they can see his eyes straying to the mock mahogany mini bar in the corner. The assorted lackeys gather up their papers and return to their desks in varying states of dudgeon. So it was this morning.

I ambushed Angela Whipple as she wafted past, shedding fragrances like a travelling Body Shop. I said, 'Angie, I've got a lead on the Tournier story, but it means a foreign.'

Angela was wary because foreigns cost money. 'Where to?'

'Sri Lanka. To Kandy.'

I could see she was perplexed. Until now, Angela thought Sri Lanka was the leader of a yoga cult.

'You know, off India,' I said.

'India! Why do you want to go to India?'

Using only small words I explained all the stuff about Candy and Kandy, and how Shirley had been murdered investigating it. My exclusive story was in our London final edition, but I hadn't expected Angie to have read it all the way through.

She didn't like the idea, asked me what I hoped to find, and I had to admit I didn't know. She said she would talk about it to the Piltdown Man, executive editor Tony Belker. That meant I wasn't going. Belker and I share a deep and abiding hatred. Every now and then he tries to have me fired for landing us with a libel writ or getting blotto. The man has no sense of humour.

I aimed a mental kick at my backside, acknowledging I'd blown Sri Lanka. What I should have done was to have taken Angie out for a liquid lunch, told her the Kandy line, hinted that the *Sun* might be on the same track and then feigned boredom. After an hour or two she'd piece the whole thing together, suggest I shoot off to Kandy and think what a clever little news editor she was.

Angie bustled off to Belker's festering lair and I treated myself to a cup of yellow tea from the machine. She returned before my first grimace and said no, and forgot me. I ambled round to our library which is manned by the biggest bunch of amnesiacs since I can't remember when. After half an hour's hunting they dug out a book on Sri Lanka that was so old it called the place Ceylon. I flipped to the section on Kandy to see what I was missing. Kandy, it said, was the former capital, much beloved by English colonists and still redolent of the Empire's glory days with its architecture and unhurried ways. It was home to the Temple of the Tooth, which housed one of the Buddha's molars. There was much to see and do in Kandy's leafy environs, the book said, like watching spectacular festivals where elephants trundle around town tarted up like Danny La Rue. In a throwaway line, my guide to the pearl of the Indian Ocean happened to mention that once a month there is a Poya Day holiday, when 'all places of public entertainment are closed and the sale of alcohol is forbidden'. I closed the manual, reflecting that maybe I wasn't missing so much after all.

Back at my desk I found a brief from Angela to do up an early page story on gun-happy teenagers. I trawled through cuttings, invented a horrified senior police officer, got him to say something outlandish, and hammered out 500 words. I was about to sneak off for a livener when the phone went. D.I. Harry Pennycuik wanted me to drift down to the Tournier incident room and make a statement. I said I'd a dental appointment and he said balls.

The statement took ten minutes. Harry didn't have any intelligent questions to ask, though he made base insinuations about the nature of the affair between Shirl and me. On the desk in the incident room was the WorldCare Foundation letter he had lifted from Shirley's bag. I tried to read it again upside down. I was thus engaged when a woodentop entered the room and said the boss wanted H. for a mo. He waddled out. I grabbed the letter, stuck it in a convenient photocopier, and dashed myself off a copy before he waddled back in. I meandered home to the office by way of Scribes and El Vino's, the letter rubbing shoulders with my chequebook.

Maybe it was missing out on Sri Lanka or maybe it was just plain ennui. Whatever, I felt mischievous. I dug out the number for Sir James's private office and gave it a call. The same man answered. I didn't bother to introduce myself. I said, 'The next time anybody asks you about Kandy, tell them it's a place in Sri Lanka.'

'What!'

'It is a place in Sri Lanka,' I said, putting big spaces between each word.

Silence at his end. 'What we used to call Ceylon,' I added helpfully.

Another stretch of silence. Then: 'That is Max Chard?'

'That is I.'

'Why are you calling? What are you saying?' His voice was higher than normal.

'I'm saying that Kandy must be stopped,' I said.

'I do not understand . . .'

I said, 'Ask Sir James. He'll explain it. Or better still, ask his beloved Emma Pearson. She said in my presence, "Kandy must be stopped – I don't care how".'

He took a breath and got himself back together. He said, 'Mister Chard, no one here has anything to say to you. I suggest you stop harassing Sir James or we shall be obliged to complain to your editor.'

I said, 'Never mind. See you in Kandy.'

He was saying 'What!' again, only in capital letters, when I put the phone down.

I edged across to News Desk when no one was looking and nicked their *Evening Standard* to see what it had about Shirley's murder. I think it was only then I began to feel anything about it. There was a small pic, taken three or four years back, of Shirley, with her hair in flyaway style. Probably tinted. There was a bigger shot of her grieving mum and dad, a middle-aged party with too much beef. The story was the usual flat tabloidese, not a patch on mine. But reading between the lines you got an idea of the ghastliness of her killing. Shirley was their only child. She lived for ice skating, and, somewhat surprisingly, was a whizz at ballroom dancing. I tried to picture Shirley all dolled up in sequins, doing the fandango with a big lipsticky smile. I couldn't. Where the story got to me was her parents' total bewilderment. Why should anyone want to kill Shirley? they asked. I'd asked myself the same question the night before and come to the conclusion she was murdered to shut her up. Possible? yes. Probable? yes. But it seemed a lame excuse for killing a girl of barely 25. She had a boyfriend, Darren, her fandango partner. They were planning a September wedding, a fortnight's honeymoon in Corfu and they'd even bought themselves a flat in Epping. Darren said the ordinary trite things about being in shock, broken-hearted, how much they loved each other. People are always trite when faced with a tragedy beyond their comprehension. They look for hard-edged words to convey their terrible loss, but all they can find is the commonplace currency of everyday life. Yet often it is the very trivia of what they say that brings it home. Her mum said Shirley bought her wedding dress on Saturday and now it hung in the wardrobe, never to be worn. I saw a bedroom, pastel pink and littered with idiot stuffed animals, and, in a corner, a wardrobe, its door ajar to reveal a fussy, frilly bridal gown, hanging there silent and accusing like an Elizabethan ghost.

The Law had weighed in with banal quotes about 'a brutal killing', 'a girl with so much to live for.'

And so little to die for. What was the awful secret that made someone murder Shirley? I flipped through my mental list of suspects. It was a short list. Sir James Tomlin. Not very likely. He would have to stand on a chair to strangle her. Anyway, why should he want her dead – because she'd discovered he had his hand in the till? Hardly. Half the financiers in the City are up to their ears in jiggery pokery as a matter of principle.

And why was Claudine Tournier tipped in the Thames? Because she had a secret lover? Because Sir James was sick of veggie meals? I realised how little I knew of the romantic financier. I studied his form in *Who's Who*, where he listed his hobbies as skiing and reading, though not simultaneously. His unlisted hobby was collecting wives. There were three of them. First one deceased. Third one likewise. But the one in the middle, a Margaret Delsey Ford, had so far bucked the trend. There was also a son by Wife One, Henry Michael James, b. July 3, 1959. Where are they now? I mused.

There were evening drinkies at the Yard for a deputy assistant commissioner who was packing it in and going straight. He kindly invited the crime hacks to join him, and as the Met were buying, we could hardly refuse. It was an amiable do, lots of foul jokes and recollections of drunken debauchery. Sometimes us crime hacks and the Old Bill have a lot in common. The difference is we get paid to drink with them.

Among the gathering was Big Ben Ashbee, the superintendent in the Tournier case. In a moment of bonhomie, brought on by free drink, I told him about the Kandy connection. Ben tugged at an imaginary moustache, brooded, and said big deal. I sniffed and said that was the last juicy titbit I brought him. Ben said he hoped so and told me the latest from his side of the divide. Shirley, he said, was topped somewhere else at least an hour before her body was dumped in the dock. She was strangled with a thin rope and the killer had not been too clever about how he did it. There were burn marks around her chin and upper neck, suggesting he bungled it first time round, or maybe she put up a fight. So far motiveless. They'd found her bag and everything, except one shoe, a low, white open-toed affair, for the record. Big Ben lapsed into the doldrums and I asked instead about the Tournier case. A bad move. I thought he was going to cry, so obviously nothing doing there. I wandered off before he could borrow my hankie.

By this time the party was getting perilously near the fall-down drunk stage and a uniformed killjoy was busy detaching guests from their bottles. A bunch of us wandered off in search of curry and lager, though not necessarily in that order. Somewhere between the tandoori tikka and the chicken passanda my bleep started yelping. 'Call me,' it commanded. Apart from me, the only other me I know has smoky eyes and a dirty laugh. Yep, Rosie.

It was gone one when I finally rang, from the back of a taxi steaming south. She said, 'You're pissed.'

I couldn't disagree because I dropped the mobile. When I picked it up she was saying, '. . . and it's too late now, so go home.'

'It's not too late, Rosie,' I said, using far too many esses.

'It bloody well is. You should have called me earlier.'

'I prefer to call you Rosie.'

She said, 'I'm asleep. Call me in the morning – if you wake up.'

I tried my usual ploy of swearing undying love and obedience, and Rosie delivered her usual rebuff. But she did say, 'Okay, me too', before switching me off.

Back in my lonely garret, actually a basement apartment off Pilbeam Gardens, I was greeted by a ringing telephone. Aha! So Rosie's changed her mind, thought I.

But it was not Rosie. Whoever it was didn't introduce himself. His voice was distorted, as if he was speaking through a fog. He sounded a perfect stranger, well, an obviously imperfect stranger, for he did not like me one little bit.

'We've got your number, Chard,' he said.

'So it would appear.'

'And we know where you live. We can get to you anytime.'

I said, 'Is this a threatening call or are you emergency plumbers?'

He said, 'Call it a warning – the only one you'll get. Leave the Claudine Tournier story alone.'

'Or else?'

'Remember what happened to the last snooper.'

I said, 'Oh, you must be the gentleman who's not very good at strangling people.'

He laughed. It wasn't one of those wicked blood-curdling laughs that makes your toes curl. It was a straightforward ordinary laugh. It made my toes curl.

He slapped the phone down. I immediately punched out 1471 and got a sing song machine to tell me where Mister Menace had rung from. It was a 730 number, somewhere in Victoria. It kept ringing for a couple of minutes before someone answered it. A man.

'Yus?' he said.

I said, 'My name is Chard. Someone there has just called me.'

'Wasn't me, mate.'

I said, 'I know. But has someone else called?'

'Don't know, mate.'

'Is that a private number?'

'Wot, this?'

I said, 'Yes – this.'

'No mate.'

I said, 'Where am I calling?'

'It's Victoria Station. It's a call box.'

I said, 'Thanks, anyway. Sorry to bother you.' We both hung up and I stood stock still for a long time thinking. I was as sober as a teetotal judge. More so.

# Chapter Six

It is never a smart move to tell a newshound to push off. It only makes him want to push on. This is a basic lesson which trouser-dropping celebs and dodgy Cabinet Ministers fail to grasp. They hide themselves from us and bleat about invasions of privacy. The upshot is we bivouac on their doorsteps for weeks and root around for further scandals in their tawdry lives. And we find 'em. What they should do, as soon as the story breaks, is invite the hacks in, offer them cups of tea – nothing stronger – and say: 'It's a fair cop. I've been a naughty boy.' Ten minutes later it's all over. You see, if they invite us to invade their privacy, it's no fun anymore. It's like telling a schoolboy to come scrump your apples. Besides, we love being hated.

Another thing people should know is threats don't scare us. We reserve all our fear and deep dread terror for News Desk. News Desk has the power to do terrible things to us, like bounce our exes or give us the boot. We wake in the night, a cold sweat upon us, hearing the voice of the Desk demand: 'How come the *Mail* got the mother?' Such is the nightmare of every true hack.

Therefore I was not all that worried about my

mystery caller. The one thing that bothered me was how he got my number, for I'm ex-directory. Not only am I ex-d, but I'm ex-d in my sister's married name, and I'm very choosy about whom I give my number. I was intrigued about why my caller felt it necessary to warn me off. I must be getting close to something and I wanted to get a damn sight closer. Close enough to understand what was going on.

I thought about my caller's voice. It was not one of those cor blimey smash-yer-face-in types which are such a lively feature of Old Bailey reporting. This bloke sounded middle class, educated, in control of his faculties, if a mite melodramatic. He had not denied choking our Shirley, but then he might just have wanted me to believe he was capable of murder. I gave up and clambered into my welcoming bed.

In the morning, after a gallon or two of tea, I rang the Tournier incident room, got Harry and told him someone was threatening to do me in. I heard him shout round the room: 'Did any of you phone Max Chard last night?' which is the closest Harry has ever come to cracking a joke. He took the details anyway, laughed heartlessly and suggested my caller might be Shirley's jealous boyfriend. H was in sparkling form this morning.

I was not so effervescent. I hung around the Bailey, knocked off a piece on a fine upstanding pillar of the community who went out and knifed three coppers. Despite the fact that the incident was witnessed by half of west London, it took the jury two hours to make their minds up.

Afterwards there was nothing else to do so I

headed back to the office and, inspired by my late night caller, started sifting through cuttings on Sir James, Claudine and the Foundation. In Tomlin's file there was a diary item about his divorce from Wife Two, an unpleasant affair by the sound of it. A year before that there was a cosy women's section interview with Wife Two at her home in Virginia Water. She was big on charity and small on talking about herself, though that might just be the interviewer's ineptitude. I tried directory inquiries. No, they didn't have any listings for a Tomlin in Virginia Water. Maybe she'd gone back to her maiden name. I phoned directory again. Yes, there were two M. Fords, both ex-d. I said, 'Oh dear, this is her son's year tutor. I must speak to her urgently about his school trip. There has been an accident . . .'

The operator was sympathetic but refused to play. I said, 'Perhaps I'd better drive round to her house. Do you have a Ford in Fairham or Fairburn Way?'

The operator forgot herself. 'No. One's in Primrose Avenue, the other in Badger View.'

Which was all I wanted. At the back of our library is a stack of reverse directories which are strictly illegal. They cost us a bundle. I turned to North Surrey and Primrose Avenue. At number 72 there dwelt an M. W. Ford. Not my Margaret Delsey. I tried Badger View. Yes, there she blew. M.D. Ford at number 26.

I told News Desk what I was up to and ventured by train and taxi to darkest Surrey. It was a balmy May afternoon with a playful breeze rippling through the cherry trees or whatever they were. Badger View gave off the scent of freshly-mown money. Big houses, big cars, big burglar alarms. Here and there the hired help toiled manfully in perfect gardens. Otherwise there wasn't a soul for miles around. I didn't view any badgers either. I tiptoed up the garden path so as not to wake the neighbours and pushed the bell on a front door big enough to cover a garage. In the middle of the door there was a bobbly glass panel. Presently a face swam into view behind it. It was hard to tell if it was Quasimodo or just the distortion of the glass. On my side I wasted a perfectly good smile. The door opened about a foot. 'Yes?' she said. She was Margaret Delsey Ford, as was, Margaret Tomlin, as she became, and was now right back to Margaret Delsey Ford again.

I said she didn't know me, which was true, showed her my press pass and asked if I could talk to her about James Tomlin.

She said, 'Come in.'

I was barely over the threshold, my brain still reeling from the shock, when she said, 'Drink?'

I think I needed brandy, but I settled for gin & tonic. She dished it up in a glass vase. She was equally kind to herself. She threw herself with enthusiasm into an adjoining chair and hoisted her vase. 'Cheers!' she said in Australian. That explained things. I knocked back a goodly sip and looked around. A big airy room, with billowy chairs and sofas, yellow wall-paper and yellow wood tables. The Tudor beams were all wrong. My eyes came back to her. I don't know what Sir James's secret allure was, but he could certainly catch 'em. He must have a certain je ne sais quoi, or what the French would call I don't know what. This version was tall and dark. In a couple of years her hair would be just brushed with grey. She had an open vivacious face and a smile that lurked on the brink of laughter. She had a toothsome overbite. She said, 'Call me Margie. Now, what can I tell you about the little ratbag?'

A woman after my own heart. I owned up and said I didn't know what I wanted to hear about Tomlin, so, could she just chatter on and we'd see what came out. She said great, and let rip a muscular laugh.

'First of all,' she said when she'd recovered herself, 'Sir Jimmy Tomlin is a snake, though that's not fair to snakes. He's a money-grubbing, egotistical, smarmy, little bastard. Those are his good points.'

If I wasn't already promised to Rosie Bannister, I would have run off with Margie Ford right there and then. I looked at her frankly. She was decked out in an outsize bright blue casual shirt with baggy beige pants. No shoes. I said, 'There's something that really puzzles me: how does Tomlin do it?'

'Beg pardon?'

'What do girls like you see in him?'

Margie drank deep of her gin and pondered this. She said, 'Have you ever read Graham Greene?'

'Not so as you'd notice.'

She said, 'Greene says when two people are in love, each is in love with the other's image of himself or herself.'

I said, 'Greene says that?'

She shook her hair at me. 'You don't get it. Let me give you a fr'instance. Fr'instance an Ozzie secretary arrives in London still wet behind the ears and lands a job with a fabulously wealthy man. Well, fabulously wealthy by Brisbane standards. Before she knows it, he's inviting her out to dinner where he spends more on the wine than she earns in a month. The little squirt looks into her eyes and tells her she's the greatest thing out of Oz since Dame Nellie Melba. He buys her flowers – fields of roses. He takes her to Ascot. Miss Nobody from Nowhere gets within spitting distance of the Queen. They go skiing. St Moritz, would you believe. They fly Concorde to the States. Wherever they go, there are people fawning and drooling over him. And her. He keeps giving her all this claptrap about how wonderful she is. Then one day he takes her to Maxim's, the Paris one, and he gives her a little box. "Will you marry me?" he says. And she says, "Just give me a sec to change my briefs." And that's what happened. I fell in love with his image of myself, just like Graham Greene says.'

I said, 'Maybe this explains Jack Nicholson's success.'

She said, 'Maybe he's got something else.'

I said, 'Yours was a whirlwind romance?'

Margie nodded. She snatched my vase and made free with the gin again. She was a shade mean in the tonic department.

She said over her shoulder, 'But we didn't live happily ever after. Two, three years at best. In the meantime I went home to mum who was pretty sick. I think it was then Jimmy started playing around.'

'With Claudine?'

Margie settled down again. 'No way. She was

absolute yonks after that. He was well in with a bunch of creeps and wowsers like Lewis Trefoyle.'

Well, well, well. Lewis Trefoyle. Isn't life funny?

Margie was saying, 'And there was that ginger guy who's a big cheese in the Jockey Club.'

'Clernthorpe?'

'Yes, Gus Clernthorpe. Now there's another weirdo for you.'

Margie sunk herself in her gin and brooded over past wounds. She said, 'Next thing I know is Jimmy's in the sack with Clernthorpe's ex. In that mob everyone was playing doctors with everyone else. And it didn't matter what sex they were.'

I said, 'Is Sir James a bit bi?'

'No, not him. But all the rest of them were at it like knives. Every time I see that smug bastard Trefoyle on the telly, I laugh so much I nearly spill my drink.'

I said, 'When you heard what Tomlin was up to, you kicked him out?'

'Flat on his skinny little backside,' she said with relish.

I said, 'You have a son.'

Margie went very still. She picked the words as if she was picking nettles. 'I had a stepson,' she said. 'He was at boarding school. He seemed an okay kid then. After uni he got a job with his father. I don't see him anymore.'

'Is that sad?'

Margie fidgeted with her cushion, looked into her glass, tugged at her sleeve and generally made it known she didn't want to talk about it. That was tough because I did. I hung back waiting.

The words came in a rush. 'It's no loss, Maxie. I don't want to see him either. If anything, he's worse than his father, and that's saying it all.'

'How?' I pushed.

'It doesn't matter how. He's weird.'

'Like Lewis Trefoyle is weird?'

Margie nodded her head but was silent. The silence lingered.

I said, 'Do you mean gay?'

'Hell, no. There's nothing weird about that these days.'

I said, 'Well, what do you mean by weird?'

She tossed her head back. She said, 'Look, let's leave this. I don't want to talk about it. They're just weird.'

So what do these geezers do? I mused. Drink lemonade or something? I backed off. I said, 'The police suspect Tomlin of having Claudine murdered.'

She was amused. 'They've got that one wrong. He's too sneaky for that. He'd just let her divorce him, pay up and move on to the next girl with beans for brains.'

I said, 'What if he had money troubles and couldn't afford to pay up?'

'Jimmy never has money troubles. That gang he hangs around with look after each other. Fleas on a dog's tail, they are. I reckon they've all got something on each other from when they were at Winchester or Eton or one of those dumps.'

I said, 'What about someone else in the pack killing Claudine?'

'Sure. They're capable of it. But why bother?'

Margie uncoiled to liberate the gin and I reviewed the story so far. She'd given me some lively stuff, but I couldn't see what use I could make of it.

I said, 'Do you know Leon Knapp?'

'What, old Crap Knapp? Yeah, he's one of the dead-beats too.'

I said I didn't see him as the public school pin-stripe type. Margie said, 'No, it's funny that. Maybe they liked his singing.' We both had a good laugh over that one.

But she didn't laugh when I threw into the conversation the story of my dead of night caller. Her big happy bunny smile vanished like snow off a ditch. She said, 'You better watch out.'

I said, 'That's what he said.'

She frowned. 'No, I'm serious. That bunch are capable of anything. I ain't joking.'

I promised to lock my doors and never to take sweets from strange men. That didn't seem to reassure her. So I said, 'Tell me about Brisbane', and the sun shone again. She chattered on for a while until I consulted my fake Rolex which said ten past five. By now I knew more about Brisbane than was necessary. I thanked Margie. She said no sweat, she'd enjoyed it, and if I fancied another drink . . .

I looked at her and she looked at me a second longer than was polite. There were flecks of brown in her green eyes. She was smiling. Then a vision of Rosie with a corkscrew came between us. I made my excuses and left.

I caught a cruddy little train where they wouldn't let me smoke but it was belting out great clouds of diesel. I phoned Rosie to let her know her loving man was homeward bound. It was a grievous blunder. It gave her time to prepare a meal. My normal practice is to pop up unannounced. That way we get to sample the international cuisine on offer down Woolaton Road. One night it's afelia with roast potatoes, the next it's spring rolls and something in chilli black bean sauce, or cod and chips. All good healthy wholesome stuff. Rosie's home cooking is a different kettle of fish altogether. She's more a gardener than a cook. Everything is green. She eats more spinach than Popeye. Tonight's bill of fare was salad with olives and the smallest plaice fillet ever caught in British waters. There was also a heap of baldy little new potatoes. Rosie tucked in and professed herself well satisfied. I lied and opened a bottle of frascati to drown the taste.

We reviewed our respective days as we hid the plates in the dishwasher: she had lunched with a Selfridge's buyer who showed interest in her lizards. She promised me a treat if the deal came through. I suggested dinner out. I told her about my meeting with the Brisbane Belle. When I'd finished, she said, 'Bloody typical.'

I said, 'What is?'

She said, 'Claudine's Foundation.'

'Eh?'

Rosie said, 'Claudine gets the idea for the Foundation to help the sick and poor; but look who runs it – her crummy husband and his old school tie pals.'

I said, 'Maybe that's because they can count, or they can con their rich friends into handing over large sums.'

Rosie said, 'Phooey', or something worse.

I said, 'How dare you impugn Sir James.'

We were sitting down now on the sofa so her punch didn't hit home. She poured the rest of the frascati into her glass. A dirty trick.

I said, 'Jimmy and his weirdos club together to give Mrs Jimmy a helping hand with her pet project. What's wrong with that?'

A snort from the south end of the sofa. Rosie said, 'I bet you all the money in the WorldCare Foundation is controlled by him. If he wanted to embezzle it, she'd never know.'

I thought about it and had to concede she might be right. It's probably all that spinach she packs away. I reached in my pocket and picked out the Foundation letter I'd copied when I gave Harry Pennycuik my statement. The heading listed the trustees. Tomlin himself, Proudhoe Veizey the alleged actor, Martin Crowley, whoever he might be, Leon Knapp wherever he might be, Gus Clernthorpe the Jockey Club joker, and one H. M. J. Tomlin. The hon. press was our old friend Lewis Trefoyle MP, PC, QC etc. Every man jack of them a bosom buddy of Sir James, unless Martin Crowley was a decent soul. I didn't think so.

Rosie draped herself across me to read the letter-head. She said, 'Told you so.'

I said, 'Who, and if so, why, is Martin Crowley?'

'The round the world man.'

It came back to me. Crowley was the toff who circumnavigated the globe in a sieve or something. It was an eight day wonder in the heavies. Having won her argument, Rosie was bored. She said, 'There's damn all on TV.'

I suggested an early night. She messed up my hair. And so the two of us rumpled the cushions for a while. Suddenly she sprung free and held me at bay with a finger stuck in my chest. She announced, 'Hey, I've found a great deal for the Maldives.'

I said, 'And who are they when they're at home?'

She said, 'You know, the Maldives. The islands. You're due for a holiday and you promised we'd go somewhere special.'

'Do they have bars in the Maldives?' I asked, wary after reading that bit about Poya Days in Sri Lanka.

'Stacks of them. Every street corner has one.'

I said, 'I don't fancy it anyway. We'd end up lying on our bum staring at the sun all day long.'

Rosie pictured herself lying on her bum staring at the sun. 'So?'

We were deep in argument when the phone broke in. Night Desk and the ever cheery voice of Vic.

'Have you seen the *Mirror*?' he demanded.

Considering his edition was hot off the presses, I considered this pretty dumb. But I just said no.

Vic said, 'We need to catch up on their splash.'

'Which is?'

He read it to me in tones which would never win him any prizes for elocution. The great thing about the *Mirror* is their stories are as short as ours, so he finished it before I could fall asleep. He said, 'We need copy in ten minutes top whack.'

I said it was a load of bilge but if he wanted it, he'd get it. The story concerned a former copper in the

Royal Protection Squad who had put a senorita in the family way when he was supposed to be guarding Prince Charles during a Spanish holiday. Gripping stuff, you'll agree.

How, you might ask, can I get the story from cold in ten mins? Fortunately there is honour among thieves. The age-old practice among hacks is to let a story run as an exclusive in your own first edition and then share it around the pack. I rang Geordie, my opposite number at the *Mirror*, and bawled at him for not telling me. He said oops, he thought it wasn't worth passing on. I had to agree. I said, 'Is it kosher?' He said as kosher as gefilte fish, which was a pleasant change from his usual drink-inspired copy. The *Mirror*'s stringer in Madrid had even spoken to Senorita Con Infanta herself. So I put the phone down, rephrased the *Mirror* stuff, for Geordie is not the most literate of men, and let Vic have it. He didn't say thanks.

Rosie was still off sunning herself in the Maldives. She spoke eloquently of azure seas and tropical palms nodding their sleepy heads in the noonday sun. I said not a word, but my silence was every bit as eloquent.

'You're a selfish git,' she said, and wrecked my hair again.

The police called a morning press conf. at Leman Street nick. Big Ben Ashbee was the master of ceremonies. He looked even sadder than usual. I put it down to a deserved hangover from last night's thrash. Ben kicked off the proceedings, saying the murder squad required the public's help in retracing Claudine's movements on the night of her shooting. A polite way of saying they hadn't a clue. For the purposes of the exercise they had a WPC with fat legs kitted out in a white mac. She was supposed to resemble Claudine. I look more like Claudine. I don't have a moustache.

We all hoofed it down to St Katharine's Dock where the pretend Claudine sauntered up and down smiling for the monkeys. Big Ben said she would strut her stuff again at 8 pm in the fond hope it would jog the memory of the evening drinkers. I suggested he got another WPC, wrap a rope round her neck and chuck her in the dock in the fond hope someone might remember Shirley's last minutes. Ben told me to go away.

I went off to the Tower hotel where I sat with a pint knocking out a picture caption.

*Dressed to kill . . . a plucky police girl walks the lonely quayside where sexy socialite Claudine Tournier was slain.*

*WPC Anne Scott bravely volunteered for the tragic role because of her uncanny resemblance to the murdered woman.*

*She wore an identical designer mac for her grim mission at the Thames marina where . . .*

And so on. You don't really want to hear it. But that line about the marina had given me an idea. I quit the hotel and navigated round to the Port O'Call where the Kiwi barmaid greeted me with dancing eyes. I reciprocated by ordering a glass of New Zealand pinot noir. The place was calm as they hadn't uncaged the city gents for their lunch yet. I inspected the walls which featured yachts the size of the *QE2* and weather-grained veterans of the briny deep. I pointed to one old buffer and said, 'I suppose you get lots of these in here?'

She said, 'The ancient mariners? Oh yeah.'

I mentioned a few names, dropping Crowley's into the pot. She didn't know half of them, which was hardly surprising as I just made them up. But Crowley she did know. He pops in every now and then. Seems a nice guy. Doesn't drink much. Her knowledge of nice guys is somewhat narrow.

And has he been in recently? I asked, as if I was making light conversation. She said no. She thought it over. She said yes. He'd been in last week. I said I'd bought his book and would love him to autograph it for me. Was he in the night I was there? And what night was that? she asked. I ordered another glass of what folks drink in New Zealand when they're feeling frisky. I pretended to think about it.

'Oh, I know,' I said brightly. 'It was the night that woman was murdered.'

'Which one?'

I'd forgotten that murdering women was a nightly sport in these parts. I said, 'I think it must have been the first one.'

'Who? Claudine Tournier?'

'Yes, her.'

The barmaid said, 'God, wasn't that awful? I mean, when you think of all the great work she's been doing in Africa and India, I mean, who would want to murder her?'

I nodded my head in sad agreement. First, Claudine gets holed in the temporal lobe, then Poland stuffs England three-nil. What is the world coming to?

Miss Kiwi was raving on about Claudine's beauty, her riches, her generosity. I called her to heel. 'Was he in that night?'

'Was who in?'

'Martin Crowley.'

She said, 'Oh, him. Yeah, I think he was. Him and another guy.'

'Another ancient mariner?'

'Naoow. The other one was a business type.'

I said, 'Maybe a weekend sailor?'

She said, 'Too soft for that. Why all the interest in Martin Crowley, anyway?'

I repeated my feeble excuse about wanting him to autograph his boring book. She said, 'Oh yeah', but didn't look convinced. I said cheerio and she winked a fond farewell. It was probably something indecent in morse code.

The Piltdown Man wanted to see me. Why? I asked Angie. She got busy with her bits of paper, averted her eyes and muttered something about exes. I straightened my tie and went in search of Tony Belker, regretting there wasn't time to equip myself with a silver crucifix, a Holy Bible and maybe a sharpened wooden stake.

He had his blinds drawn because he was watching TV golf. He immediately clicked to CeeFax when I entered. 'Siddown!' he commanded. He stood up. I suppose this is a trick they learn on power management courses. Lesson One: How to make your staff feel inferior. I took a look at his paunch and felt infinitely superior. I sat, one leg hooked over the other, and switched on a 100-watt smile. He frowned at his bitten fingernails. Belker is living proof that man and warthog must never again mate. He's got little piggy eyes set deep beneath a chevron of bushy brows. There's maybe an inch of forehead before the hairline begins. He's florid, fat, fifty and, with a bit of luck, should keel over with a heart attack any day now. I sat there thinking what I would write on his wreath while he rummaged in a drawer. He produced my expenses, slapped a paw on them and said, 'How do you account for these?'

I said, 'Ah, I'm glad you mentioned them. I forgot to charge for phone calls.'

He said, 'You've charged for everything else you could think of.'

He didn't mean it as a compliment but I nodded gracious acknowledgement. Belker picked up the exes, turned his back on me, and shook them in a fury. He never looks you in the eye. He said, 'Extortionate claims like these set my teeth on edge.'

I said, 'Oh yes. I forgot the toothbrush. And the toothpaste.'

'What?' A porcine squeal.

I said, 'It was a rush job. I didn't have time to pack. I had to buy a toothbrush.'

Belker's shoulders trembled in Neanderthal rage. He still had his back turned, affording me a wide panorama of his backside. Fat-assed men should wear overcoats at all times. He said, 'I will not tolerate expenses fiddles. You have charged for two interpreters.'

I said, 'Noblesse oblige.'

'What?'

I explained my French was not up to coping with the heady accents of Geneva or Brittany. Belker flung a glare over his shoulder. He sucked air through his teeth and tried to regain his bestial composure. He returned to the fray.

'I accept foreign exes can be high, but they are not there for reporters to defraud the paper out of hundreds of pounds. This sort of claim rips the arse out of exes.'

I said, 'And Y-Fronts. I forgot to claim for underwear.'

Belker goggled in outrage. He flapped his arms wildly, bounced off the wall and pointed at the door. I uncrossed my legs, smiled at him again and quit the world of the undead. Behind me, Belker got his voice back. He yelled, 'You've really blown it this time, Chard. You'll regret ever daring to submit these exes.'

And he was probably right. I resolved to keep my nose clean and sleep with a string of garlic around my neck.

# Chapter Seven

Next morning the bunch of dysfunctionals which passes as an Old Bailey jury retired to consider their verdict in the Silence of the Crams case. Half an hour later they were back, in solid agreement that Stan Cram and his haggish wife Vi were guilty of the murder of their au pair. I think it was the fact Stan used to be an estate agent that swung things.

Mr Justice Seamley got on his high horse and described the couple as wicked, villainous, and generally a bad lot. Stan got life with a recommended minimum of 20 years. Vi got life, which meant she could be out barbecuing au pairs again in seven years. Justice was seen to be done.

The gentlemen of the Press adjourned to Harry's Bar to look at their notebooks. Most time our shorthand is so atrocious that we get together and make up quotes, but today there was a hackette from the *Telegraph* who had a verbatim note of the proceedings. The snag was that it took her half the morning to go through her brimming notebook and dig out the lively stuff. It wasn't as good as the quotes we make up.

Armed at last with all the guff and a gin, I sat down to compose. Reporters, the tabloid hacks especially, work to a rigid formula. We take a news event and revamp it as a piece of soap opera. We are basically playwrights. We have a set cast of characters and a simple plot. General news reporters are luckier than crime people because they get to play with a slightly larger cast. Our playlets feature a baddie, a goodie and a victim. Sometimes, as when a have-a-go hero gets himself killed, the goodie and victim are rolled into one, leaving us with a cast of two. We sift through the wearisome hours of courtroom blarney to furnish our actors with their lines. We re-enact the dirty deed, editing out the humdrum bits, and there you have it. A tale of murder most foul told in 500 words, not counting the by-line.

In the Cram case we had a couple of ace baddies. The tabloid crime journo's favourite word, evil, fitted them like a wetsuit. Plus, he was a furtive, oily, little weasel, while Vi Cram had all the native charm of a meter maid. The victim was another great character – a 21-year-old Kurdish refugee who had fled Saddam's waves of war only to be grilled on a Surbiton patio. She would have been better still had she not looked like Mahatma Gandhi, right down to the specs.

The Crams deserved more than the standard 500 golden words. They got about five times that. The gruesome twosome had belted their au pair with a claw hammer last Whitsun for reasons unknown, but it was widely assumed she was threatening to tell the police that Stan had raped her. Afterwards Vi chopped her in chunks and burned her on the barbie. In custody they never once coughed or said oops, despite hours of Plod interrogation – so that gave us the Silence of the Crams motif.

Besides my lead story, featuring Mr Justice Seamley's 'heartless and horrific' crack, I supplied a handful of pre-written background pieces on the killer king and queen of Stirton Close. We unearthed an ex-wife – 'Stan had mad, staring eyes', and Vi's broken-hearted mother – 'I Hope my Daughter Rots in Hell', and a clutch of neighbours – 'The Monsters Next Door'. Neighbours often serve as sort of spear carriers in our dramas. They march on stage, deliver their asides, and get to hell off so that we can concentrate on the real stars. The victim's family were unable to come up with any good lines, largely because they didn't speak English. That didn't stop us attributing the odd red-blooded quote to them. Dad apparently said he'd give the world for a blunt breadknife and five minutes alone with Stan Cram. Mum said Vi was more cruel than Saddam. It made a rattling good yarn, just the thing our readers like served up with their cornflakes.

I phoned my copy through and asked to be put on to News Desk. I got Norbert, our dithering foreign editor, which meant that Angela Whipple and all the other empty vessels were off somewhere getting tanked up.

I told Norbert I was seeing contacts but would keep in touch. Norbert said he wished he could join me. I said yes, that's too bad, but I'd have a drink for him anyway. We were running out of pleasantries when he remembered he wanted to tell me something.

He said, 'You know your friend, Leon Knapp?'

I said he wasn't my friend, but what about him?

Norbert said, 'He's turned up.'

'Dead?' I asked hopefully.

Norbert treated me to a tolerant chortle. 'No, no, no. He's alive, but not terribly well.'

'That's bad,' I said, inspecting my empty glass. 'I'll hear about it later. Where was he?'

Norbert couldn't remember. Somewhere in the Middle East. Oh yes, Amman.

I bade him bye bye and pondered. Amman. What on earth was Knapp doing there? Jordan is hardly renowned as a mecca for coke snorters. Maybe he was doing a Cat Stevens and turning Moslem. The hackette from the *Telegraph* tapped me on the shoulder and said it was her round. I forgot Leon Mustafa Knapp.

I made it back to the office some time late in the afternoon. No one wanted me and I needed a cup of boot black coffee with extra sugar before I remembered why I had bothered to show. The case of the unvanishing Knapp. I switched on my console, typed in my password, *crippen*, and began ploughing through the tapes. It wasn't on staff copy, freelance, foreign stringers or Reuters. I finally ran it to ground on Associated Press who didn't think the story particularly riveting. Their staffer in Oman – not Amman – had filed as follows:

*OMAN, Friday – The former English pop singer,*

*Leon Knapp, was admitted to the American Hospital here today, said to be suffering from acute stomach pains.*

*A medical spokesman at the hospital said that Knapp required emergency treatment but his condition was not listed as serious. The 48-year-old singer, an overnight celebrity in the Seventies, was en route to London when he was taken ill.*

*An ambulance met his plane at Oman International Airport, and paramedics carried Knapp to a waiting ambulance. He was said to have been travelling alone.*

*In London, England there has been recent concern for the singer's welfare following reports that he had failed to fulfil several long-standing commitments.*

*In the Seventies, Knapp, from Birmingham, England sold millions of records worldwide. His most famous song, 'Bananas For You', was simultaneously a number one hit in Britain and the United States.*

And that was it. Not a word about where the lonely Leon had picked up his bellyache, no mention of drugs.

I'd like to say I had a hack's hunch. But I cannot lie. I just had a sudden whim. I rang AP's London office, said we were doing up the Knapp story, and could I have the number for their man in Oman. I certainly could. I phoned the sunny sheikhdom and got a lady who was on the first disc of her Berlioz course in English. 'Jus' mommem pliz,' she instructed. A mommem later on came the author himself. Nope, sorry, he knew nothing more of our Leon. The plane was a KLM 747, winging home to Amsterdam. I said fine, but where did it come from.

Even before he opened his mouth, I knew what was coming.

Sri Lanka.

Call it a hack's hunch.

Hotfoot and panting, I charged up to News Desk and broke the glad tidings to Angie. She was in the middle of dictating her schedule for evening conference so she was not pleased to see me. She made it clear she cared as much about where Knapp had been hiding himself as she did about European sugar beet subsidies. Talk to me later, she said, hoping I'd go off, have a drink and forget about it.

I was not to be put off. Angela sighed and said, 'All right. Go and talk to Belker and see if he falls for it.'

I began to regret yesterday's tête à tête with The Man With Two Bums, but I summoned up my nerve and battered on his door. He was peeved at having his TV golf interrupted again. When he saw it was me, he was even less delighted. I spelt out the story for him, mentioning Kandy every third word.

He let me run through my whole spiel. Then he smiled. It was not a 'Great idea, Max!' smile; more of a 'You are a worm beneath my feet, Chard, and you haven't got a hope' smile.

He made me wait for his answer. He reached in his top drawer and withdrew my exes claim. He poked it with a sausage finger. He said, 'You are a luxury we cannot afford. If I was sending to Sri Lanka, which I'm not, I would not send you. I wouldn't send you as far as Clapham Common – not after this.'

He hoisted my exes aloft and let them fall, fluttering forlorn to the floor. I said we might be missing a great story. Belker said he could live with that. I said he was a loathsome, fat, foul-breathed, pompous imbecile with the news judgement of a baboon. But I said it to myself so he kept on smiling. I closed the door on his smile and trooped back to my corner of the news room. Around me merry hacks hammered out stories, pausing only to ask questions of each other: 'Who's the Prime Minister?' 'How many v's in evil?'

For once I did not help them out. I rang The Stone dive bar, told them to set me up a pint and I was gone like a thief in the night.

I got home early and mooched around the place with nothing to do. I stuck a Bob Marley disc in the player but it made me think of sunny places: places like Sri Lanka. I pressed eject. I was debating whether to slit my wrists or overdose on milk when the phone warbled. Rosie. 'Coming round?' she asked.

'We eat out?'

'You paying?'

'Why not?'

We settled for Thai. Beef in green curry sauce for me, oodles of noodles for her. She listened to my tale of woe and called Belker a few things I hadn't thought of. I had just got round to thinking what a wise and wonderful woman Rosie is when, ever so casually, she slipped it in. She said, 'Thought any more about the Maldives?'

I told her I had thought considerably less about the Maldives. She pouted at her noodles and said a holiday was just what I needed to stop me turning into an old grump. She dived into her bag and whipped out a travel brochure. It represented the Maldives as paradise minus the bad bits. Sun, sand, sea, snorkelling and lots of other things beginning with S, though it didn't mention sex, sunburn or scotch.

'It doesn't say anything about bars,' I said.

Rosie pointed at a mixed quarter of nutters grinning out of the page. 'They're drinking,' she said.

'It might be water.'

She clicked her tongue. 'Honestly, drink is all you ever think about.'

'Not entirely all.'

She turned on the famous dirty laugh and an adjacent voyeur poured lemon grass soup down his shirt. Rosie said, 'Are you staying with me tonight?'

We have a very simple arrangement which I do not understand. Three, sometimes four nights a week she lets me share the duvet down in Battersea. The rest of the time she chooses to live alone. Alone, apart from her toffee-nosed cat, Blue, who eyes me askance and shimmies his backside at me. At least I have the satisfaction of knowing that all my private parts are where they ought to be.

Rosie never explains why half the time she doesn't want me around the place. I don't think she and I could ever marry, because I'd have to spend every other night kipping in a bus shelter. There is no forward planning to our arrangement. She simply says, 'Are you staying tonight?' and I stay.

As always, I told her I'd be there to hold her hand through the long night watches, but first I had to leg it back to my place for a fresh supply of clothes. I paid the bill, persuaded a reluctant Thai into parting with a couple of blank receipts, kissed Rosie au revoir and semaphored a cab.

My place is surprisingly neat. I like clothes, so I hang my suits up every night, regardless of what state I'm in. Similarly, I unknot my ties, drape them on the rack, consign my grubby shirts etc. to the laundry bin. I even have a few pairs of shoe trees for my Loakes. I don't spend a lot of time in my flat, regarding it rather as a hotel bedroom with a kitchen tacked on. There is also the lounge and beyond it a patch of mouldy grass where one might sit enjoying the sun. Two might find it a bit of a squeeze. Inside, the overall mood is a pensive grey, which I find least distressing in the mornings. There's little in the way of decoration. Rosie says that's because I haven't bonded with the flat and don't feel like sharing my identity with it. I said she might be right because I don't share my drink with it either. But apparently that's different.

When I got home I tuned in the answerphone. Tommy, my partner in crime from the *Express*, reported he had tickets for the England visit to Landsdowne Road, and did I fancy a drunken weekend by the banks of the Liffey with a rugby match to boot. Indeed I did. I made a mental note to call him soonest. There was also a rather subdued call from Ross Gavney, saying he wanted to talk to me urgently. I glanced at my watch and phoned his Magpie Court flat. I heard seven rings before his answer phone chipped in to tell me he was not available at present but would I leave my message after the beep and he would get back to me. I told him I was the competitions manager of the *Reader's Digest* and I was calling him, Mister Ross Gavney, as a valued customer, to let him know he hadn't won a thing. Just on the off chance, I called his office. The phone rang on and on unheard.

It was getting late now, and Rosie becomes fractious when I'm late. I shot off to the bedroom, unhooked a lightweight black and grey two-piece, a Sea Island cotton shirt with a hint of apricot, a Paco Rabanne tie of misty blue. I keep an overnight bag stocked to the gills with socks, underpants, notebooks, pens, a tape recorder, batteries and aspirin. I was dragging it off the shelf when something disturbed me. It wasn't a noise. It was more a movement in the air. I paused and cocked an ear. Nothing, apart from the usual background sounds of all-in sumo wrestling from the flat upstairs. I stood still and wound back my memory, wondering whether I had locked the Chubb security before I went out this morning. Us crime reporters are all too aware of the burglary statistics in London. We are even more aware of Plod's manifest ineptitude at catching burglars.

I pictured myself returning to the flat. No. I had just used the Yale key to get in. So there might be someone else in the vicinity. I eased off my shoes, wrapped my keys around my hand like a knuckleduster and went exploring on tiptoe. The lounge was asleep and empty. I parted the curtains across the patio doors. No lurkers out there. But there was still a vague sense of something wrong, that someone else was sharing my space. I tried the bathroom and peered into the shower cubicle. Not a soul. If I had an intruder, it wasn't Psycho. I was padding down the narrow hallway towards the kitchen when my supersensory perception detected something which did not belong. A faint but distinct whiff of petrol. I do not have a car. I stopped in mid-stride and considered the petrol motif. If someone is planning to torch your flat, there is a set procedure to the way they go about it. The routine is they lift the letterbox, squirt a jet of petrol through it, light a match and retire to a safe distance. That's the way they do it. Secure in such knowledge, I wheeled about, tramped back up the hallway to the front door and got down on my hands and knees for a good sniff. Alas, the petrol merchant was not au fait with the rules on torching people's flats. For even as I knelt there, snorting at the berber, he sneaked up behind me and smacked me on the head with a refrigerator. My teeth bit the carpet.

My brain said, 'Sod this for a game of soldiers' and did a runner. I dragged it back and got my eyes working. They couldn't see much because they were flat against the floor, but they registered that the beige pile was turning reddy brown. Meanwhile, to my rear all was quiet, causing me to wonder whether her upstairs had fallen on me. My ears had gone on the blink and what feeling I had was concentrated on a great lump of crimson pain in the back of my head. If my sense of smell was operating, it had nothing to contribute to the proceedings. I waggled my tongue about and tasted that heady mix of salt and copper which doctors call blood.

After a while decked out in the hallway, I heard a groan, a long, aching, Gawd-help-us groan. It came from me. Apart from the pain in the head I felt warm and cosy and ever so sleepy. I was even getting to like lying there. Then something grabbed me by the ankles and I began to be towed backwards towards the lounge. My chin bumped along the floor leaving a muddy wake through the tufts. My shoulders, arms and hands stayed where they were. After a while they got the general idea and followed suit. It was a boring journey with not much in the way of scenery. I nodded off.

When I awoke I found myself sprawled in my Conran lounger. The world was a shade gloomy and black round the edges. I let my pupils sidle from side to side. Just off camera there was a fuzzy noise which I eventually worked out was the opening and closing of doors. A man appeared before me. I didn't know him from Adam, apart from the fact I don't believe Adam wore a ski mask. I gave the stranger my deepest concentration. He was of average height, average build and had a more than average penchant for black clothing. Sweater, trousers, gloves, the lot. I didn't think he had slipped in to give me a box of Cadbury's Milk Tray because the Milk Tray man doesn't wander around with a wheel brace in his mitt. I eliminated as suspects most of the men and some of the women I knew. My brain started playing Smart Alec. 'Aha!' it said. 'This geezer has just applied that wheel brace to your cranium.' I said thank you brain. I'd already figured that out myself. I studied him hard to see if there were any Clues I could pass on to the rozzers. I couldn't tell whether the wheel brace came from a BMW or a JCB. There wasn't even a Marks & Sparks tag sticking out the back of his jumper.

Burglar Bill paced around the lounge with average sized paces, poking in my nooks and crannies. He had a lot to learn about good housekeeping. He scattered books and tapes willy-nilly in his path. I moaned again, possibly thinking about all the mess I'd have to clean up. His head pivoted round and he glared at me. I'm guessing it was a glare. He disappeared from view and returned clutching a Clue – a black sports bag emblazoned with the legend Adidididadadadadasas. I subbed it down to Adidas. He ripped back the zipper and began stowing all the loot inside. It was about now that I realised my visitor was not the usual breed of burglar. He ignored the video and CDs galore, opting instead for every scrap of paper he could find. He was doing his burglar business when the telephone pealed out. He froze. I froze. Or at least I just sprawled there like a squid on a rock.

Brrriinnnng-brrriinnng! went the telephone. He let it. After a due interval I heard my tinny recorded voice inform the caller: 'I'm not here at the moment, or if I am, I'm in no state to talk to you. But feel free to chat to my machine.' The burglar and I listened to the message all the way through. So did the caller. Then he/she hung up without saying a word. Don't you just hate it when people do that? My burglar didn't like it either. He ripped the phone off the wall and trussed me to the chair with the cable. I thought it was time we got acquainted.

I said, 'The cheque's in the post.' My voice had a built-in echo.

No response from my captor. So he wasn't from American Express.

I had another go. 'I've never met your wife, and anyway, she seduced me.'

The burglar was as chatty as a dumb Trappist monk with laryngitis. I was not getting through here. A sudden flash of inspiration hit me like a wheel brace. I said, 'You are the Kandy Man and I claim my five pounds.'

That worked. He smacked me across the shins with his favourite toy. Through the pain I heard him say, 'You were warned.' His voice was blurred, or it might have been my hearing. He returned to his labours. He opened my briefcase and decanted its entire contents into his bag. I watched aghast as dozens of dodgy taxi bills and dinner receipts vanished from sight. I wondered briefly if he was a fellow hack with a lot of expenses to do. He paused to flip through a notebook full of my pidgin shorthand and about as readable as a Booker Prize winner.

He was not in any hurry. Every now and then he nipped off to scour the neighbourhood for hidey holes. At length he zipped up the bag and stood before me. I suspected he was about to clunk me with the wheel brace again, but no, he disappeared kitchenwards and returned clutching a gallon can of petrol. Or it might have been five litres.

He unscrewed the cap and began splashing it over

me and the chair. Oh hell, I thought. He slipped from vision again and I heard the cheery sploshing of four-star unleaded all over the place. I tested my bonds. There was some give. I squirmed a little and estimated I could wriggle free without much problem. But there was a big black question mark over whether I had the strength to stand up. I discussed tactics with myself. My brain suggested I feign unconsciousness, wait until my visitor had cleared off and then flee like the wind. I didn't argue.

When next my burglar flitted into view, I followed his movements through knitted eyelashes. My mouth was drooped open in vapid stupor. My breath came light and slow. He stood barely a yard away. I saw his arm swing back and he gave me another playful slap on the bean with his wheel brace. It didn't hurt at all. I wasn't being brave or anything – I just passed out. I passed back in, in time to see him scoop up the holdall. He was halfway out of the room when he remembered the wheel brace. He came back for it, presumably in case his JCB sprung a puncture on the way home.

I waited until I heard him fiddle at the front door before I began wrestling off the telephone cord. Then I heard a noise which put the fear of God into me. The rattle of a matchbox. I was out of the chair and on the floor even as he struck the match. The front door slammed and there was a Whooosh! from the hallway.

As feared, my legs refused to play and I pitched forward on my face to the floor. The sweet treacherous stench of petrol hung over everything, me especially. I forced my arms into action and scrabbled my way towards the patio doors. I think I ripped the curtain down because I got snagged up in it. The glass reflected a wall of flame behind me. I freed the bottom bolt and pushed. The door gave an inch. The top bolt said if you want this bloody door open, you're going to have to deal with me first. I gazed up at it in anguish. I could feel the heat now. I pushed at the door again. It stayed put. I looked around for something to smash the glass. The only weapon to hand was a paperback. Probably *Bonfire of the Vanities*. I gritted my teeth, closed my eyes, forced myself upright against the wall and grabbed that damn bolt. The agony was bloodcurdling. For a moment the door refused to budge and then it flew open, throwing me onto the patio. I clawed to the middle of the lawn, at which point there was a great hollow Booom! behind me and all the glass in the doors shot out.

I fought out of my petrol-soaked jacket and trousers and didn't bother to hang them up. There were little licks of flame racing across the lawn towards me, following my tracks. I salvaged the mobile from my pocket and dialled 999. The operator, a chatty type, asked me which service I required – fire, police or ambulance. I was feeling reckless. I ordered all three.

I squirmed back to the fence, tore off my shirt and waited for the sirens. I thought of the intruder and what he had done to my suits, my silks, my legs, my poor head. 'You bastard!' I screamed at the night. 'You filthy lump of dog turd. You vicious, stinking shit.' There was lots more of this. After a while I calmed down and started thinking about what I should do next. I could hardly wander the world in Y-Fronts and spotted socks. Fortunately Rosie allows me to keep a small stash of casual gear at her place. I thought about Rosie. I'd better tell her why I was late for the date. I called her number.

'I've been tied up,' I said wittily.

'You bastard,' she said wittily. And hung up.

# Chapter Eight

That night I slept in the stiff sheets of St Thomas's hospital. Doctors have a rule: if anyone ever bangs their head and loses consciousness, even for a fraction of a second, whoever owns the head must spend the night at the mercy of the National Health Service. I enjoyed myself.

They carted me off half naked to Casualty, my stretcher accompanied by a bulky Boy in Blue. He came in handy, explaining to the paramedics that I was not the victim of a foiled suicide attempt. I was, he told them, the skin-of-the-teeth survivor of a fire bombing. The nurses looked at me with awe and I reciprocated. I was wheeled down fifty miles of squeaking corridors where somebody zipped off x-rays, another white coat embroidered my skull, a third took my blood pressure (normal), a fourth applied cooking alcohol to my legs. I wasn't up to licking it off. A nurse with breasts like zeppelins slipped a thermometer under my tongue, nearly suffocating me in the process. My temperature was surprisingly normal. I put it down to shock.

They wheeled me backwards and forwards for an hour until they found a bed which was not already occupied. They gave me something vile to drink, possibly water, and a lethal cocktail of painkillers and sedatives.

They all went off to play with somebody else and I used the interlude to give Rosie another call. I had a hard job getting her to shut up and listen. It was worth the effort. In the end she came over all tearful and contrite. She was rotten and selfish, she told me, and that was a first. How could I forgive her? She'd make it up to me. I lay there on the crackling sheets having a whale of a time.

Rosie said, 'Are you badly hurt, love?'

I put on a stiff upper lip and moaned, 'Yes.'

Rosie wailed, 'I'll be right over.'

I whispered 'Okay' in a way that suggested she'd better hurry if she wanted to see her darling Max before St Peter did.

I also rang News Desk. Vic answered. So that's one suspect down the Swanee. He wanted to know every nasty little detail about my ordeal. I had a sneaking suspicion he was rooting for the burglar. He made me dictate a first person story: 'Our Crimebuster Beats Hellfire Murder Bid.' It's odd, reporting about yourself. It's also a bundle of fun. I lied about my age, and invented loads of exciting tosh that made the copytaker go 'Wow!' I verballed the burglar. He said he'd fry me like a slice of bacon. I dreamed up a few heroic quotes for myself. I spat defiance and told him to change his deodorant and where to stick his car jack. A pop-eyed sergeant sat by the bedside while I was dictating. After I'd done he got me to make a statement. And after that he was a disappointed man.

'So you didn't kick him in the groin?' he asked, ballpoint hovering.

'No.'

'But you just said . . .'

'Don't believe everything you read in the papers,' I said.

'And that bit about trying to rip off his mask?'

'Ditto.'

The sergeant looked as if he wished I'd gone whooof! in a blaze of glory instead of lying here making up porkies. I asked him if he had any drink concealed about his person. He said no. He probably had half a bottle of vodka tucked down his trousers, but he wasn't going to share it with some phoney hero. He cleared off, leaving me with a taciturn woodentop for company. I was grateful for his silence. It gave me time to think about the evening's adventure.

I had no doubt that Burglar Bill was up to his eye teeth in the Claudine Tournier affair. Why else should he belt me for mentioning Kandy? But why did he break in? His final intention was clear enough. He planned to torch the flat. Intruders don't cruise the streets of our city with jerrycans of petrol unless such is their intention. But then why was he tooled up with a wheel brace? Maybe that was in case he bumped into anyone. And why did he nick all my papers? There was nothing in the flat that would land anyone in trouble, apart from me. I keep a lot of info in my head. My contact book was in my pocket. The pocket of the jacket untidily discarded on my singed back lawn. I ticked myself off for leaving it behind. A hack's contact book is absolutely vital to him. For starters, that's where he keeps his pin number for the hole-in-the-wall beer token dispensers. Mine also contained hundreds of names and numbers, some of them very sensitive indeed. For instance, there's a man who used to be in Special Branch but now earns his keep in MI5 and who sometimes . . . maybe we'd better not go into that.

I thought about what else was in my jacket. My passport. Not so long ago a passport was an essential accessory for every proper hack. If you turned up in the office without it, you could be fired on the spot. And justly so. The principle was that if the office wanted to send you somewhere at a moment's notice you had to be ready. That was in the days when newspapers had news in them. You also need a second passport, one without a Tel Aviv entry, in case you're sent to Beirut, Damascus or one of those places where evidence of a visit to Israel is proof you are a Zionist spy. What else had I left on the lawn? Chequebook, credit cards, at least a hundred quid in readies, the Thai restaurant receipt. Oh yes, the WorldCare Foundation letter. Christ, I had to get that back before the Old Bill spotted it. I reflected that my burglar was downright careless in not frisking me. It suggested that Plan A was merely to toast the flat.

The questions chased each other down the back alleys of my mind until I heard the skippety-skip of heels heralding the arrival of Rosie. She was as fragrant as a meadow at dawn, flushed and fantastic. She leaned over me and poured kisses of sweet bounty on my fevered brow. I forgot the nurse with the zeppelins. Rosie kissed me on the lips, which was bloody painful as my teeth had gone halfway through them when the burglar bashed me. Every couple of seconds she broke off to tell me how much she loved me and that I was a poor thing and she would take care of me and cater to my every whim and how much she wanted me to be home with her. She was warming to her theme and I thought any minute now she's going to hop into bed beside me. I wished the nurse had left a couple of spare sedatives.

She lifted her hair out of my face and gave me a look of heart-tugging sympathy. I said, 'Have you brought a first aid kit?'

She bobbed her head, fished in her bag, and produced three miniatures of whisky. That would do for a start. She propped them on my bedside locker and added forty Bensons to the pile.

'You're a treasure,' I said, deeply moved.

I unscrewed one of the dinky little bottles and reached for a glass. I heard a loud 'Harrummph!' from the other side of the bed. The silent policeman had given voice. Maybe he wanted a tincture himself.

He pointed at the golden bottle. 'You're not supposed to touch that.'

I said, 'What?'

He said, 'It's dangerous to drink after taking sedatives.'

Rosie said belligerently, 'Are you a doctor or something?'

My bodyguard conceded he wasn't a doctor, but he had Experience of This Sort of Thing. Rosie said it was none of his business, and why wasn't he out catching the man who thumped me? PC 49 got to his feet and yelled, 'Nurse!'

Before I had time to stash my scotch under the pillow, a ministering angel appeared and trousered the lot. She wagged a finger at me. 'Sedatives and alcohol don't mix,' she said. 'And smoking is forbidden.'

I wanted to be home, or better still, at Rosie's place. I wagged a finger back at her. 'If you'd given me whisky, I wouldn't need sedation.'

She brushed an imaginary germ from the sheets and said, 'You've also had some very strong painkillers.'

'They're not working.'

Rosie did her Florence Nightingale bit. 'Are you very sore?'

I grimaced. 'All over. My head, my shins, my knees, my tonsils.'

The Angel of Death fluffed up my pillows. She said, 'What you need is a good night's sleep. That'll cure your aches and pains. You'll wake up feeling much, much better. Won't he officer?'

PC Spoilsport said that's right, sleep cures everything. It doesn't do much for sleeping sickness, I said, but I was too tired to argue the point.

The nurse turned on Rosie. 'Now, Mrs Chard. It's time you left. Your husband has just been through a great deal. I think we should let him rest, don't you?'

I don't think Rosie liked being called Mrs Chard, and I'm not sure she liked having me described as her husband. At any rate she nodded in dumb obedience. I wish I could get her to do that.

She flung her arms around my aching head, planted another juicy one on my lips and off she went. I watched her trim little bottom wiggle away and half of me went chasing after her.

Now she was gone I felt bloody awful. Wracked with pain is the expression that came to mind.

The nurse was scribbling something on the chart at the foot of my bed.

'How am I?' I asked.

'You're all right. You're not in any danger, if that's what you're thinking.'

I winced away a tidal wave of pain. I said, 'When people ring the hospital, what condition do you tell them I'm in?'

She smiled the smile of the truly insane.

'We tell them you're comfortable.'

They woke me at dawn with tea from the office machine, shovelled pills into me, and asked me how I was. I told them. They smiled in tender sorrow and went on to the next unfortunate. It was a small ward, about a dozen patients in varying states of decay. One man had a bandage like a turban all round his head. Another was encased in plaster and hanging from the ceiling. I didn't even have a strip of Elastoplast to show for my troubles. I felt aggrieved. My silent partner of the night before had gone, taking his considerable medical lore with him. If there was still a copper guarding me, he was either dolled up as a nurse or swathed in bandages.

I closed my eyes and sought sanctuary in sleep. A

nurse prodded me awake by popping a thermometer through my broken lips.

'My, my. You're quite a celebrity,' she said.

'Mmpphh?'

'Don't talk until I've taken your temperature. Yes,' she continued. 'I've been reading all about you in the paper.'

'Ooofwhumphuh?'

'Mouth closed, please. You can see it yourself in a minute. Read it over breakfast. You'll like that.'

I nodded vigorously. The back of my head fell off. She saw my agony and gave a cheery laugh like the tinkle of falling bedpans. She patted my lifeless wrist. 'Don't worry. We'll soon have you up and about.'

I said to myself, 'You bet. As soon as the pubs are open.'

She lied about me enjoying breakfast. I pushed it away so that it didn't put me off the paper. There was a short on page one about our ace crime reporter escaping death by a whisker. Full story: see page five. I saw page five. I beamed back at myself from a two column pic. I certainly didn't look like someone who had been almost frazzled. I read my glittering account. It was not bad, but for the fact that some halfwitted sub had seen fit to embellish my quotes, the ones I'd invented in the first place. I read: The raider smirked and said, 'Right, Chard, you know what happens to nosey parkers – they end up on a slab.' What he actually said was, 'Burn, baby, burn.' And I never said he smirked. How could I tell what his face was up to under the ski mask? It really pisses me off when newspapers get things wrong. I tossed the paper aside in disgust.

The morning dragged on like a *Sunday Express* intro. Occasionally someone would come up and have a butcher's at my legs or head, scrawl on the chart, and wander off. The main man and his posse of juniors spent a good 20 seconds peering at the chart. I don't think they noticed me.

I was slipping into slumber when my first visitor hove into view. Big Ben Ashbee, the super. He gave me his undertaker's smile and a bunch of grapes.

I said, 'I usually get my grapes from a bottle.'

In my story I was careful not to mention the Kandy line. I didn't want to tip off the rest of Fleet Street. I hinted instead that my attacker was linked to a drugs racket and had been sent by that well known baddie, Mr Big. But I told Ben the full bit. He tugged his ear and said, 'Umm humm', which I took to mean he thought it a sensational item.

I told him not to bother lining up an identity parade because one geezer in a ski mask looks much like any other geezer in a ski mask. Ben said forensics had taken a look at the ashes and found nothing significant. Now they had a couple of men doing door-to-door stuff. So far no one had seen, heard, suspected anything until my flat lit up the neighbourhood. Ben remembered he had some bits and pieces for me. He handed over a Tesco's carrier bearing my once beautiful suit. I took a peek inside and it didn't look as if Ben had nicked anything. My suit still reeked of petrol and for the first time I thought there might be something in the hospital's no smoking rule.

Ben asked me if I knew anyone who might want to do me in. I said yes, there's Tony Belker, and one of the monkeys, and a certain sub, and an old girlfriend, and the neo-Nazi in our library, and . . .

Ben said Umm humm again and away he went.

The battery on my mobile was dead but I coaxed the ward sister into wheeling up a pay phone. I rang the world to let it know I would live to write again. The world was unimpressed. I got Mac on the golf course, practising his cheating.

'Are you well there, boy?' he asked.

Holding my own, I assured him. He said I'd go blind. Ah, the old ones are the best. He said, 'I hear tell you've changed your name from Chard.'

I fell for it. I said, 'What's it now?'

'Max Charred.' He spelt it out. It still wasn't funny.

I put the phone down on his cackle and lay back to await the Seventh Cavalry. They showed up around lunchtime while the locals were packing away grub that looked as if it had already been eaten. Angela Whipple led the charge, bearing a hamper as big as a wardrobe. I whisked it open and there, ripe green and glorious, was a bottle of Moët. She prised the cork out, giving Tutankhamun in the bed next door a minor heart attack. We knocked it back like cossacks and rooted around for more goodies. The hamper was a get-well-soon prezzie from the Editor. Angie coughed up with a bottle of Gordons. The NHS doesn't stretch to providing tonic so we drank it with borrowed Lucozade. After a while you get used to it.

Meanwhile other hacks showed up like ghouls at a plane crash. Cigars, cigarettes, bottles and flasks built up on my locker. I could have opened an off-licence. Everyone was most concerned, particularly the ward sister who kept trying to throw out my beloved brethren as they were giving the casualty ward a bad name. I was sitting up, chewing a chicken and quaffing red biddy, when the dear noisy crew suddenly hushed. The Editor himself had arrived. Now this was an honour. Not as good as a pay rise, but an honour just the same. The foot soldiers slipped away like wraiths and I was left grinning at the boss. Normally he doesn't speak to me. He brushes past in the corridor, evincing a deep interest in his shoelaces. But newspapers are funny things. Most of the time editors and the rest of the executive rabble spend their days dreaming up ways to make life miserable for you. They're pretty good at it too. I've seen them drive droves of hacks to the looney bin or the bottle. Sometimes both. I could rattle off the names of a dozen good men who died before their due, thanks to editors and their ilk. Those who survive the daily round are tortured souls with shattered marriages and jangling nerves. You can hear the Valium rattle as they pass. Editors look on the destruction they've wreaked and they are well pleased. It's their way of exercising power.

But if someone else does something nasty to one of their hacks, by God, they're for it. And the abused hack finds himself on the receiving end of a generosity that would make the prodigal son feel hard done by. So it was with me. The Editor asked after my limbs, my head, my happiness. He said the paper was putting up a five grand reward for info leading to the arrest of The Petrol Can Kid. I blushed and nearly spilled my wine. Furthermore, said the Editor, I was to take time off, as much time as I wanted. And when I was fit enough, say in a month, the paper would send me somewhere nice and sunny for a holiday.

'With my girlfriend?' I asked.

Only the slightest hesitation. Yes, with my girlfriend. The Editor recommended the Caribbean or Bali, places with which he is uncommonly well acquainted. He folded up his half moons, told me if there was anything, anything, I needed, I just had to call his secretary. He departed, leaving me to think I must thank my burglar, if ever they caught him.

Rosie interrupted my kindly thoughts. She swooped, dived, hugged, kissed, caressed and mauled my mangled body. The ward's bandaged peeping toms stopped licking their wounds and began fighting for a ringside seat. We were forced to draw the curtains. Alone at last we grinned at each other like a pair of idiots. Beyond the screen the zimmer frame brigade listened to a chorus of ooohs, yumms and the occasional Arrrrghh! when she hugged too hard. We were rudely interrupted by a staff monkey who wanted an up-to-the-minute shot of me. He also persuaded Rosie to pout provocatively over my injured skull. And who can blame him?

After he'd gone, we took time out to talk. I was careful not to say a word about the Editor's freebie holiday for I knew what Rosie would say. The Maldives. She poked around in my hamper and finished off the glazed fruits while I told her of the lazy days of recuperation ahead. She said super, she would help me shop for a new wardrobe. Oh no you won't, I thought. But I said that would be nice and I would lodge in her flat and help her draw lizards. Rosie said, 'Oh no you won't.' We breezed away the afternoon until a nurse parted the curtains and turfed Rosie out on her ear.

The next day I was set free. They were glad to help me on my way. I exchanged the hospital shroud for a pair of jeans and an Elvis Costello tour tee shirt and limped around Rosie's place with an air of heroic suffering. Rosie insisted I stay and I got the impression that meant permanently, or at least until I was fit to walk the streets.

The Law paid me a couple of visits but we didn't have much to say to each other. They were getting nowhere on the Claudine Tournier/Shirley Ham killings and I think they'd lost interest in my pyromaniac. The paper ran a shortish follow-up on my status, with a pic of Rosie and me, and some hamfisted quotes. Friends popped up every few minutes, largely because it was a great excuse to get out of the office. Whenever things went quiet Rosie would feed me an improving book. She reads some weird stuff. I started at A for Allende (Isabelle), hurriedly moved on to B for Brookner (Anita), and by the time I hit C for Colette (no first name) I must have read at least a dozen pages and my head was hurting. I surrendered myself instead to the pleasures of daytime TV. There is much to be said for the medium. It does not require your intellectual participation. Therefore I was able to watch *Neighbours* while thinking of something else altogether, which the actors were also doing. Mostly I thought about The Man in Black. He had left me with a pair of multi-coloured shins and lips like Mick Jagger's. What manner of man was this, I mused, who could callously incinerate two dozen exquisite suits and God knows how many shirts? What did I know that made me worth burning?

I pondered while Rosie played with her crayons. All was domestically blissful apart from the grub. Whole fields of spinach were laid waste for my delectation. It didn't make me any smarter. Rosie said it was chock full of iron. I soon had metal fatigue.

On the third night of convalescence the phone shrilled while she was doing something nasty with bean sprouts. I was hoping it was meals on wheels. It was Vic on Night Desk. He didn't ask after my welfare. He said, 'A bloke's been on three times to get your new number. I've told him we don't give out personal details, but he keeps on ringing. He also wants your new address.'

I said, 'Does he call himself the Masked Marauder?'

'No, he calls himself . . .' Vic broke off and went on a paper chase around the desk. He picked up the phone again. 'He says his name is Gitney or something.'

I didn't know any Gitneys. I said, 'Might it be Gavney?'

Vic said it might be. He couldn't read his notes. I said it was very kind of Vic to ring me and he said that's okay, he was doing nothing anyway.

I rang Ross Gavney at his Magpie Court number and he snatched up the phone.

'Yes?' he demanded.

I said, 'You're supposed to say: "This is the Gavney residence; how might I be of assistance?" '

'Max!'

I said, 'A lucky guess.'

There was what they call a pregnant pause. I reflected this was a shade odd. He was supposed to be dying to talk to me. He cleared his throat and said, 'I've been trying to get your number but the paper wouldn't let me have it.'

I said, 'I know.'

A three beat silence. He said, 'I feel very bad about this.'

'I feel a hell of a lot worse,' I said. I asked him why he felt bad.

Ross said, 'Well, it's my fault really. If I hadn't made that stupid bet, you'd be okay.'

I said, 'I don't think I'll ever forgive you. But if you were to buy me a large steak I might just weaken.'

Ross laughed. It was a tense little heh-heh. A laugh you could do without smiling. He said, 'You haven't eaten yet?'

I said, 'I don't eat any more. I graze.'

Another snippet of laughter. Ross said, 'Well, I'm doing nothing tonight. If you like, I'll pick you up and treat you to dinner.'

I said, 'I'm beginning to forgive you already.'

His voice picked up pace. He said, 'Tell me where you're living now and I'll collect you.'

For some curious reason I didn't feel like giving

him Rosie's address. I rolled over the question and said, 'Don't bother – it's just as easy for me to pop round to Magpie Court.'

'Half an hour, say?'

'Half an hour.'

Ross said, 'Great. Look forward to seeing you.' He didn't sound as if he meant it.

I cast an appraising eye over the few garments in my cache at Rosie's place. The nearest thing I had to proper clothes was an ecru linen jacket and a pair of navy slacks. I tried on a faded lavender shirt and I looked too precious for my own good. I settled for a navy crew neck, slipped on my black loafers and kissed Rosie goodbye.

I got to Magpie Court fifteen minutes later than promised. Ross was on the phone to Tokyo or Wall Street, checking up on his pork scratchings futures. I was welcomed instead by his idiot brother, Euan. I have never felt too fond of Euan ever since he nearly took my eye out with a homemade air pistol when I was fourteen. He must have been all of twelve. He's still mad keen on shooters though these days he prefers potting pheasants to people. Tonight he pretended the Great Eye Incident had never happened. I fingered an imaginary scar over my left eye to remind him. He said hello and stuck a whisky in my hand so maybe he's improving. I limped towards a nearby chair, taking care not to spill a single drop. Euan is another of those City types who consider it a wasted day if he hasn't knocked up a million before breakfast.

He's got a mansion in the shires with all the adornments, including a wife who could steal your breath away and twin daughters who look like they belong in the Hitler Youth kindergarten. But Euan's old lady has recently told him to pack his pyjamas and clear off. A fling with a floozy, I gather. Now he's cluttering up Ross's guest bedroom and looking very down on his luck indeed. We didn't have a lot to say to each other.

Ross got off the phone and said, 'Here's to the Great Escaper.'

The Great Escaper smiled bravely and stuck his nose in his glass. Euan mumbled his best wishes and sloped off. Ross said, 'How do you feel?'

I said, 'Like I look. Only worse.'

He said, 'You don't look too bad. A bit pale maybe.'

He was looking a trifle peakish himself, and edgy with it. I had the feeling he wanted to confide in me but couldn't make up his mind.

I said, 'Where are we going?'

Ross said, 'I thought perhaps John Dory's.'

I said, 'But that's a fish restaurant.'

'Where, then?'

I said, 'I have a desperate craving for roast beef and Yorkshire pudding without the Yorkshire pudding. Maybe I'm pregnant.'

Ross laughed and this time he was more relaxed about it. He suggested a place by the Tower and we drained our whiskies and went. The restaurant was knee deep in Japanese tourists, thirsting for Merrie Englande at very unmerrie prices. Judging by their dress, they evidently thought the place had a golf course upstairs. I didn't feel so bad about my outfit.

I waited until we got to the port and Stilton stage before I asked, 'What's on your mind?'

Ross swallowed a nugget of cheese and went into a coughing fit. I topped up my glass and passed the port to the left. Ross got his larynx working again.

'Mind? Nothing. I was just very worried about you. I felt responsible, and . . .'

'And balls,' I said. Ross blinked but didn't say anything. I took my time lighting a cigar and admiring its glow. I started. I spoke in flat, undramatic tones, all the while locking my eyes on his. I said, 'You and I, Ross, go back to the birth of time. You've copied my English homework, I've copied your maths. You've bled my nose and I've punched your head. You wrecked my bike, and I stole your girlfriend. You've got drunk with me, I've chased women with you. What's yours is mine, and vice versa. If ever I marry, you'd be my best man, and if ever you have children, I'll dandle them upon my knee. We are as close as brothers. We don't have secrets.'

I paused. Ross was listening intently, but not giving anything away. I said, 'And now we have a secret.'

'A secret?' he said warily.

'A secret. It begins the night you bet me there was a story behind a stiff in the Thames.'

He said, 'I didn't know—'

I stopped him. 'No, you didn't know it was Claudine Tournier. None of us knew until we saw her face. I thought: "Hello, it's Claudine Tournier." The Old Bill thought: "Hello, hello, hello, it's Claudine Tournier." But you didn't.'

'I didn't?'

'You didn't. You said, "My God, it's Claudine!" Just Claudine. As if there was only one Claudine in the whole wide world.'

I stopped to see if Ross wanted to say anything. He didn't. I said, 'You also started acting like a zombie. You stopped talking. When we went to that wine bar you stood there knocking it back and staring at the wall. If I hadn't been so busy I would have got it out of you there and then. It was only later I thought about it. You said, "It's Claudine." That meant you were on first name terms with La Tournier. Nothing wrong with that. But you didn't want me to know about it.'

I took a lazy draw on the cigar. I said, 'So, you see, Ross, we have a secret.'

He was looking down at the table, rolling a crumb of Stilton across the linen folds.

I said, 'But that was only the start of the secret.'

He glanced up. 'The start?'

I said, 'Oh yes, there's more. We'll pass over the day I rang you, when you couldn't stick a sensible sentence together, and we'll move on to tonight.'

'Tonight?' It was like talking to a parrot.

I said, 'This very eve. You were desperate to get hold of me. Why? Because you felt guilty about me nearly getting fried alive. Because you knew that it was all tied up with the killing of Claudine. You said, and I quote: "It's all my fault. If I hadn't made that stupid bet you'd be okay"'.

I took in a centilitre of port. Ross sat hunched over the table, his eyes hooded. He didn't seem inclined to talk. I exhaled a blue billow of cigar smoke. I said,

'Now that was a very interesting thing to say. And it puzzles me. You see, when I wrote the story on my arsonist, I deliberately implied he was an underworld villain, a straightforward gangster. I never for one moment suggested he had anything to do with Claudine's murder.

'But I knew he was up to his balaclava in it because of something he said at the flat. I know that, he knows that, and nobody else knows that. Nobody except you. I haven't the faintest idea how you know. That is your big secret, Ross, and I'd like you to share it with me.'

I sat back. I hadn't blinked an eye throughout my little monologue and I was still intent on every reflex, every nuance from my good old mate. The cigar smoke made pretty spirals in the air, otherwise we were frozen. I waited a long time. When he spoke, he didn't look at me. His voice was so low I had to lean forward to hear him.

He said, 'I can't.'

I said, 'You can't tell me the secret?'

He made a sort of shrug which could have meant anything but added up to no.

I said softly, 'Ross, I very nearly died in there. I don't even know why.'

He said, 'I'm sorry . . .'

I was silent, forcing him to go on.

He tasted his port and looked across the glass at me. He said, 'Max, it's not what you think. It's different. It's something I want to tell you, but I can't.'

I felt betrayed and vicious and I still didn't know

what was going on. I said, 'You're full of crap. Maybe you'll tell the police.'

He said, 'The police!'

I said, 'Yes, those blokes in the funny hats.'

He said, 'Christ, Max, don't involve them. Please.'

I laughed without humour. I said, 'Maybe you'd prefer it if I stopped nosing round this whole affair.'

His eyes told me he would like that very much.

I said, 'Well that's tough, Ross. I'm sticking with this one all the way through. I want you to tell your friends that. Tell them I'm going to turn them over and wring them dry.'

He said, 'Look, it's over. Just trust me. I just can't . . .'

I said, 'Why don't you pick up the bill and get out of here. And any time you feel like calling me – don't.'

He sat for a few minutes. His face was pointy. Then he stood up slowly and gave me a last look of entreaty. My eyes were cold as death. He turned and walked away. We didn't say goodbye.

I stayed on with the port and a new cigar until I couldn't stand the taste any more. I got them to call me a taxi and I returned to the land of the living.

# Chapter Nine

First thing next morning I moved house again. It was my fourth address in a week. I felt like giving Salman Rushdie a ring and comparing notes. This time I hid myself away in the Barbican. My brainy brother Dominic keeps a second-floor flat there. But as he prefers to earn his living in Vancouver, teaching the natives all they need to know about social anthropology, the flat lies vacant ten months a year. I phoned his log cabin in the middle of the black Canadian night, got Dominic out of bed and told him my sorry tale. Supportive as ever, he grouched, 'You deserved it.' But he got on to the Barbican concierge and arranged for me to squat. I liked the thought of the Barbican. Its name means a fortified tower, and a fortified tower suited me down to the ground right now. I tried to persuade Rosie to pack up her lizards and move in. She said, 'Has it got a studio?' I lied and said the flat had its own art gallery, get-slim gym and beach. Rosie doubted my word and stayed put in Battersea, borough of my dreams. I think I was secretly glad she wasn't sharing my bolthole.

I gave Rosie and nobody else my address and number. I told the office if they wanted me they just had to bleep my pager. I didn't want News Desk knowing where I was in case the Black Blazer phoned and some loon gave him the details. It's happened before. I armed myself with a couple of extra batteries for the mobile phone and pulled up the drawbridge. It was a clean, well-lighted place with soft hued walls and a stack of golden pine furniture. Dominic had left behind a rainbow of grey suits which were presumably too bohemian for the backwoods of Canada. They fitted me after a fashion. His taste in ties was atrocious, as was his musical inclination. I thumbed through CDs by Simple Minds, Mike Oldfield and Jean Michel Jarre before I found a Bonnie Raitt album. I stuck it on the player, helped myself to Dominic's gin and put my feet up on the dwarfish table. I was home and dryish.

There's not much to do in the Barbican, unless you're lucky enough to have a flat facing out on the local roads, where you can sit counting taxis. Dominic's faced inwards. I counted five trees. His books made Rosie's look like a rattling good read. I survived until Bonnie Raitt stopped warbling. Any more of this and I'll start talking to myself, I said. I picked up the mobile and called News Desk. Angela Whipple was sweet and solicitous. I said, 'Can you get me a laptop, Angie?'

'No problem. Where do you want it sent?'

I thought about it and remembered a bar behind Smithfield. I told her to give me half an hour and I'd be there to meet the messenger. She was feeling perky. She said, 'How will he recognise you?'

I said, 'Tell him to look for the man with his flies undone.'

I was on my second G&T when a young freelance who does shifts for us shambled in looking bemused. Maybe it was his first time in a bar. I waved a mitt and he sighed with relief. He handed over the laptop and I offered him a drink. But he wanted a half of lager shandy instead. Signs of a grievously misspent youth.

I got myself home, brewed up a jug of coffee and kickstarted the laptop. I keyed in DLIBFILE, which in English means our electronic library. I wasn't sure what I was looking for and I wasn't particularly hopeful. The real editor of a newspaper is often its lawyer, which is why you rarely get to read the dirty stuff. Oh, the stories I could tell you would make your eyes whizz round like Catherine Wheels.

My general idea was to splash around in the backwaters of all the leading characters and see what rippled the surface. I locked on to the little green screen and embarked on my task.

There is a convention among cops and crime reporters: they don't write stories, we don't investigate murders. Possibly an awful lot more murderers might be caught if it were the other way around, but then your newspapers would be extremely boring. This is the price you pay for your daily tabloid.

There are occasions when we do play Plod. Imagine, for instance, that a top spook at Cheltenham spy centre is found dead, wearing nothing but a suspender belt and a silly smile. Naturally the public has a right to know what's been going on here, especially as Those In Authority have not the faintest intention of telling them. So us hacks beetle off to Gloucs. and start acting all steely-eyed. After a few hours of this most of us get bored, write some guff about a sinister conspiracy and repair to the bar. You do get the occasional oddball who makes the career his lifelong vocation. He usually works for the *Observer* or one of the other tomfool heavies. Months, even years after the event, he still churns out great reams of impenetrable copy. Still, it keeps him off the streets.

When it comes to common or garden murder, such as Claudine's or Shirley's, we all stand back and leave it to the Old Bill. That's what I should have been doing. But I was a bitter and twisted man. Besides, I wasn't entirely convinced that the Law would ever collar the man with the itchy matchbox finger.

But even before the bonfire I had been acting the super sleuth. It took me a while to work out why. It was all Ross's fault. He'd bet me the unknown corpse in St Katharine's Dock was a story. So he'd won the bet. But I wanted to prove I could get a bigger and better story than he ever imagined. I suppose it comes down to ego. I needed to show off, to demonstrate that I'm smarter than the average hack. It's pathetic but it's true. So that was why I was acting like a gin-fuelled Miss Marple. As well as that, I was enjoying myself.

I had a list and I worked my way systematically through it from Cowley to Veizey via Tomlin. I worked all afternoon, pausing only for the occasional screen break and coffee. I appropriated a sheaf of creamy notepaper and made notes in a large, clear longhand so I didn't have to decipher them afterwards. The clock on the bookshelf winked out 18.37 when I at last switched off the laptop. I made myself a proper drink. Dominic favours Plymouth gin, but I'm not picky. It was a grey evening towards the fag end of May, so I lit the chairside lamp before I settled down to read my findings. They didn't impress. I felt I'd missed *Neighbours* and *Home And Away* for nothing. I read:

LEWIS TREFOYLE: 51, Junior minister at Home Office, previously junior min. Welsh Office. MP for Butterley since '84. Marginal seat. Political leanings more Con than Lab. Keen on hanging and forced repatriation of immigrants, providing they're black. Outside interests: non-executive director Chalencidon Properties, also minor consultancies. Rumoured holiday home in Cyprus, the illegal part. Wealthy but not openly so. Married once, divorced once. Viewed by his colleagues as a cold fish.

LEON KNAPP: aged 47/49/52. Born Leo Knapowlski. Founder member of Rotors teenybop band. Made and squandered a fortune. *Sunday People* bought up roadie's tale of drugs and depravity – 'Road to Ruin'. He didn't sue. *Mirror* earlier paid ex-wife for 'Life with Leon the Louse'. Seems he liked blacking her eyes and wearing her knickers.

PROUDHOE VEIZEY: 53. Born Proudhoe Veizey. Ham actor typecast in string of Brit films as pompous duffer. Overacts even in kids' panto – 'Veizey's Widow Twankey is nothing like a Dame' – *Evening Standard*.

Confirmed bachelor, as the diary writers say. Oft seen in the Garrick molesting stray Tories in fond hope of a knighthood.

MARTIN CROWLEY: 46. Ex-marine commando and Falklands veteran, possibly with Special Boat Service. Messes about with boats and not much else. Briefly linked to woman golfer. Affair bunkered after he kept sailing off into the sunset. Tough and tetchy.

GEORGE 'GUS' CLERNTHORPE: 51. Big light in Jockey Club until unseated over links with fugitive tycoon. Lavish party thrower. Less lavish about where the money comes from. Hints of shady property deals. His ginger locks said to be a rug. Gossip writers call him Gorgeous Gussie, but don't say why. Lawyers no doubt.

SIR JAMES TOMLIN: 50. Low profile City moneybags. Hangs around with Square Mile's premier division. Likes women and firing people. Has son, Henry Michael James. Nothing known. Whispers of cash flow problems for Sir J. Educ. Harrow & Cambridge.

I read through my research and tacked another name to the list. I didn't have to dial up our library.

ROSS GAVNEY: 36. Educ. St John's PE, Littlemere, Holly Hill comp. Exeter college. PPE. Dapper bond dealer. Enjoys his money. Occasional girlfriend,

Chloe. Mixes well and widely. Skis and golfs. Secretive bugger.

I sat back, thought about that one, and added, 'Arsenal fan.'

I poured myself another stiff one and read through it all again. Now, I said, spot the man who murdered Claudine and poor Shirley. More to the point, find the evil monster who set fire to my suits. The only one who fitted that description was the unlovely Martin Crowley who used to be paid to kill people. I recalled that my matchbox man had a blurred voice, as if he were trying to disguise it. That meant he was someone I knew. I wouldn't know Martin Crowley if he sailed through the door. Then I recalled that my hearing was not too clever at the time. So maybe his voice wasn't disguised. That left me nowhere.

Sir James was in Geneva when Claudine was topped, Knapp probably in Sri Lanka for all three events. I couldn't picture the flabby pink Trefoyle getting his hands dirty. Proudhoe Veizey would faint clean away at the scent of petrol. I didn't know enough about Gus Clernthorpe. I pencilled a question mark against him. Ross had a surefire alibi for Claudine, thanks to me. I think he was taller than my arsonist. I scratched my tummy and cogitated. There was always the possibility that a couple of them had clubbed together and hired themselves a hitman. Why? Because of a common threat. I ran through the suspects. What did they have in common? Barring

Ross, they were all close mates. Nothing sinister in that. I was about to chuck my notes in the bin when I remembered. They were all linked to the WorldCare Foundation. Whatever mischief they're up to, I reasoned, it involves Claudine's pet project. But Ross has nothing to do with it. Or has he? Ross has a secret, and a big one to boot. It must be a lulu if he's prepared to spike a 20-year friendship.

All this thinking made me hungry. There was no point in calling Rosie because she had shot up north to Huddersfield or Halifax or some place beginning with H to flaunt herself at a textile exhibition. I didn't know they still had textiles up there.

I showered and picked out a suit that made me look like an insurance salesman minus the charisma. I sashayed round to a sushi place off Broad Street. I ordered up a plate of raw fish. I'd gone off roast beef. I was fiddling with my chopsticks when the bleep went off. CALL TROPPER, it said. Who he? I said. I gave Night Desk a ring. 'Have you just bleeped me, Vic?'

'Um hum. A bloke called Tropper wants you to give him a bell.'

I said, 'Did he leave a number?'

Vic did his usual Mogadon-inflamed rumple around the desk and came up with an 0181 number. Somewhere in the outer darkness. I rang it. 'Mister Tropper?' I said.

'Trotter,' he corrected.

'My name's Chard: you want to talk to me.'

He said, 'Yes. It's about Shirl. Shirley Ham.'

He spoke in Estuary English, sticking an r in yes

and dropping the t in about. Maybe he was a trendy TV talk show host. I asked him what about Shirley. He said, 'I'm Darren. I'm her boyfriend.'

Not any more you're not. I waited for him to elaborate. He said, 'Hello? You still there, Mike?'

'Max,' I corrected.

'Oh yes, well, I was thinking, like maybe we could get together and talk about it.'

I said, 'And what do you want to talk about?'

He said, 'Well, I knew what she was up to, working for you, didn't I? I mean, I'm her fiancé, so she told me things.'

I remembered the *Evening Standard* story. Darren was the man who skipped the light fandango with her. I said, 'You've talked to the police?'

'Yes, well that's the problem, innit? They think I did it. I need to talk to somebody because Shirl's been murdered, and I don't know what it's about.'

I asked him where he was. 'Dagenham.'

Dagenham! If south Essex is the backside of England, Dagenham is the pimple on its unlovely bum. I said warily, 'Where do you want to meet?'

'Here's okay with me. How about you?'

Not bloody likely. I sent my brain on a pub crawl. It remembered the Scimitar down the Mile End Road. No, that would be tasteless, considering Shirley was bumped off just before we were due to meet there.

'The Scimitar,' I said, and told him where it was. He wanted to know how he could recognise me. I told him I'd be the one standing by the snapshot of Al Capone. That satisfied him.

I was there by nine. Judging by the mood of the

customers, I must have hit the unhappy hour. Darren arrived along with my first drink. He was much as expected. A crinkly-haired specimen in jeans and tee shirt. His leather jacket was too new so it looked plastic. Maybe it was plastic. He asked for a pint of bitter. We found ourselves an empty snug and sat facing each other. He was nervous and tugged at his fingers.

I said, 'You have something to talk about?'

He said, 'Well, yes, Shirl told me she was pulling this job for you.'

I said, 'She offered information to my newspaper.'

He said, 'She was trying to dig up the dirt at Claudine Turner's place.'

'Tournier.'

He said, 'Yes, well, her. Shirl phoned me that day and said she'd got some great stuff that'd be worth a bundle.'

I said, 'Did she tell you what?'

'No. I thought, well, you'd know.'

I said, 'She was supposed to meet me here but never showed.'

Darren looked around as if he expected Shirley to pop up grinning. He said morosely, 'The police think I murdered Shirley because they don't believe where I was.'

'Where were you?'

He said, 'I was at home. On my own, watching telly. The first thing I know was them knocking on the door and telling me she was dead. They just came out with it. I was choked.'

Not half as much as Shirley. He took in a huge

gulp of beer. I said, 'Did she give you any idea what information she had?'

'No, she got it from someone she knew at the Foundation. She was all excited because we needed the money. We was getting married in September, you know.'

I bought him another pint. He brooded aloud: 'I was doing overtime and all. I was looking forward to getting married even though my mum said I was wrong. I didn't mind about it.'

'Didn't mind about what, Darren?'

He looked embarrassed. 'Well, Shirl was pregnant, like.'

I said, 'Christ! That's really tough for you.'

Darren said, 'No, no. It wasn't my kid or nothing.'

I offered him a cigarette and said casually, 'Who was the dad, then?'

He said, 'Shirl never told me, she said it was all over – with him, I mean. She never said his name but I think it was somebody in her office.'

I said, 'When was the baby due?'

'November. That's why we was getting married this year.'

I counted backwards. 'So she must have met the father only a month or so back.'

Darren said, 'Yes, well, we was split up then. We'd had a real up and downer at Easter and didn't see each other for a few weeks. It happened then. It was nothing serious or nothing. She just got pissed one night . . .'

'You planned to keep the baby.' I made it a statement.

'Oh yes, sure we was going to keep it all right.'

I said, 'And the real father would never know.' Another statement inviting confirmation.

Darren looked shifty. He took in a mouthful and wiped his lips. He said, 'Maybe not.'

'Maybe not?' I pushed the words back across the table. You've got to do better than that, Darren.

He tucked his chin in like a boxer and started pulling his fingers again. I sighed. 'You might as well tell me.'

He owned up. 'Well, Shirl had a plan, see. She was going to go to him when the baby was born and make him pay up. She reckoned she could sting him hard. And he couldn't do nothing about it because she could always go to the Child Support Agency and make him pay.'

I said, 'Did he know Shirley was pregnant?'

'I don't know, do I? It don't matter anyhow. Shirl's dead.'

I said, 'And maybe he killed her.'

I left Darren mulling this one over. It hadn't occurred to him before. I was in desperate need of company. I flagged a cab and told the driver to take me to Hampton's. I was that desperate.

The bar was thronged with Fleet Street's hopeless cases. They welcomed me back to their bosom, asked after my injuries and made tasteless cracks about legovers. I smiled with a touching fortitude and limped to the corner where Mac was chatting up the new barmaid. He gave me his Mafia kiss and ordered up a glass.

He said, 'Jesus, boy, you've got a face on you as long as a Lurgan spade.'

I took his word for it. I said, 'I'm bored with my own company.'

'I always said you were a boring old fart.'

I raised my glass in gracious salute. I said, 'What's new with the world?'

He said, 'Not a lot, apart from that barmaid. She's Finnish, you know. She could finish me off any day.'

Mac has a way with words. I said, 'She probably will. Underneath that blonde wig is a bald man.'

He cackled, 'Sure they're all the same in the dark.'

The conversation made its usual headlong plunge into the abyss and the glasses kept coming. Half way down the second bottle Mac interrupted his own obscene observations to say, 'Here, have you seen they've found the murder weapon?'

'What murder weapon?'

'Claudine Tournier's, you eejit. It was caught up in some fella's anchor chain or something. He was pulling up the chain this morning when the gun fell out.'

I said, 'What was it?'

'A wee toy thing. A thirty-two,' Mac said.

Or what we in the trade like to call a ladies' gun. Czech-made, evidence of our burgeoning trade links with our old Commie foes. It had bits of a makeshift silencer still stuck to the barrel. The rest was blown away. There were no prints, no track record of any prior hits.

At this point the door to Hampton's shot open and the Wildebeest shambled in leading a conga of like-minded reprobates. All hope of sensible conversation was gone. I didn't mind. I'd been sensible all day long. It was too long for a grown man.

I settled into my castle keep with ease. There was an open-all-hours mini-mart within limping distance and I stocked myself up with instant meals, cigarettes and the other essentials of life. It was Thursday lunchtime and I was eating Bird's Eye cod mornay and tender sliced baby lamb plus hot 'n' spicy rice. That's the only trouble with instant meals. You need five of them before you feel a thing. I had my feet up and was deeply engrossed in *Coronation Street* videoed from the night before. I was thinking what a God-awful boozer the Rover's Return is when a wisp of a question drifted across my mind. Why, it whispered, don't you ring the Foundation and ask them straight out what they've got going in Kandy? This was the sort of question that any proper hack would have asked on Day One. I watched *Coronation Street* all the way through – by heck, lad, there's some reet ugly lasses oop north – before I called the Foundation. I wanted to get them before their lunchtime drinkies wore off. That's a tip to aspiring journalists. Between 2.30 and 3.30 is the best time to catch them unguarded. Get on first name terms as fast as you can. That way they forget themselves and think they're still talking to a mate in the bar. The only snag about this cunning ploy is you have to interrupt your own lunch break to do it, so it's useful only if you are a teetotaller or you're trying to impress the boss.

I got them to put me through to the Foundation's press office where a five-year-old girl squeaked a hello. I donned a Scottish accent, Edinburghian, I think it was. I said my name was Max Bygraves. I was a freelance journo who'd been commissioned by the *Big Issue* to do a bit on Claudine's Legacy of Love, and how the Foundation was functioning on, even though its founder had foundered.

The child identified herself as Jo Earley – 'But call me Jo.' She said super, and what did I want to know? She sounded too young to drink, so I abandoned my bar room mate approach. I went at Kandy from an oblique angle, starting off in Mozambique, shooting up to the Sudan and winging way out east to Vientiane. Jo kept up a running travelogue. I pretended to be taking notes, asking her to spell out place names or expand on a particular item. We travelled on. I guided Jo India-wards. Her voice went off the scale into batspeak as she enthused over a street clinic in Bombay. She'd been there! She'd seen it for herself! It was true! Gosh!!! And I could have written a book about the Foundation's literacy programme in Bangladesh.

I asked in that laid back way of mine: 'Anything else on the Indian sub-continent?'

I had to explain what that meant. Yes indeed, said Jo. Much more. Self-help projects in Uttar Pradesh, ante natal care in the Punjab, birth control education all over the shop. I marvelled at the sheer scale of Claudine's empire and wondered how she ever found the time to go and get herself murdered.

Jo had run out of places and she still hadn't said a thing about Kandy. I directed our footsteps further south. 'Haven't you got something in Colombo too?'

A fluffy-headed pause. 'Where's Colombo?'

I said, 'In Sri Lanka.'

'Oh, there! No, we've nothing in Colombo, but there's a project in Kandy and I think that's in Sri Lanka.'

I sounded as if I didn't much care either. 'What you got there?'

Jo said, 'I'm not up to date on that one. I've never been there. But my boss has been to it several times. He could tell you all about it but he's out of the office right now. I'll just see what I've got on it.'

She was flipping through papers. 'Ah, here it is!' she yipped. 'It's a handicraft centre. That's all it says. Wait a minute, you're in luck. I can see my boss coming back now so you can talk to him, Mister Bygraves.'

'And what's his name, Jo?'

She said, 'Tomlin. Michael Tomlin.'

Well, well, well. You could have knocked me down with an 11-stone feather. I said, 'Sorry, Jo. I'll have to call him back. There's a call from New York holding on the other line.'

I brewed myself a Douwe Egberts decaff and did a think. A handicrafts centre? I couldn't picture Leon the Louse scooting off to the far reaches to buy himself a wooden elephant. Maybe the place turns out terrific saris. But none of this explained the panic in the Tomlin camp every time someone mentioned Kandy. Well, let's see what else the handicraft centre might keep under the counter. Drugs? Highly possible. Colombo is a handy stopover port for clippers plying their nefarious trade in unprocessed poppy juice from the Gulf of Bangkok. What else? Elephant tusks? Exotic but unlikely. I didn't know if Sri Lanka had any tigers worth bumping off and grinding up as aphrodisiacs for Chinese gents who have never heard of Kir Royale. Money laundering? For all I know, in Kandy they wash your dirty money in the street and pin it up to dry. But why bother going all the way to Sri Lanka? There are enough shysters within half a mile of the Barbican, tripping over each other to offer you their discreet services. There are even a couple of companies who make a bomb out of laundering IRA funds.

So what was so special about Kandy? I knew there wasn't much point in ringing up Sir Jimmy, inviting him out for a pint and asking him the score. If I tried Lewis Trefoyle, he'd probably get MI5 to lace my gin with an Undetectable Poison. I wandered around the flat kicking the chairs. When some stranger dressed like Zorro pours petrol down your trouser front you have a natural inclination to ask why. The answer to that one, I knew, lay way down there in Kandy.

I had a vague suggestion of an idea nibbling away at the back of my hand-crocheted head. I know the exact moment it slipped in. It was that afternoon when the Editor sat down by my hospital bedside, peeled himself a grape and suggested I take my wearisome bones off to Bali or some other place full of sunshine and drink at 5p a gallon. Surely, I reasoned, Sri Lanka was such a spot.

I hauled out the mobile and phoned our Travel Ed, Rick, a seasoned traveller who gets car sick on the way to work.

He said, 'Hi, Max. I was wondering when I'd hear from you. I've got a nice surprise.'

It was a surprise, and it was very, very nice, but not for me. A fortnight for two shacked up in a Barbados pleasure palace where the blue Caribbean licked the private beach clean every morning. A privileged resort where one could bask, bathe, scuba dive and walk on the water.

I said, 'Sounds magic, Rick. But to tell you the truth, I'd really love to go east.'

Rick sounded hurt and baffled. He said, 'Everything's built in on this one. Eat all you want, drink all you want. You don't have to pay a penny.'

I admit I was tempted, but my inner resolve held. The things I do for love. I said, 'You've gone to a lot of trouble setting it up, and thanks a million, Rick. It's my fault really. I should have let you know before, but I didn't feel well enough to ring.'

This was designed to have a triple-pronged effect: to stroke his ego, tell him I was an idiot who didn't know a gift horse when he saw one, and to elicit his sympathy. It hit the target on all three.

'No, I understand,' said Rick. 'I kept this one for you because it's such a gem, but if you don't want to go to Barbados, that's that. Now tell me where you are thinking about and I'll see what I can do. Thailand? Bali?'

I said, 'Sri Lanka, actually.'

He muted his surprise. 'Sri Lanka? You know

they're still having trouble with the Tamil Tigers? Tourists aren't allowed in the north.'

I said I knew, but crazy little fool that I was, I had my heart set on it. Rick thought aloud: 'I don't think the Sri Lanka tourist people lay on any press trips. Maybe Air Lanka does. Or some of the better package holiday companies. You want a trip for two, don't you?'

I said I did. He said he'd try. I put the phone away feeling a right little clever clogs.

Normally I don't care a fig for freebies. There's a grave danger you might end up on a trip with the agony aunt of the *Basildon Bugle,* wittering on about the grub. I'd best explain how freebies work. Travel companies, airlines, cruise lines and so on deluge newspaper travel eds with offers of free holidays. In the office the prime trips are shared out among those the Editor loves. That leaves me out for a start. It's a sobering thought that I had to get myself nearly flambéd before I was allowed to join the club. The Editor's pet pets get all the top junkets – *QE2* cruises, China, bloody Bali etc. Then you come down to the middle rankers who get to roast their bums in Kenya or freeze their tootsies off in Iceland. Lower still, the office toadies clamour for a gîte in the Dordogne or a week off-season in a farmhouse in Tuscany. At the bottom of the pile are the menial minions who are content with a weekend in the West Country. Self catering.

All of these souls, be they a night editor golfing in Augusta, or a features sub caravanning in Wales, are charged with the same awesome responsibility: they have to write a travel feature – anything up to 800 words of unmitigated claptrap. Naturally it's in everyone's interest to keep the freebies rolling in, therefore if you had your wallet nicked in Naples or developed full-blown dysentery in the Dominican Republic, you tend to brush that aside and write about the friendly folk and the delicious food.

Freebies come with several strings attached. Often the donor company invites a group of journos. This is the Press Trip. If, as so often happens, you find yourself saddled with a bunch of social lepers, you get homesick pretty quickly. Sometimes you end up in the company of travel writers who are even worse. Many years back I did a story which the Editor actually liked. He sent me off to Malta for revenge. My fellow travellers were all travel writers. All the day long they talked of nothing else but last year in Marienbad or the jaunt to Aspen, Ho Chi Minh city, wherever. They went to bed at ten with Agatha Christie books. I don't think they even knew which continent we were in. Tour companies aren't bright enough to invite a bunch of horny-handed hacks together, so you don't have any drinking mates. I became an expert on Malta's singles bars.

When you're safely home in England and receiving medication, then you start thinking about the 800 words you have to write. The best way into it is through an anecdote, usually invented. Here's how it goes:

*It is not often you stroll along a sea-kissed beach, scented by frangipani, and chance upon a golden doubloon.*

*I came across several, one too many in fact, and had to retire to my hammock in the shade of the whispering palms to regain my bearings.*

*For on Bloggoland, the idyllic isle where Captains Blood and Blackbeard once buried their booty, a golden doubloon is not what it used to be.*

*These days it's the name of a swashbuckling cocktail – a large jigger of rum with a generous drop of brandy, topped off with grenadine and lime.*

*If Blackbeard were still holding court in Bloggoland's pretty harbour, I'm sure he would happily exchange his golden doubloons for the 20th century version . . .*

Now all you need is a linking sentence, say something along the lines of – *The buccaneering tradition of this enchanted Caribbean paradise lives on in its lively carnivals and street parties.*

After that you pick up the tour company's brochure and tap in whole chunks of it, right down to the stuff about the island's happy, innocent ways. You conveniently forget that Bloggoland is the Numero Uno refuelling point for planes weighed down with Colombian cocaine.

That's the way you do it. Pick up any tabloid on Saturday and you read whole pages of sheer garbage that would set your teeth on edge.

But then maybe I'm just ethical.

# Chapter Ten

I was ferreting around in my brother's drawers looking for salacious stuff (the nearest I came was a pair of lilac boxer shorts with big pink hearts) when my bleep let me know it was still working. News Desk desired concourse. It was Nigel, Angela Whipple's deputy.

'Nothing important, Max. Just thought you'd be interested – Leon Knapp is back in Britain.'

I said, 'He must have come via Lourdes. Last I heard he was sick as a pig.'

A matey laugh from Nige. 'Seems he had a bleeding ulcer.'

I said, 'I've got a bleeding headache but I don't make a song and dance about it.'

More sounds of hilarity. I said, 'What's he got to say for himself?'

Nigel said, 'He's not talking. He got into Heathrow and they drove him away airside.'

Airside is the private bit. Hacks aren't allowed into it except by special arrangement.

Nigel said, 'His manager came out with a statement. Let's see. Where is it? Ah, here we are: "Leon, as everyone knows, is a true professional and he is very upset that he missed engagements. He hopes to resume his career in the very near future. He has returned to his home and we ask that the Press respect his privacy until he is fully recovered".'

I said, 'The manager's not saying what Leon was up to in Sri Lanka.'

Nigel said, 'No, but showbiz asked him if Leon had a nervous breakdown.'

'And?'

I could hear the shrug. 'He just said the ulcer was brought on by stress.'

I had an idea. I was having a great day for ideas. I said, 'Nige, put me through to showbiz.'

I got on to the luvvies, let them know it was me and asked for Knapp's home number. 'Why?'

They can be ever so precious, showbiz reporters. I told them I was a Leon fan from way back. They didn't believe me. I pulled rank and said it was none of their business. They squealed and fluttered but they gave me a number. Somewhere way out in the Berkshire badlands.

I gave it a call. Brriinng-brinnngg, brriinng-brriinnngg it went without answer. I switched off the mobile and thought about it. Maybe he was there, but didn't feel like talking to strangers. But how did he know it was a stranger calling? I remembered ex-Sir Anthony Blunt, former keeper of the Queen's pictures and well known traitor. When the story broke about him Blunt stayed in his flat, refusing to answer the phone. Yet we knew his chums had been able to get through. Finally one of us, not me this time, had a brainwave. He called Blunt, let the phone ring out three times and he put it down again. Then he called back immediately. Blunt picked it up immediately. 'Hello,' he said. And the hack got a quote or two.

It's a wheeze I've used many a time since. It works once in twenty times. I used it today on Leon Knapp, alias Leo Knapowski.

'Hello,' he said in fluent Brummie.

I positively gushed, 'Leon! You're home! Thank God for that!'

He said, 'Who's that?' There was a thin edge to his voice. Tension or native dialect. I couldn't tell which.

I elbowed the question aside and pushed on, showering exclamation marks down the phone. 'We were so worried! Poor you! It must have been such a shock! I was absolutely horrified when I heard you were in hospital!'

'Is that Ted?' The edge was sharper.

I rushed on heedless. 'I've been talking to my dad and he had ulcer trouble some years back. He said what really did the trick for him was yoghurt. Not ordinary yoghurt, but that lovely, thick, creamy Greek yoghurt. You can get it from any Waitrose or Sainsburys. You get a tub of that, stir in a big, big spoonful of honey, the clear honey, and it does you the world of good, and . . .'

It didn't sound as if I was doing Leon's ulcer any good at all. He cut across me tetchily: 'Who are you? Why are you calling?'

'Me?' You could see my eyebrows arch in astonishment. 'This is Bobby. Bobby Maxwell. I know Sir

James. That's how I got your number. But as I was saying, it's great to know you'll soon be up and about . . .'

Our Leon was a suspicious cove. He accused: 'I don't know you. What did you say your name was?'

I chimed a peal of laughter. 'Of course you don't know me. It's Bobby. Just ask Sir James about me. By the way, I was at his place in Switzerland recently and I had *a great* time. You should ask him for the loan of it. You could get yourself fighting fit there, and the great charm of it is it's very private, well away from all those snooping reporters.'

Knapp said, 'Look, Bobby, whoever you are, it's kind of you to call, but I'm trying to get some rest. Goodbye.'

I jumped in before he could get the phone down. I said, 'You've been eating too many Kandy curries.'

I had his attention again. He said warily, 'What about Kandy?'

'Kandy? I'm going there next week.'

He poked at the statement with his toe. He said, 'That's funny. I've never heard anyone mention any Bobby.'

I lit a Bensons and puzzled over what to say next. When I answered I sounded even more guarded than him. I said, 'You know the form, Leon. We've all got to be discreet.'

He didn't answer but he was still listening. He needed something more. I said, 'There were plans to close Kandy down, you know.'

An edgy 'Yeah?' Nothing else. But I was headed the right direction. I thought back to that moment in

Switzerland when Sir James and I glared at each other while his little piece of mischief, Miss Emma Pearson, went haywire on the hall phone.

I said, 'I was in Switzerland with Jimmy and Emma when the balloon went up. He was livid.'

'Yeah.' Stripped of any nuance.

I took a shot in the murk. 'You weren't flavour of the month, Leon. But I expect you know that.'

I held my breath waiting for him. I was turning purple round the ears when he finally said, 'I'm out of it.'

Out of what? Out of his minuscule mind on coke? Out of the white slave trade? Out of clean underwear?

I said, 'That's a shame, Leon. I was hoping you could give me a few traveller's tips on Kandy and the handicraft centre.'

'The what?'

Hellfire and damnation. I'd said the wrong thing. We were right back to his impersonation of a brick wall with paranoia. I tried an all-mates-together laugh. 'You know what I mean. The set-up.'

Leon said, 'Who are you?'

That was the third time he'd asked me, and the third time I didn't feel inclined to tell him. I said, 'I know we've never met, but just call me a friend.'

I think he wanted to call me something altogether different. He said, 'I've told you: I'm out of it. If you want to know something, ask the others.'

And the phone went down with a clatter and a clunk.

I slid off to the shower to think things over. Big brother Dominic pampers himself in the hygiene department. I splashed myself all over with Givenchy bath oil and plastered my locks with lashings of creamy lanolin. I smelt so sweet I could almost fancy myself. All the while the high-powered shower battered me senseless. I emerged fresh and pink and somewhat eroded. I wrapped my fragrant form in Dominic's robe, uncorked the Booths and draped myself across a chair.

The ulcerous Leon is the talkative type by nature. His every sentence begins with a capital I and carries a me or two, with the odd myself thrown in, just in case the listener forgets who the star is around here. But he'd been curiously reticent during our little chat. He'd doled out a few dozen words at most. Strange. Taken on their own, Leon's utterings were about as meaningful as anything he ever sang. But when I dovetailed them into what little I knew, he had blabbed his head off.

First, whatever was going on in Kandy it was not the sort of thing you talked about in front of the children. Second, Sir James and the 'others' were embroiled in it. Third, there had been a major flap, and Leon was the cause of it. He was no longer a part of the Kandy club. I guessed he hadn't left of his own accord. He'd sounded miffed when he said, 'I'm out of it.'

My paisley patterned shins poked out of the paisley patterned robe. I frowned at them. I wanted to be on the next plane to Sri Lanka. But not on pins like these. And certainly not togged up like Noel Coward. I started my preparations anyway. I spent the next hour ransacking Dominic's wardrobe for suitable gear.

He had a couple of lightweights and a drawerful of casual stuff. I made my selection, packed a baby Samsonite, adding razors, soap etc. Big Brother didn't have a camera, or if he did, he was off somewhere snapping beavers with it. I said, 'Never mind, you can always buy yourself an Olympus in duty free.' And then I said, 'Balls, you're not a monkey.' I got on the phone again, this time to ace lensman Frankie Frost. I know precisely what makes Frankie happy. I said, 'Fancy a little trip to a land of dusky maidens and curry galore?'

'Wot – Bradford?'

Sometimes you despair. I told him. He gibbered with delight and climbed a nearby wall.

'Frankie,' I said, when he'd got himself down again, 'this is real secret squirrel stuff. You mustn't tell anyone in the office.'

He had difficulty taking that one in. I tried again. 'No one must know. Nobody. Not even your girlfriend.'

He seemed to latch on. I don't think he tells her much anyway. I briefed him to get himself a visa, to grab my spare passport from Foreign Desk and do likewise. Frankie said, 'Done. Why all the secrecy?'

I said, 'Walls have ears.'

He said, 'You all right, Max?'

I felt out the bump on my head with tender searching fingers. It was still in the same place. 'Yes, I'm hunky-dory. Do me a favour and meet me tonight in the Ball and Chain. About eight.'

Frankie assumed the monkey's traditional role of penniless artiste. He mumbled, 'I'm broke.'

I said, 'I'm buying them.'

That did the trick.

I had a reason for pouring drink down his throat. I knew Frankie would dearly love to pack up his gizmos and come play with me in Sri Lanka. But I also knew he would want to do that only if the office was picking up the bill. If he thought he might have to reach in his own laden pockets he'd have conniptions. I had to hit him when his resistance was low.

We met up in the Ball and Chain. By day it's awash with lawyers, the Old Bill, hacks, murderers' alibi witnesses and similar scum. In the evening it is a quiet, half-civilised place where they even wash the glasses sometimes.

Frankie handed me a stack of mail. Get-well-never cards, I suspected. I pushed the pile aside and asked him about his week. He was in fine fettle. He'd had a good one. Monday he was at Gatwick, snapping the girl whose boyfriend got shot on their New Orleans honeymoon. The *Mail* had bought her up so she wouldn't be posing for any pix. But all the papers sent people just to give the *Mail* minders a hard time of it. We do that a lot. It's great fun.

Frankie started a rumpus in the arrivals lounge, punched a *Mirror* hack on the nose and sent the tearful widow sprawling. This might be seen as a touch heartless, seeing the poor girl had just lost her bridegroom. Normally we would be more considerate. But once someone sells their story to another paper, they become a legitimate target for all the others.

Those are the rules. And she was a star player in the game. If she didn't like it, she could always give the *Mail* their twenty grand back and the hacks would behave like the proper little gentlemen we are.

She was still sobbing as the *Mail* boys hustled her out of the terminal and threw her in the back of a limo. They'd blown it there because they forgot to get one with tinted glass. The widow wanted to sit up but the *Mail* heavies kept nailing her to the floor so no one else could get a shot of her. Every now and then she fought free to stick her head out the window and hurl obscenities at the pursuing pack. Then the *Mail* muscle would sit on her again. The upshot was everybody got a pic, and a far better pic than the *Mail*'s. The three-day bride made a four-column show on all the tabloid front pages next day, looking hysterical, haggard and ravaged by tears. Everyone stuck made up quotes on top of the snatched pic. 'Bring Back My Billy' (*Mirror*). 'Our Honeymoon Hell' (*Star*). 'Bill Bonked My Bridesmaid' (*Sun*). 'Man Has Cabbage Heart Transplant' (*Sport*). The only losers were the *Mail* who showed the ex-bride all noble and grieving, a single tear trickling mascara down her chops. They had sent one of their Sybil Fawlty weepie writers who penned 1,500 words of slush.

Anyway, back to the Ball & Chain and Frankie. I let him spin out his over-egged account of the day, ensuring his glass was never empty. He finished his ripping yarn and remembered me. 'What's this hush-hush trip about, then?'

I checked the bar for eavesdroppers, bugs and lip readers just to impress him and led him to a corner table. I told him the score. All he and I stood to gain from it was a couple of free flights, I said. After that we paid our own way. If we got a story, we could rip off the office hand over fist in exes. If not, we had each sacrificed a week's holiday and whatever it cost us in food and lodgings. I didn't mention drink. Frankie knew I'd take care of that.

When I'd finished he looked a stricken man. I didn't blame him. Now that I'd spelt out the deal it didn't sound that attractive to me either. I woke the barman and got another two drinks in. Frankie gulped a gollop of London Pride. He slid me a nervous glance. I could hear his little monkey brain thinking. It was thinking: 'Max is mad. It must be that bump on the beam.'

I said, 'You think I'm crazy.'

He didn't even try to humour me. He said, 'You're bloody bananas. Why should we fund the office on a story? What do you expect to get anyway?'

Two unanswerable questions. I force-fed him a cigarette to shut him up. I said, 'Frankie, you know you're the best snapper we've got. That's why I'm asking you. If anyone can get the story, it's you.'

Frankie is by no means our best monkey. There are at least three up the tree ahead of him. But he's a good foot-in-the-door man, and he's easily led. Not this time. He gave a sour laugh. 'That sod Belker knocked a hundred off my French exes. And you're saying we should do a foreign for free. No way.'

I argued this way and that. Frankie was unmoving. In desperation I hinted he might even win an award if he landed the story. Hacks and monkeys alike go all funny whenever anyone mentions awards. Our official line is: 'Awards? Who cares about them?' Unofficially we live in the pathetic hope that we might land one. And if our dreams are realised, we say: 'This silly old thing? I never wanted it. The Editor forced me to enter.' I remember the quote from a gnarled hack who late in his years finally bagged one: 'Awards are like piles. Sooner or later every bum gets them.' Only he didn't say bum.

Thus far Frankie had not even picked up a Highly Commended. No doubt this irked. I let him chew on the idea that Sri Lanka might eventually fill that gap on the lavatory wall while I ripped into my mail. American Express had sent me a wrist-slapping billet doux over the matter of an unpaid £1,264. The next missive was more interesting. It read:

> Hello Max,
>
> I'm really sorry you feel I'm holding out on you. I am holding out, because it's something I cannot bring myself to tell you. I don't know if I ever shall.
>
> I did not have anything to do with the attempt on your life. That is truly unthinkable. Whether you like it or not, I still regard you as my nearest and dearest friend.
>
> You may be in danger, but most certainly NOT from me. If you need my help in any way, just call.

The big scrawl at the bottom of the page said Ross. I laughed. It was one of those hollow jobs. Across the table Frankie looked up. 'All right, one for the strasse,' he said proffering his empty glass.

I tottered over to the bar where I was greeted without enthusiasm. I eyed myself in the mirror while the barman jiggled the optic. My face didn't look happy and it felt the same. Frankie was not falling for my wizard wheeze. I was still at the bar, double-checking my change, when I heard an amazing Whisssh-bisssh-BOOOF! From the corner. I swung around and there was Frankie running for cover. The middle of the table where we had been sitting was ablaze. Either American Express was doing a new line in blistering reminders or my private mail had self-combusted. I snatched up a water jug, shot over to the corner and splashed it on the bonfire. It blazed on. Frankie poked his head up by the fruit machine and started yelling for a fire extinguisher.

The barman rolled out from behind the counter armed with another jug. An interested bystander thoughtfully kicked the burning pile off the table, thereby almost setting the whole place alight. Frankie joined in the fun, jumping up and down on anything that glowed. Together, splashing and stamping, we beat the hell out of the fire, and mightily proud of ourselves we were too. The barman went off to phone the Law while Frankie and I fished ash out of our drinks. I turned over the charred debris with a delicate toe. The guilty party was a manila Jiffy bag, or what used to be a manila Jiffy bag. Now only a couple of singed corners remained. Them and a scorched contraption with wires protruding.

'What the hell's that?' asked Frankie, keeping his distance.

'That,' I said, 'is a warning.'

'What warning?'

'A warning to keep away from Sri Lanka.'

Frankie licked a burn mark the size of an amoeba on his hand. He was not used to letter bombs going off mid-drink. The experience made him a truculent and vengeful monkey. He gave the letter bomb a boot.

I flicked burnt paper from my sleeve. 'That settles it,' I said.

'Settles what?'

I said, 'There's no way I can ask you to go to Kandy if you could get hurt.'

Frankie said, 'Bollocks. Try keeping me away.'

'But, Frankie,' I said in angelic tones, 'I could never forgive myself if something happened to you. These buggers aren't kidding about, you know.'

He pointed at his invisible scar. 'See that? Nobody does that to Frank Frost.'

I murmured a weak protestation. He steam-rollered it down. He stuck his uninjured hand in a bulging pocket. He said, 'Right, let's have a drink and talk about Sri Lanka.'

We were savouring the first sips when an idea suddenly struck a match in his beady eyes.

'You know something?' he said. 'This is the kind of story that wins awards.'

We had to wait a week before Rick the Travel Ed came up with the trip. I fretted and kicked my heels, or Dominic's heels anyway. I needed something else to fill my waking hour. Which was why I fled the fortress one fine morning to seek stimulus at East London coroner's court. On the menu today was the item of Shirley Patricia Ham, late of Loughton, in the county of Essex. It was just the formal opening. Normally hacks don't bother to cover these. They don't provide copy. What happens is a copper gets up and says the corpse of the deceased was found at such and such a spot and identification was made by so and so. I was the sole hack present and the coroner gave me a fishy look. I heard a subbed down version of the autopsy. Shirley died from asphyxiation, the coroner's clerk read out. I blinked. A portly middle-aged man with a scrubby moustache paddled in, followed closely by a woman who looked just like him, minus the whiskers. I recognised them as Shirley's mum and dad. You don't usually get family at inquest openings. They sat very close to each other at the back of the room while D.I. Harold Pennycuik got up on his hind legs and said inquiries were continuing. The coroner said thanks a lot folks and adjourned the inquest until July 23.

I grabbed Shirley's dad as he emerged blinking in the sunshine. He was dry-eyed, but you could see he was not quite with us. I poked my hand out. I said who I was and how sorry I was. Mr Ham stepped back and looked me up and down. He was considering whether I might have murdered his only child. After a moment's careful appraisal he declared me not guilty.

He said, 'Shirley didn't meet you that night.'

I said no, that's why I'd called him. I asked if she'd told him what she planned to tell me. He hesitated, trying to get it right. 'No. She just said, see you later, I'm just going to see Mike about something.'

'Max,' I corrected automatically.

'Max,' he said.

I said, 'But she never hinted what her information was?'

Mr Ham waggled his head. He said, 'I can't remember. But she was expecting to get something from you.'

Yes, large wads of fivers, I thought. I said, 'Shirley had been selling us stories.'

Mr Ham looked at me hard. 'I hope my daughter was not murdered just for helping you get a cheap story,' he said.

And off he walked, leaving me feeling like whoever it was who killed Cock Robin.

I was in a bar in Cheapside, trying to convince myself I wasn't such a bad sort after all, when my bleep bleep-bleeped. At first I didn't know it was mine. The place was stacked to the rafters with City white collar criminals, each armed with mobile phones, pagers, parking alarms. There was also the electronic trill of the till plus the microwave timer adding to the gaiety of the moment. When my pager gave voice, half a dozen adjoining drinkers dived into their pockets. It took me a moment to suss out I was the wanted man. My neighbours glared at me. I pressed the message button and said, 'Jesus Christ!' Right out loud. I read the message again. It still said the same thing: 'PSE CALL SIR JAMES TOMLIN SOONEST – NEWS DESK'. I didn't. I ordered another gin soonest and did a spot of pondering. Why should the mighty midget feel the pressing need for my conversation? Maybe they'd watered the gin, or else they'd beefed up the tonic, because I didn't come up with any answers. I sought out the gents, locked myself in a cubicle and dialled the Tomlin number. My old chum, the snotty twerp in Sir James's private office, answered. He recognised my voice too. He asked me where I was calling from and I told him precisely where. I don't think he believed me but he was ever so polite. He said, 'If it is convenient for you, Mister Chard, Sir James would very much like to see you.'

'Why?'

'I believe he wishes to have a conversation with you.'

'Where?'

'Wherever is suitable for you.'

I said, 'Maybe he would like to meet me at my convenience.' It wasn't a great joke, but it deserved at least a ripple. He ignored it.

He said, 'Sir James is free now. He's here, of course.'

I said, 'Where's here of course?'

He gave me an address in Victoria Street, a ten minute limp from my present address. I said I was having a drink with a murder squad detective and would be there shortly. This was a subtle way of saying that if my body turned up in the Thames, the Old Bill would know where to point the finger.

I took my time ambling round to the premises of Freleng-Bourke. It was a slabby office block with mauve windows. It looked like it had liver trouble. A sallow individual, decked out as a security guard, shepherded me to reception, where a Miss Jamaica lookalike turned on a smile that warmed the cockles of my heart and much more besides. She led me like a puppy down a flecked marble corridor to a flecked marble lift. We were alone. Miss Jamaica hit the top button. She was cool and spicy and delicious. I was none of these. I joked feebly: 'You're going all the way with me?'

She gave an easy languid laugh. 'All the way.'

By the time we hit the penthouse floor I was a grinning imbecile. She didn't seem to notice. Off she tripped down another marble corridor, pink this time, with me panting a yard or so in arrears. She knocked on an acre of pink tinted ash. A voice commanded: 'Come in.'

We came in. She said, 'Mister Chard to see you, Sir James.' And she was gone. I felt as if someone had turned off the sun.

Tomlin said, 'Won't you sit down, Mister Chard?' He indicated a fragile settee with spindly little legs. I eased myself down. He was already seated, but he got up from behind his desk and opened a cupboard knee deep in bottles and glasses.

'Care for a drink?'

I said I cared for a gin. He did the business and helped himself to a thimble of sherry. He handed over the glass and pulled up an ancient chair to face me. It was higher off the ground than my chi-chi settee so our eyes were level. But his were half hidden behind his tinted specs. They went with the mauve windows.

I sampled the gin and inspected the privileges of high office. Floor to ceiling roman blinds across a panoramic window. Bland walls, dotted here and there with shots of bods in dinner jackets smirking at each other. Squidgy buff carpet littered with antique chairs and sideboards. It didn't look much like an office.

'Care for a cigar?' he pushed a silver box my way. I shook my head.

'A cigarette?' Another silver box.

I was wondering what he was going to offer me next. Miss Jamaica? I accepted a cigarette and eyed him through the smoke. He said, 'I'm sure you're wondering why I asked you here.'

I indicated that a certain perplexity had crossed my mind. He had his lips set in a benign smile. The sort of smile that doctors in looney bins wear to work. He tacked one leg over the other and regarded me fondly. He said, 'I believe we started off on the wrong foot, Mister Chard, or may I call you Max?'

I said, 'Okay, Jimmy.'

The smile slipped off the edge of his mouth. He said, 'When we met in Switzerland, I was understandably upset. My wife had just been murdered and I suspected that you were a muck-raking reporter.'

He got that one right. I nursed my gin and didn't say a thing.

Tomlin said, 'So I hope you will forgive my brusqueness at our first meeting. I am not by nature a discourteous man.'

I thought that one deserved a smile.

He pushed on. 'I have subsequently learned that you are a highly respected crime journalist and that you were engaged in the legitimate pursuit of a news story. I know you have since tried to contact me and have been, ah, fobbed off. I'll be honest with you, Max. I was still upset about the incident in Switzerland.'

I tipped my cigarette in an ashtray the size of a soup tureen. I said, 'So what's changed?'

He flipped over the palm of a hand. 'I felt I was being unreasonable. I have asked you here so that we can speak without rancour. I believe you wish to ask me some questions about my late wife's work. I understand this. You are involved in reporting a story: my only interest is to see my wife's killer brought to justice. The two are not incompatible. I have already spoken at length to the police. However, I feel your persistence is to be welcomed. Investigative journalists can sometimes succeed where the proper authorities have failed.'

It was a lengthy speech. It made me feel thirsty. I peered into my empty glass. He took the hint and gave the gin bottle another squeeze. He sat himself down again, switched on the smile and said, 'Now, what do you want to talk about?'

I said, 'Kandy.'

His voice drifted up a semi-tone. 'Kandy? I gather you are referring to my wife's WorldCare work?'

I said he had gathered correctly. He eased back in his chair and studied the distant ceiling.

'Kandy,' he said, 'is the location for one of her many projects.'

So far he hadn't even stuck a name on Claudine. I said, 'And what's so special about it?'

A light cocktail party laugh. He treated himself to a little sigh. He said, 'You see, I am perplexed, because to be totally frank, the Sri Lankan operation is a very minor part of the Foundation's programme.'

I sipped my gin.

Tomlin said, 'In various parts of the Third World, the Foundation has specific projects which are intended to focus on self help. For example, in Mozambique there is a rural farming project . . .'

I said, 'And in Kandy?'

'In Kandy there is a cultural crafts centre. Its aim is to encourage local skills by producing and selling traditional handiwork. Batiks, hand-woven silks, jewellery. The island is rich in gem stones, you know. The centre sells its products to tourists and the money helps to fund other local activities.'

I said, 'It's a souvenir shop.'

'If you like, yes.'

I said, 'But what makes it so popular?'

Tomlin frowned. 'I'm afraid I don't quite understand.'

I said, 'Leon Knapp speaks highly of it.'

He said sharply, 'You've spoken to him?'

I said, 'Oh yes. At length. I got him when he came home and we had a good natter about what goes on in Kandy.'

Tomlin forgot to smile. He sat rock still, his specs scanning my face.

I said carelessly, 'Seems like Leon had a great old time of it in Kandy. But he didn't say much about arts and crafts.'

Tomlin sat there holding his glass tightly. He got up and toddled off to the drinks bar to top up his sherry. He called, 'Care for another drink?'

People should never say: 'Care for another drink?' It makes you sound like an alco. They should say: 'Let me top you up', or, better still, just snatch your glass and splosh drink into it. I overcame my distaste. 'Thanks.'

Tomlin said, 'What did Leon say?' He still had his back to me. The words came out as hard as little stones.

I went coy. 'I'd rather not go into that.'

He returned with a gin, a miserly sample this time. He attempted a laugh. 'Leon can be quite a joker.'

'He said some very funny things.'

Tomlin was working out how to follow this when there was a brisk knock on the door. It sailed open before he had a chance to say come in. A man in his late twenties entered. He eyed me suspiciously.

'My son,' said Tomlin.

He grunted. 'Pleasedtomeetyou.' I knew the voice. This was the stroppy herbert who answered my calls. He didn't offer to shake hands.

Little Tomlin senior said to big Tomlin junior, 'We were talking about the Kandy project.'

Junior looked baleful but didn't speak. Tomlin turned back to me. He said, 'I think that's all I can tell you. If you have any further queries, please don't hesitate to call. Michael and I would be delighted to help.'

I felt all hurt. Sir James didn't want me around any more. I emptied my glass and stood up. I said, 'Thanks, but I'll get all I want when I'm out there.'

'Out there?' This from Tomlin junior.

I said, 'Yes. Didn't I say? I'm going to Kandy next week.'

I showed myself out. The Tomlins had suddenly developed rigor mortis.

On the way out of the building, Miss Jamaica and I dazzled each other with our smiles.

# Chapter Eleven

We caught an early One-Eleven out of Heathrow. It was the first of June but it looked like the thirty-first of January. Neither of us felt like talking. We met up in the departure lounge, had a beer apiece and opened our papers. I was reading a fun-filled story about a gym mistress who had run off with her star pupil. Her star girl pupil. But my mind wasn't on it. I don't quite know where it was. Sometimes it was back with Rosie who wasn't speaking to me any more ('You rotten sod – we were supposed to be going on holiday to the Maldives'). Sometimes it was with the Old Bill and the letter bomb ('Seems like somebody else doesn't like you' – D.I. Harry 'Horselaughs' Pennycuik). Occasionally it strayed to that glorious moment in the office, the day I dropped in to pick up my exes. I'd been zipping down the corridor when the bog door popped open and out bulged the evil Belker. He put on a slimy smile and asked after my health. I said I was feeling wonderful, just to piss him off. He said that was great, but what was I doing in the office? Was I back in harness already? Oh no, I responded. It was much, much too soon for that. I gave him the sunniest of smiles and said the Editor had insisted I go on a nice freebie. And whither was I bound? he inquired, in the fond hope it was someplace renowned for its malarial mosquitoes and rabid bats. I said, 'Do you remember that time I asked you to send me to Kandy?'

He nodded dumbly, his lizard eyes sick with premonition.

I said, 'Well, I'm off to Sri Lanka in the morning.'

The Beast Belker paled beneath his pallor. His eyes went squiffy and his jaw froze. I stood there beaming at him, watching his lips grind out: 'Have a nice time.'

'I will,' I assured him. 'I will.'

And off I swung down the corridor, whistling a breezy tune.

It was a happy memory. Less happy was the memory of my flaming hate mail. They'd called in the anti-terrorist gang to see if the letter bomb had the stamp of the Animal Liberation Front, the IRA or similar headbangers. It didn't. It was a homemade affair with a couple of ounces of gunpowder, a battery and a crude trigger. The general principle was for it to go pop as soon as I ripped open the envelope. Fate didn't like the idea. It had a better plan which involved Frankie pushing the envelope into a beer puddle while I was off buying yet more drink. The beer soaked through the envelope, short circuited the electrics and set the thing off.

I asked the anti-terrorist ace what would have happened if I had opened it as planned. He said at worst I might have lost my typing finger. So it was just a nuisance bomb, a way of letting me know the baddies still hadn't forgotten me. I went through the whole Claudine Tournier/Shirley Ham story with them. The anti-terrorist blokes got bored and went off to practise drilling holes in cardboard men. Big Ben Ashbee, the super fronting the murder inquiry, listened sadly and told me to watch my step. His cliché, not mine. I suggested he lock up Sir James Tomlin and his brigands for my protection. Nothing doing. But did I want someone riding shotgun on me in London? I pictured a large Plod sharing my Barbican retreat and boring me senseless with his colourful memoirs of booking desperado motorists who hadn't paid their road tax. I said no thank you, Ben. I'd just sleep with a loaded ballpoint under the pillow. He seemed to think that would do the trick.

The airport speaker went bing bong and a girl who had gone to elocution lessons announced the departure of KLM 338 to Amsterdam. Would passengers kindly get off their backsides and scurry along to Gate Thirty-six. Frankie and I were in devilish mood so we hung on for the final call.

The flight was half empty. Our fellow fliers were business types with personal organisers and stripey ties. They took the *FT* or *Der Telegraaf* from the courtesy trolley. The flash ones took both. None of the suits looked capable of anything more violent than slapping the temp's rump.

I wasn't really in the mood, but I had a Dutch gin, noblesse oblige and I read the duty free tariff with the fascination of a connoisseur. Frankie fell asleep with his mouth open and his legs across the aisle. We skimmed down into Schipol, taking care to avoid the high-rise flats. It was coming up their lunchtime. Just gone my breakfastime.

Frankie and I legged it over to the long haul terminal where he found a kiddies' room littered with space invader machines. He pushed a couple of blond infants out of the way and started blowing green blobs to purple bits. I'm not sure if he was even looking at the screen. He just wanted to press buttons. Monkeys are suckers for that sort of thing. A blissful smile wrapped itself halfway around his face. The machines were for free. There was also a video cartoon channel, but that was probably beyond his attention span.

I left him playing in the kindergarten while I converted some of my pounds into guilders and cruised the duty free mall. Schipol has a great reputation as a happy shopping ground, but I've never figured out why. If ever I feel like blowing seventy quid on an Armani tie, there's a friendly psychiatrist I know.

We had three hours to kill before the Colombo flight. I treated myself to some muddy coffee, a hunk of rubber cheese and croissants which tasted marginally less interesting than balsa wood. I had an Amstel beer to placate my aggrieved palate. Ten quid, thank you werry much. Our flight flashed up on the departures board. I went and detached Frankie from his machine. His pupils were scooting around like space invaders on warp factor five.

There was a double security check, which meant everyone bound for Sri Lanka had to stand by clicking their tongues for five minutes while Frankie demonstrated that his various geegaws were not ingeniously disguised bombs. I don't know why they bothered.

Anybody could see he was too tall to be a Tamil Tiger. A Tamil Camel, maybe.

On the plane our seats were about three inches from the in-flight movie screen. Besides which my earphones didn't work. I explained our predicament to a blonde concealing her naked body in the blue uniform of a KLM stewardess. She laughed gaily and said tough titty. Hacks do not take kindly to being treated without due respect. We started a row. She called up reinforcements in the shape of her twin sisters. They roped in the head steward who was hiding in the galley. Pretty soon the whole plane was in uproar as they scoured it for alternative seats. We rejected their first suggestions out of hand. They were in the no smoking ghetto. We eventually got what we wanted, a pair of seats near the galley, so that we could summon up refreshments more easily. It's a terrible thing to admit, but hacks get a buzz out of starting petty rows like these. It keeps our adrenalin on stream.

The 747 swung out wide over Amsterdam and hid itself in a cloud a thousand miles long. I'd exhausted the papers. The only thing to do was follow our progress on the screen map. They waited an hour and stuck on a movie. It was some candyfloss effort about a sexy pizza girl who teams up with a lunatic chef to bilk the Mafia out of fifty zillion dollars. She kept her clothes on, otherwise I might have enjoyed it. Six miles beneath us Greece slumbered while I snoozed. Frankie went into a coma. I woke up in Oman in brazen sunshine. So this was where Leon Knapp was stretchered off. It didn't look a jolly place to have a bleeding ulcer, or even a head cold. Frankie slept on.

Off we flew again, out across the Persian Gulf and tacking south east over the Indian Ocean. Sri Lanka finally put in an appearance. I gazed down on a green and sunny isle and wondered what dark secret lurked beneath its leafy canopy. I was feeling melodramatic.

They poured us off at Colombo about ten in the morning. Everyone seemed delighted to see us. We flashed our cheesiest smiles and charmed through immigration. I sent Frankie to change £1,000 into coin of the realm while I sought out a taxi. The cab bosses lived in a cubby hole by the information desk.

I said to one: 'Mount Lavinia.'

He gave me a dirty look. I wondered whether he had a sister called Lavinia. Another driver came to the rescue. 'No Mount Lavinia, sir,' he said happily.

I had a brochure in my pocket which promised paradise at 'the magical Mount Lavinia hotel'. I also had two ocean-front rooms booked there. I showed them the brochure.

'Ah, Mount Lavinia,' said bloke one.

'It's closed,' said bloke two.

'Yes. Closed,' said the first bloke. 'But we have very good hotel in Colombo.'

'Much better than Mount Lavinia. Special price for you,' said the second one.

Frankie loomed over my shoulder. 'What the hell's going on?'

I made the introductions. 'Frankie, these are a couple of con artists; con artists, meet Frankie.'

They flashed their teeth at the pleasure of

meeting him. I said, 'Now, I want you to take us to the Mount Lavinia. We always stay at closed hotels.'

Number one glanced at number two. Number two glanced back. Number one said, 'It is very far away, sir.'

'Very far,' I agreed. 'Eight miles south of Colombo. That far.' I had read my brochure.

Frankie cut in, 'How much?'

More silent communion as they weighed up how much they could skim us for. Number one said, 'Forty American dollars. Thirty English pounds. Air conditioned taxi, sirs.'

Frankie and I laughed hysterically. I said, 'Let's call it five pounds.'

Now it was their turn to roll about in merriment. We haggled on amid convulsions of outraged laughter until they agreed to do the biz for fifteen quid. It was still a rip off but we were getting thirsty. We bounced off in the back of a dusty Datsun towards the chaos that calls itself Colombo. The chief industry hereabouts is the making of noise, and very good they are at it too. Tuk-tuks parped, trucks blared, bikes and trikes ting-a-linged and in the shade of whopping great trees buddhist monks tinkled their bells so as not to be left out of things. We bumped around for an hour until we fetched up outside a hotel of sparkling brilliance. 'Mount Lavinia,' said our driver, as if he'd built it himself. It was open and it had welcome writ large on the mat.

We checked in, ordered a brace of Goldbrews and stretched ourselves on the terrace. Far below, boisterous waves slapped the rocks about.

'This is the life,' said Frankie.

'I wonder what the poor are doing,' I mused.

'Drinking better beer than this,' said Frankie.

But he forced himself to down a couple more Goldbrews before shambling off to his room, returning in a pair of Bermuda shorts of rare and hideous design. He said, 'I'm going for a swim', just in case I got the wrong idea and thought he was offering himself up for seduction.

I retired to my room and began poring over maps, brochures and guidebooks. Kandy came highly recommended. There was a botanical garden with 4,000 plants, and there was a huge lake, a colourful bazaar and the celebrated Tooth Temple. It was up in the hills, 70 miles north of Colombo, and the most interesting way of getting there was by train. The brochures suggested first class in the observation car of the Intercity express. That was the way to do it. I've always been a sucker for trains, especially those kitted out with buffets. Such was the Intercity express. I wandered down to reception where a Miss de Silva made all the bookings. I was about to head for the bar when a sudden thought assailed me. I said, 'Is it a Poya day tomorrow?'

Miss de Silva assured me it wasn't. I drifted off again. I got five yards when she called after me: 'Even if it was, you could still drink in the hotel.'

Clever girl, that Miss de Silva.

Frankie and I went walkies in the evening. He had burned his shoulders basking by the pool. The pain was hellish, he said. I said, 'Is it as bad as the time you got burned by the letter bomb?' He didn't speak to me for half an hour.

We found a restaurant before he died and tucked into a motley assortment of things. At least I did. Frankie had a pizza. We embarked on the local fire-water which was alcoholic and drinkable, which, I suppose, is the same thing. But I was glad of my bottle of duty free Glenfiddich back at the hotel. The bill for our excursion was on the nice side of £10. Frankie was delighted. I wasn't so tickled. The owner refused to hand over any blank receipts.

Back in my room Frankie kindly helped me with the Glenfiddich. I told him the plan. At the crack of ten we were to get up, breakfast and voyage north to Kandy on the famous express. He didn't like the idea.

'Why don't we hire a car and drive there?' he demanded.

Because I wasn't going to risk my life with all those jay-walking buffaloes around, that's why. He grumbled a bit but bowed to my superior wisdom.

Life moves at a different pace in the tropics. Things are slower there. Nowhere is this more true than on the Intercity express train from Colombo to Kandy and vice versa. If there'd been a copper on the track he would have booked us all for loitering. We sat in the observation car, watching myopic butterflies bat into the rear window. 'Great way to travel,' snorted Frankie. And the buffet car wasn't quite what I had in mind. It offered chipped blue cups of milky tea. There were also unidentifiable things to eat, but it seemed a shame to disturb the flies. Otherwise it was a jolly outing. We were surrounded by amiable Sri Lankans, determined to make us enjoy ourselves. They pressed their services as bearers, guides, interpreters. I said, great, we were Serbo-Croat. They shut up.

One man, who had been sitting silently watching us, broke into a laugh. He came across, dipped his head in a bow and said, 'Hello, I'm Varun.' He was about thirty, slimmish, neat and looked just like anybody else. We said hello Varun and returned to watching the jungle unfold inch by inch. Varun was not to be put off. He squeezed in beside us and launched into a long catechism of his remarkable talents. He could drive, guide, translate, show us the best bars, the plushest hotels, the most complaisant young women. Somewhere along the line I got interested. And what would his inestimable services cost us?

He measured us out carefully. 'Fifty pounds a day.'

I said, 'Call it thirty.'

We called it forty and shook hands. When the train finally clawed its way into Kandy, Varun snatched our luggage and told us to follow. He stormed his way through the reception committee of vendors and beggars, telling them to bugger off. Varun had us sussed. He led us directly to a leafy cafe, ordered up a couple of Singha beers and left to get a car. He returned ten minutes later with something that looked suspiciously like our battered Datsun of the day before. Varun thought it the bee's knees.

He said, 'I will do all driving. You must have very special knowledge to drive in Sri Lanka.'

This very special knowledge was apparently attained with the help of a large shot of arrak.

Varun scoffed a couple and then said, 'Now you want very special hotel with all amenity. I take you to MacDuff hotel. There is everything you desire. Swimming pool, very fine restaurant. Very clean. All rooms Ay Cee.'

I said, 'What's Ay Cee?'

'Air condition. Everywhere air condition. It is a hotel for gentlemen.'

We didn't like the sound of that. Frankie said, 'How much?'

Not very much at all – twenty-five quid for a double room, with a view over the lake thrown in. We parked our stuff and went walkabout. On first acquaintance Kandy seemed to live up to its advance hype. A civilised but colourful burgh, peopled by snake charmers, monks, fortune tellers, musicians and individuals selling things made from coconuts – mats, carved masks, arrak, mandolins, cures for impotence, money boxes, pots, coconut treacle, coconut pickle. The less imaginative simply flogged coconuts.

Varun, a man who liked his arrak, called a drink stop. We took our ease and watched the rich tapestry of Kandyian society unscroll around us. There were plenty of shysters and knaves on view, but I've seen worse in Rio. I've seen a damn sight worse in Oxford Street. But I didn't see a soul who looked as if he might have a hand in Sir James Tomlin's funny business, whatever it might be.

Varun, dipping into his third arrak, felt it was time

he earned his keep. He said, 'Now I show you how to save the fifty pounds a day you pay me.'

'Forty pounds.'

'Okay, forty pounds. First you ask for the bill and I show you the five-card trick which people play on the tourists.'

He had our undivided attention. We got the bill, presented inside a leather-look folder. Varun produced a pair of specs with one arm missing and perused it.

'First card is they charge you too much,' he said. 'Then they put on the bill something you do not have. Third card is they add it up wrong. Fourth card, they give you wrong change.'

He stopped. I said, 'And the fifth card?'

He smiled slyly. 'You see in a minute.'

It took about fifteen times that. In the meantime he got the prices knocked down, wiped three mystery brandies off the bill, corrected the waiter's arithmetic and made him cough up the right small change.

'Now,' said Varun, still looking like a fox, 'you tell me if everything is okay.'

It all looked kosher. Then I counted up the big 100 rupee notes the waiter had placed on top of the bill. There should have been eight. There were seven. I summoned the waiter. Where's the other note? I demanded. After all, it was worth seven quid. The waiter's face was a study in outraged innocence. He picked up the bill, and there lying under it in the folder was the missing 100 rupees.

'I gave you right money,' he shouted and stumped off in a huff.

Varun said, 'That is the fifth trick. He was hoping you pick up the money on top of the bill and walk away. That way you never know he has stolen 100 rupees. That's the biggest trick of all. You see? Pretty soon I earn my fifty pounds a day.'

'Forty pounds.'

'Forty pounds.'

We had a guide, we had transport, we had lodgings. What more could a man want? Well he could do with a decent meal for a start. Dish of the day at the MacDuff was not a decent meal for man or beast. It was billed as special curry. I asked a deliriously happy waiter what was so special about it.

'Wenison,' said he.

'Wenison?'

He spread his fingers and poked them out like antlers above each ear. 'Wenison.'

If they could build cars from deer they'd last forever. I pushed Bambi's remains around my plate and picked at the rice. What I would have given for a decent Ruby Murray down Soho.

Later in the lounge we settled ourselves in vast clubbable armchairs and lit into the arrak. Varun insisted on the Polgoda Walauwa premium version, at a price to match. 'What every gentleman drinks,' he said. Just for the novelty of it, we decided to be gentlemen. The arrak was peppery and sweet at the same time, but thinned out with soda you could almost get to like it. Varun was an expert on liquor. He told me something I had never known before.

'Inside every barrel of White Horse Scottish whisky they put the head of a white horse,' he vouchsafed. 'That is why it has a very fine taste. That is why they call it White Horse.'

I absorbed this information. I said, 'So, when they're making Johnny Walker do they go around looking for blokes called Johnny Walker to stick in it?'

Varun regarded me as if I were an idiot. He changed the subject. 'Tomorrow I show you all the famous sights in Kandy. I take you to the Tooth Temple and we go to watch the elephants in the river.'

Frankie said, 'What are the elephants doing in the river?'

'They are getting washed, of course,' said Varun, regarding Frankie as if he were an idiot.

It was time to let our trusty guide in on what we were up to in Kandy. I didn't fill in all the fine detail but I said there was mischief afoot. Varun dropped his smile. He listened with his head cocked and his gaze steady on me. When I had done he said, 'There are many things in Sri Lanka which people do not speak of.'

But he was prepared to speak of them. There were the mothers who twist the feet of their newborn babes to provide them, the doting mums, with a living begging bowl. It paid well until the kid was about seven or eight, by which time the mother had usually produced another crippled little earner. There were drug dealers in the south, rent boys and prostitutes on every beach. And then there were the baby farms. The government had rooted out most of them but they were still operating in the backwoods. The farms were big money, said Varun. A country girl could earn herself £200 just by giving birth. Her child vanished into a flaky orphanage while middlemen scouted out likely buyers. The biggest market was among childless Scandinavian couples.

Varun said, 'They come here and see the child. They want it. They say to the middlemen: "Okay, we give you two thousand pounds." Everybody says that is fine. They give the child a western name, so now she is not called Saliya. She is called Mary. They go home, but they do not take Mary with them. When they are home they put her name on their passport. They have papers which say it is a legal adoption. They come back to get their baby. When they are leaving Sweden or Denmark no one says to them: "Where is your baby?" Many tourists leave their baby at home. When they come here, the baby sellers play their five-card trick. They say the price is now two thousand more. The man and woman pay because they want their baby. But the sellers say they must pay for medicine because she has been sick. And they must pay for her clothes. Now they have their baby and they are happy. But the seller plays his last card. He says he needs to bribe immigration fellows. He needs another two thousand. They are desperate, but they want to go home with their baby very quick. They give him the money. Total bill is seven thousand, not two thousand. Next day they fly to Sweden with little Mary. When they come to immigration in Sweden, the officer looks at their passport and sees her name. Everything seems okay. He lets Mary in. That's how it's done.'

'Wow!' said Frankie.

Varun helped himself to my cigarettes. He was

enjoying his role as racket buster. He said, 'Maybe you do not believe me? If you want to see, you just go to airport and watch for white couples with a brown baby. You ask them how they got their baby. They don't talk to you.'

I said, 'Does the baby trade go on in Kandy?'

Varun shrugged. 'Maybe. I don't know. I will ask for you.'

I thought of the various low lifes associated with Tomlin and tried to picture them flogging hot babies. Morally they were capable of anything but realistically this wasn't their style. There had been nothing in our files on any of them being the proud possessor of a heavily tanned son or daughter. And the financial rewards were small beer. Varun might see £7,000 as megabucks, but Tomlin dealt in millions. There was something more to it than imported infants.

Frankie was thinking along the same lines. He said, 'Maybe they get the kids to swallow bags of heroin.'

Eh? I said, 'Yes, Frankie, and maybe they stuff their nappies with stolen elephants.'

'Don't be bloody stupid.'

'I won't if you won't,' I promised.

Frankie was aggrieved. 'All right, maybe it's not heroin. But they could hide a stack of diamonds in the nappies.'

Diamonds. I hadn't thought of that. I asked Varun if there was a thriving trade in under-the-counter sparklers.

'Most certainly yes, Mister Max,' he said, reaching for his arrak. 'There is illegal trade in everything. In diamonds, in drugs, in gold. You name it and there is smuggling. Anything. Absolutely anything.'

'Coconuts?' queried Frankie.

And thus ended that particular meeting of the Brains' Trust.

# Chapter Twelve

The Alahaka arts and culture centre perched itself on a hill road just outside of town. To get there you drove through trees the height of skyscrapers, their branches bowed down with chittering macaque monkeys. The arts centre was in a cleft cut into the hillside. Behind it there was dense jungle. Beneath it, a spectacular fall to Kandy. You got a great view of the much-vaunted lake and the Mahaveli river – 'The longest river in Sri Lanka,' boasted Varun. This is like a Dutchman singing the praises of the highest hillock in Holland, but we did the decent thing and gaped with awe.

Frankie had gone overboard with his camera gear and looked like he had mugged a coachload of Japanese tourists. I was Mr Cool in my borrowed suit. I had a tape recorder with a hidden mike tucked under my watch strap. I also had a small notebook and pen. That's all I needed.

We were the first visitors of the day to the centre and were greeted like kings by a bevy of lissom lovelies with fluttery eyelashes. They pointed out brass lamps and perfume sprays, silk scarves and ties, the many and several products of the good old coconut palm, filigree silver and pretty-pretty gems, squat little boxes of tea, rugs to stick on your floor, rugs to hang on your wall, saris, wood carvings and all manner of things. I bought Rosie a postcard depicting a fresco of a topless beauty with a thirtyeight double-D frontage. On the back of the card was an apposite poem. I quote:

Ladies like you,
Make men pour out their hearts,
And you also,
Have thrilled the body,
Making its hair stiffen with desire

I wrote the message: Wish you were Her, and handed it to a salesgirl with a peek-a-boo sari. She licked a stamp with a delicate pink tongue. That fairly made my hair stiffen. I don't think Frankie had noticed a single artefact on display. He was just standing there leering at the girls. Varun was wandering around picking up doodahs, examining the prices and saying: 'Oh dear me, no,' with a rueful laugh and a scrunched up face. I went for a long browse through the shelves, shadowed by a girl with a hole in the back of her frock. Whenever I paused to look at something she would dart forward and assure me, 'Very good price. Extremely popular with all our customers.' She had lovely eyes so I believed her, despite Varun's derisory hoots.

I asked her name. Malini. I said, 'The centre is a charity, yes?'

Malini bobbed her head, yes, then shook her head,

no. 'It is self help. It promotes Sri Lankan traditional craftsmen.'

I said, 'So the money goes to them?'

Another bit of bobbing and shaking. 'Some yes. Not all. Much is raised to help the local community.'

I said, 'What does it help?'

Malini frowned in concentration. She said, 'You wait here.' She skipped off. I waited holding a pink wooden elephant in my hand. It gave me a sour look.

'Can I help you Mister Charrod?'

I turned around to find a slim, dapper man standing two inches behind me.

'It's Chard,' I said.

'Yes, Mister Charrod. How might I be of assistance?'

I said for a kick-off I'd like to know how he knew my name, or an approximation thereof. He flashed a double-decker smile.

'I was told to expect you, Mister Charrod. Mister Tomlin said you are coming.'

I said, 'And you are . . .?'

'I am Mister Hector Samarsinghe,' he said. 'I am very pleased to meet you.'

The feeling was not mutual. Mister Hector Samarsinghe looked the type you wouldn't buy a new car from. He had funny eyes, a mix of nutty brown and sea green. This might sound a happy blend. It wasn't. You didn't really notice the brown bit. What you did notice were the green centres, as cold, as empty, as dead as a stuffed snake's. He was dressed according to the fashion of the isle, that is in a pastel shirt with trousers which looked as if their matching jacket was hung up elsewhere. He was suave and at ease. He stuck out a ring-bedecked hand and waved at his wares.

'You like our centre, Mister Charrod?'

I said I was speechless with admiration. My soul thirsted for every detail of its operation. Samarsinghe invited us all to his office for a chat. It was a spacious room, decorated in a mix of the mysterious east and the moneyed west. Our host ordered Malini to get cracking with the teapot. He took up residence in a swivel chair behind the desk. He was facing me head on. I was in a rattan chair with no arms. Varun in another off to my left. Frankie was drifting about somewhere in the background.

Samarsinghe pressed his fingertips together and dipped his head in a sketchy bow. He said, 'Now, what would you like to know, Mister Charrod?'

I didn't answer immediately. I looked around. Here is another tip to those lost souls who hanker to become hacks: You can sit the long day through, interviewing someone who blocks your every query with a no comment, yet all the while his surroundings scream out to be heard. They tell you more about the man than he knows himself. By the props on view I could see that Mister Hector Samarsinghe was one rather in love with his bathroom mirror. On the desk was a twelve by ten snap of him presenting or accepting something from Claudine Tournier. The left wall was given over to a whole album of such shots. Hector looked exactly the same in each. Only his partners were different. Here he was gladhanding Sir James Tomlin's snotty son, there another with Leon

Knapp. The goldfish mug of Lewis Trefoyle goggled out of a third, Proudhoe Veizey in a fourth, and so on. There were also about half a dozen heads whom I did not recognise. I flicked a glance out of the corner of my eye at Frankie and he flicked one back. We had just said to each other: 'We must snatch shots of these.'

Malini swayed in with the teapot. Samarsinghe slung her out and started playing mummy. I waited until the spoons had ceased stirring. I produced my notebook, unsheathed the Bic and poised it an inch above the virgin page.

I asked him how he spelt his name and I wrote it down in whopping great letters. I laid the notebook on the desk so he could read it upside down. I asked him was he the manager? No, the director. And how old was he? For the record he was 44. His first lie. And when did the Foundation become involved? Two years back. And where did he come from? Dambulla, wherever that might be. And how do you spell that? You could spell it with an H on the end or leave the H off, said Hector. It's amazing the sort of thing we journos pick up. And what did the arts centre promote? He went into his spiel and I wrote bits down, still in huge infantile letters. I sensed that Varun was rapidly losing faith in my skills as an ace investigator. But how was he to know I was up to my very favourite trick. It is one of such simplicity and beauty that I commend it to all. What you do is stick your notebook – and every single word you write – on plain view. The victim reads exactly what you have written and he thinks: 'We've got a right thicko here.' This is what you want him to think. Every now and then he inadvertently lets slip something interesting. You do not write it down. You lay your pen aside, feign disinterest and move on to some other block-buster question, like is he married? Gradually he becomes emboldened. He lets a little more slip. Sometimes the victim does this just to test what a dummy you are. He's even having fun at your expense. Or so he thinks. What he doesn't know is that the little bug under your wrist strap is picking up everything he says.

Thus it was with Hector Samarsinghe. I asked him where the coconuts came from, did Leon enjoy his visit, how many hours a week was the centre open, were the sales girls his daughters, how often did Tomlin drop in, what was the most popular item, did the Tamil Tigers deter tourists, was Proudhoe Veizey a customer, could I buy cheap glasses locally, who were those other geezers in the photo gallery, were the four-legged monkeys dangerous, how much profit did the shop clear, was the Tooth Temple worth a visit, how did he feel about Claudine's murder, would he care for a cigarette, why did so many big shots visit him, could I have another cup, please, did his wife work at the centre and more. Much, much more.

I wrote it all down, except the bits about the Tomlin fraternity. Frankie meanwhile knew precisely what I was up to and he sat in the corner with a look of utter boredom wrapped round his face. Varun was still in the dark. His eyes sliced from me to Samarsinghe and back to me as if he was watching a Wimbledon final.

I was almost through with the questions, but I broke off to pull a little stunt. I said, 'Hector, you've got something on sale I wanted to ask you about. Do you mind having a look at it?'

Samarsinghe fired a glance at Frankie. Frankie was deeply engrossed in a leaflet about silkworms. Samarsinghe said, 'Now?'

I stood up as if he had already agreed. He followed. We left the other two in the office. I knew that the moment we walked out the door Frankie would be banging off snaps of all the pictures on the wall.

I looked around for something interesting. I saw a pith helmet in a fetching pinkish shade. 'Ah, this is it,' I declared. 'I was wondering if this was an antique, you know, something left over from the days of the Raj?'

Samarsinghe laughed in his sorrow. 'I am sorry. No. This is modern, made just this year. You like it?'

'Yes, I do. How much is it, Hector?'

He turned on a generous display of his molars. 'For you it is free. It is a gift from me, Mister Charrod.'

I squeaked in protestation. He insisted. I took it. I lingered over a shelf of ghastly shell ornaments just to give Frankie time to do his dirty work. Samarsinghe was anxious to get back to his office. I said conversationally, 'I love this pith helmet – was it made locally?'

'Yes. Our children at the orphanage.'

He turned away and said quickly, 'There is a Missus Charrod perhaps?' He stuck out his hand at a rack of scarves. 'Or perhaps you have a lady friend?'

The great salesman won me over. Rosie might

indeed like one of these wrapped round her neck. I patted him fondly on the arm. I said, 'This time I'm paying for it, Hector. It's money in a good cause.'

He eased up. We argued amiably over the price. I was trying to pay the full whack and he was insisting I pay less. An unusual experience in Sri Lanka. After a brief struggle I won the day. I also chipped in about £20 towards his Good Works. By God, there are times when I make me want to throw up.

Samarsinghe had a glitter in his hard little eyes. As far as he was concerned, our interview had been bland, boring and totally unrevealing. We strolled back to the office, each laughing up his sleeve at the other. Frankie was still comatose in his corner. Varun was playing with his car keys. I asked a few more daft questions and Frankie took a sunny shot of us together, then one of Hector looking heroic. We took our leave, but not until Samarsinghe made me promise to call him if there was anything more I needed. I promised, for I am ever anxious to make others happy.

Frankie, Varun and I didn't speak until we were back in the Datsun. Varun said, 'He is a crook, Mister Max. He is not telling the truth to you.'

Frankie said, 'Got the pix. Let's get a drink.'

As we were cruising down the hill, I showed Frankie my purchases.

'What's that?' he said, poking a finger at my hat.

'That is a pith helmet.'

'What do you want that for?' he asked.

'To wear when I'm pithed.'

Varun drove us past a hotel. We bollocked him and

made him reverse us right back to it. We had our drinks by the poolside, where a couple of Parisian housewives displayed that bikini tops are being worn off the bust this season. Frankie poured beer down his chin and licked his lips. Varun, normally the life and soul of things, was gloomy. He thought I'd come away empty handed. Well, let's just see what we got.

The cluster of unknowns on the office wall were mostly City money men. They came, they saw, they contributed. Samarsinghe had described Michael Tomlin as 'a dear friend'. The implication was he was a frequent visitor. Leon Knapp likewise. Samarsinghe had shot off into the undergrowth when I tossed his name into the pot. Martin Crowley had been there twice, going home each time with buddhist figurines. Them and something else, I bet. The florid thespian Proudhoe Veizey and the Right Hon. Lewis Trefoyle showed their all-abiding interest in the Third World by banging on the centre's door every now and then. But at least the natives had been largely spared Sir James Tomlin. He had been here only once.

According to Tomlin, Kandy was but a dot in the WorldCare Foundation empire. Let us pretend that is true. Let us also remember that the Foundation press officer hardly knew it existed. Here we have some insignificant offshoot of Claudine's labours. How then do you explain why all these money-crazed City slackers are so damn keen on going there? It couldn't just be the repro pith helmets.

But hold a moment. They didn't come to see the centre. When I'd mentioned it to Knapp, he'd gone cold on me. They came for something else, some place else.

Samarsinghe had told me the box office takings were doled out among local needy causes. A maternity unit, craft workshops, a paediatric clinic and all that. So what. Where's the funny stuff?

The waiter wheeled up with another round and I counted my change like a clever boy, for I knew all about the five-card trick. BONG! The brain lit up. The old five-card trick. That's what Samarsinghe had tried to pull. He told me more than I ever wished to know about sundry deserving causes. All but for one. The big note was lying under the bill of goods. And I knew just what it was.

An orphanage. I remembered that one brief moment when he forgot himself and broke cover. He said, 'our children at the orphanage.' And then he changed the subject so suddenly it jarred. For he knew he had mentioned the unmentionable.

I lay back in my lounger and patted myself on the back. They can't outfox Max. I'd hit it smack on the head. The orphanage. That's the scene of sin and shame.

I looked at the topless sunbathers, they looked at me. Then I looked at their faces. They smiled, I smiled. A man could be happy here.

My innocent reverie was broken by a shout from Frankie who was looking over the fence at the world outside. He seemed excited, as if he had just discovered a nudist colony serving free drink. I traipsed over for a peek. The prospect was unspectacular, a view of the road we had just descended. You could see the Alahaka arts centre on top of the hill. You could also see the fair Malini stepping daintily forth. We watched her shimmer down the road in our direction for a couple of hundred yards. She fetched up under a giant tree. She stood there as if she was waiting for a bus.

'She's waiting for a bus,' said Frankie.

I said, 'Stay here. I want to talk to her.'

I hoofed off with the sun burning a hole in my head. When I got to Malini I was hot and sticky and pink behind the ears. She was as cool as an ice cube in an Eskimo's freezer in winter. She bowed her head and showed her teeth which looked like they'd been made from the white bits of coconut. She was pleased to see me.

I said, 'Hi, Malini. There's something I forgot to ask Hector; I wonder if you could tell me.'

Her eyes said, 'Come be my lover and we will dwell in paradise all our days.' Her lips said, 'Of course. If I can help you.'

I said, 'I didn't get the address of the orphanage. Can you give me it?'

Her eyes flashed, her chin wobbled, her nostrils flared. 'The orphanage! Go away! Go back to England! I do not want to speak to you.'

I got the impression I'd said something wrong. I tried again. 'I just want to visit it, to see how it's run.'

'Ha!'

In just two letters she managed to convey that I was lower than a submarine's bum, that I should be horsewhipped, boiled in oil and forced to listen to Barry Manilow records.

I said, 'What's wrong with me seeing the orphanage?'

She didn't spit in my face, but the thought went through her mind. She said, 'You're like the rest of them. I thought you were nice men. Go away!'

I might have tried to press my credentials as a nice man but for the noisy arrival of a rusty, dusty bus. She hopped aboard, throwing a venomous glance back. The driver tooted his horn and off she went, hotly pursued by a dust storm.

I didn't mind. I ambled back down the road whistling to myself. My next stop was the orphanage. That's where whoever it was was getting up to whatever it was.

# Chapter Thirteen

The guidebooks are strangely silent on the subject of Kandyian orphanages. We were forced to boot Varun out onto the street to quiz the locals. He came back tired, thirsty, but with a big self-satisfied smirk. He'd earned his thirty quid for the day.

We were now back in the hotel MacDuff and deeply engrossed in our bright red feet. This is something else the guidebooks don't think worth mentioning: in Sri Lanka they smear hotel corridors and steps with an inch of vermilion polish each new morning. Whole armies of lackeys are engaged upon this ritual, and it is very enjoyable watching them at their task whilst you sip a Singha. The effect of their labours is pleasing to the eye, and, for all I know, keeps at bay ants, Bengal tigers and yuppie flu. There is alas a slight drawback. If you pad barefoot from your room to the pool, as we had just done, your feet look as if they have a terminal case of scarlet fever. So there we were in the lee of the poolside palm, examining our flaming tootsies when Varun panted into view. He handed us a list. Kandy, it appears, has orphanages the way Switzerland has mountains.

There was one each for the Protestant and Roman

Catholic foundlings, one for Hindus, another for Moslems, a third for Buddhist babes. I didn't spot any for atheists. There were also various private affairs. These looked the most likely. We still had a couple of hours to go to dinner, so we got ourselves dressed and went knocking on doors. I had a carefully thought-out strategy. It involved me saying, 'Hi, we're friends of Sir James Tomlin' and seeing how things went from there.

'Who?' said the bewildered matron at the first orphanage.

'Who?' said the suspicious manager at the second.

Soon the entire countryside was saying 'Who?' like a bunch of owls in an echo chamber. The wearisome day wore on and our driver stopped speaking to us. But Frankie and I know that stories are like passionate women. They don't drop in your lap and say, 'Take me, big boy. I'm yours.' You have to go wooing them. We kept on knocking. Frankie, minus his beloved necklace of cameras, looked almost human. But I could see his hand hovering over the pocket holding his little Olympus idiot-proof shooter.

It was the seventh, maybe the eighth place we visited. The Perelawaya Children's Refuge. I said to the fat lady in the front office that I was a chum of Sir James. She said who? I turned and started trekking back to the car. 'Hello! Hello!' someone yammered behind me. I turned right round again. A weedy bloke with a malnourished moustache sought my attention.

'Yes?' I asked.

'You are a friend of Sir James?'

We'd hit it. This was the spot. Dig here. Out of my

left ear I could hear Frankie uncoiling from the car. I advanced on the small man. I said, 'You must be . . .'

'Niaz.'

'Niaz! Of course. Leon Knapp told me all about you, Niaz.'

'Ah, Mister Leon,' Niaz sprung a joyful smile. 'He is very much liked here. I don't think so in England perhaps?'

News travels fast in these parts. I said, 'Perhaps.' We both laughed, though God knows why. I gave him a full up and downer. If he'd been six inches taller he'd have been a six footer. He was in his early forties but he fidgeted like an adolescent. His thick black hair was plastered with thick black grease. He was ever so anxious to please. So far I'd got away with my bluff, but I reckoned I might have ten minutes at most before he wised up and told us to naff off.

I said, 'Martin Crowley was right: this is a beautiful spot.'

Niaz said, 'You know Mister Martin?'

I said, 'Know him? We went through commando training together.'

Frankie rolled his eyes. But Niaz believed me. We had a good chuckle about Martin Crowley too. Just when I was thinking Niaz must be on the old nitrous oxide, he stopped beaming. A nasty, suspicious look started descending from his hairline.

He said, 'Mister Samarsinghe did not say you were coming.'

I had taken the precaution of arming myself with Frankie's duty free litre of Glenfiddich. The bugger had made me pay him for it too. I whipped out the bottle, stuffed it in Niaz's hand and said, 'I know. I should have called you first. But we just got into town and thought we'd pay you a visit.'

Niaz ogled the Glenfiddich. I'd done something right for a change. He said, 'I do not know your names.'

I said, 'We're business partners of Sir James. I'm Sebastian du Maurier and this is my friend, Joe Soap.'

Frankie glowered. Niaz presented a welcoming hand. 'Come, come,' he urged. 'I am very pleased to welcome any friends of Sir James.'

He shepherded us to a bungalow half screened by trees. It looked out on the main block, another bungalow, but one that sent out shoots in all directions. Niaz told us to make ourselves comfortable in his lounge. It had a TV set, cane furniture and a grubby air of bachelorhood. No pictures.

'Drink?' offered Niaz.

'Yes please,' said Frankie, eyeing his former whisky.

Niaz disappeared behind a curtain, returning with three glasses of arrak. It wasn't even the premium version. We toasted each other and did some more laughing.

'Sir James has been very good to us,' said Niaz. 'He sends many friends to visit us.'

I said, 'The refuge is very dear to his heart. He wanted to come with us but he couldn't spare the time. You know what it's like in big business.'

Niaz nodded sadly. We sipped a while and pondered the heavy sacrifices one must make in big business. He brightened up. 'Never mind, Mister

Sebastian, I want to ask what I can do to make you and Mister Joe happy.'

Tell me what's going on, that's what.

I said, 'My friend, Lewis, you know Lewis Trefoyle, said he had a very interesting time here. But of course we had to come to see for ourselves.'

Niaz said, 'Ah yes, Mister Lewis. He is a very kind man.'

I took that to mean Trefoyle made free with his wallet. I hauled mine out. Niaz was aghast. 'No! No, please, Mister Sebastian. Sir James always pays for his friends.'

Does he now? And what exactly does he pay for?

I said, 'We were hoping to have a quick look round the refuge first. Unless that is inconvenient.'

I still had my wallet on show. I fished out a chunk of Sri Lankan rupees, around two hundred pounds in orange and blue notes. It was way over the top and it was meant to be. I said, 'I know Sir James pays, but I'd like to make a small private donation, and I wouldn't want you to tell anyone.'

Niaz snapped up the money like a magpie. I got the impression the orphans wouldn't see much of it. He said, 'It is late, but we have a little time to show you our refuge.'

We said nice things about each other and raised our glasses in warm tributes. Frankie was a mite fretful and I knew what was knocking around in his monkey mind: the light was going. If he wanted snaps, he'd soon have to shoot flash and that way everybody would know what he was doing.

I said casually, 'How many children do you have in the refuge?'

Niaz counted them up. 'We have nine. We had ten, but there was an accident.'

'An accident?'

He didn't like that question. He just repeated, 'An accident.'

I said, 'How old are they?'

Niaz had it off by heart. 'The youngest is Ajit: he's seven. Lalin is the biggest. He's twelve, so he will be going soon.'

Going where and why? I rolled the arrak around like mouth-wash, puzzling over what to say next. If I hit one wrong button, he'd tell me to sling my hook, and I wouldn't get my money back either. I had to pick on something seemingly innocent. I waved my glass at the walls. I said, 'You don't have any pictures.'

That was the wrong button. 'Pictures? What pictures? Photographs are not allowed – you must know that.' Our host was very narked indeed.

Frankie got there before me. He said, 'No, not photographs, pictures. You know, pictures. Everywhere we've been, there are all these lovely paintings of Sri Lanka.'

Niaz let his jaw muscles droop in a smile. 'Ah, paintings. I thought you meant photographs.' He laughed at his own foolishness and we joined in heartily. He said, 'Of course I do have photographs of the children here – I took them myself, with my own camera.'

'Oh yes?' Frankie again. A little too keenly.

Niaz stuck out an arm, flipped open a chairside

cupboard and produced his prize. It was an eight by ten of a bunch of kids squinting in the sun. They were all boys. They didn't look as if they were having the time of their lives. I said, 'They look very happy children.'

'Oh yes,' enthused Niaz. 'All very good. All speak good English.'

I wanted to know which one was the 'accident' victim. I said, 'And they're all here now?'

Niaz shook his head. 'This boy, Janath, is not here. The accident.'

'Of course.' I studied the child he had pointed out. He looked about seven, or maybe an underdeveloped nine-year-old. He was the least happy of a hapless bunch. His face was at odds with his grinning Mickey Mouse tee shirt. I passed the snap to Frankie, my index finger pinned on Janath. I tipped back the last of my drink.

Niaz said, 'Would you like one?'

I thought what the hell and held out my glass. Niaz had a fit. He chortled and roared and whinnied while Frankie and I looked at each other, trying to figure out the joke. 'No, not an arrak, Mister Sebastian,' he said between convulsions, 'No, no, no. I mean a boy.' And off he went roaring again.

Dear God in heaven.

All along I had known there was something nasty about Kandy, but not exactly what. Now here was this little man, spelling it out callously, as carelessly as if he were selling cheap lighters. Frankie, still holding the picture, popped his eyes. If Niaz had not been wiping away tears of laughter he would have seen our horror. It took me half a minute to get my breathing back in synch.

I said, 'A boy? Why not?'

Niaz said, 'Okay Mister Sebastian. You pick a boy. You too Mister Joe.'

Frankie was still not quite with us. I took the photograph from him and pointed to the oldest looking boy. Frankie, after a little pause, chose another, a child of maybe six or seven. We were both operating by instinct. I was going for the boy who'd give me the best words, Frankie for the one who'd make the best shot. Niaz congratulated us on our discernment. He said, 'Now you finish your drinks and we go and see them.'

Frankie said he'd had enough arrak. He was still white. I whopped my glass back. Niaz said, 'We go now.'

I remember entering a room that was part dormitory, part playroom. Every single child looked up when we entered. None of them smiled. I remember that very clearly. The room was clean, but you felt the children were somehow neglected, as if each had to make his own way in the world. I cannot remember much of what Niaz said. I just recall him prattling on and on and urging the boys to look pleased to see their visitors. They didn't.

Then I was alone in a room with a skinny sad-eyed boy. He said, 'Do you have batteries for my Nintendo? Do you have any Mario games?'

I shook my head. He lost interest and began scratching the back of his leg. I took the tape recorder from my pocket and turned the cassette over. I said, 'What is your name?'

'Lalin. You call me Lal.' He didn't look up.

I didn't recognise my voice, it was so quiet, so edgy. I said, 'How old are you, Lal?'

'Eleven.' He did not want to talk to me.

I said, 'Men come to see you, Lal. What do they do?' He was a strange mix of resentfulness and submissiveness.

I said, 'I do not want to do anything to you. I just want you to tell me about the men.'

He glanced at me sharply but did not speak. I let him think about it. I inspected the room. The walls were whitewashed and bare. There was a big bed in the corner, a settee, a drinks bar and a TV set with a video. A door led off to a bathroom. The fittings were simple yet after the children's room they looked lavish.

I said, 'Are you happy here?'

Lal studied his trainers. I said, 'Where are you from?' His mouth was set in childish stubbornness.

I said, 'Lal, I am not like the other men.'

He shot me another glance. We were both standing. I was by the door, he beside the bed. I did not move closer. A terrible sadness overwhelmed me. I thought of this room and the awful things that had happened here. I looked at this child, as slim as a fish, with eyes as old as the world.

I said in hardly even a whisper, 'Sweet Jesus Christ, what have they done to you?'

And he told me. He gave me their names. Mister Martin and Mister Mike – Michael Tomlin, Knapp,

Trefoyle and all the rest of that sordid freemasonry. He told me of the 'accident', that a man – he didn't know who – had suffocated his friend, Janath. Janath was ten. Soon he, Lal, would have to leave the refuge. And go where? He shook his head. Maybe Galle, for the tourist men. Maybe Negombo. Niaz had other places for boys when the men here tired of them.

I said, 'Soon my friend Frankie is going to come in here and take a photograph of you.'

Lal shook his head vehemently. 'No. You are not allowed photographs. Mister Leon took photographs and they were very angry.'

I said, 'Listen to me. I am a journalist. You understand? I write for newspapers. I want to write about what these men are doing. I want to stop them.'

He gave me the merest glimmer of a smile. 'You will say they are bad? You will say they killed Janath?'

I said, 'I will say they are very, very bad. Maybe they will go to jail. But they will never come here again.'

Lal shrugged his shoulders carelessly. 'Okay. You take my picture.'

Something was tugging at the hem of my conscience and shouting, 'Oi!' I listened to it. It was the rarely-heard voice of decency which told me that I too was using Lal, abusing him after my own fashion. He was just a story for me, a great big bold by-line, something to make all my Fleet Street peers say: 'Nice one, Max.' I told my conscience to stay out of it.

I said, 'Lal, you must not say anything to anyone about this. Not even your best pal. If you do, Mister

Niaz will hear of it. You will be in danger, very serious danger.'

Lal absorbed this with eyes that had already seen so much wickedness. He understood.

I said, 'When I am gone you must say I asked you questions but you refused to tell me anything. You got that?'

He nodded. I said, 'Now, when the bad men leave, what do they do? Do they give you a present? Do they give you money?'

I had my wallet out and was rifling through the notes. Lal said, 'Yes, they give me money. Sometimes ten rupees. We give all the money to Niaz.'

Ten rupees. Just seventy pence. And they took even that away from him.

He said, 'Perhaps you will give me more? I will say I did not tell you about the tourist men. I'll pretend you were angry with me because I did not say. Do you want to beat me?'

He just stood there and said it. I said, 'God Almighty, no. Just say you told me nothing.'

There was a light, urgent tapping on the door. I edged it open and Frankie squeezed in. He was yellow in the 40-watt hall light. He said, 'I'm going to kill those bastards.'

I said, 'Later, Frankie, later. Say hello and goodbye to Lal. Take his snap and let's get out of here. We'd better move it before Niaz catches on.'

I whipped the blankets off the bed and rigged them over the thin curtains to keep Frankie's flash from showing outside. He knocked off half a dozen shots. Lal sat on the edge of the bed in his white shirt and shorts. His face was dark and sombre. He made a great pic. We re-made the bed, took a deep breath and ventured out into the corridor. Behind us Lal sat where he was, holding a 100 rupee note. I said, 'I promise, I'll do everything I can for you and your friends.'

A sad smile turned the corners of his lips. He said, 'Okay.' I don't think he believed me.

Frankie grabbed my shoulder. 'Quick, Max, here's Niaz.'

He was skipping down the corridor towards us, his face split in a grin. He was actually happy in that place. Beside me I could hear Frankie's teeth grind. He was trying to return the smile.

Niaz said, 'Good? Yes?'

I said, 'Very good, Niaz. I couldn't believe it.'

He was pleased with himself. He said, 'When you come back tomorrow you must bring small gifts for the boys. Just a little toy or a pen. They always like pens. That is all you need.'

He guided us back down the corridor. We passed the open doorway where the other boys played. There was something eerie about them. I think it was their silence. Their passive eyes regarded us as we passed and they returned to their wordless games. They never smiled.

Niaz kept up the patter all the way back to his bungalow. I don't remember much about it, except him extolling the honesty and happiness of his children. Then he said, 'Soon they will have new friends.'

I said, 'Oh?'

'Yes. Sir James says some of his friends prefer the girls, the young girls.'

It is hard to act conversational when you're talking to someone you'd like to see strung up by the neck. I managed it somehow. I said, 'Really? And where do the girls come from?'

Niaz pointed towards the window. 'From north of Trincomalee. Orphans from the Tamil Tigers.'

So the waifs of war who had lost their mums and dads to terrorists now stood to lose their last shreds of innocence and hope to European paedophiles. I wanted to be away from there. I gave an elaborate yawn. I said, 'You must forgive me, Niaz. We had a long flight in and I'm rather tired.'

He was kind and thoughtful, which made things worse. He said, 'I am sorry. I talk too much. When I see you tomorrow, I will be more quiet. You are staying at the Citadel of course?'

I said, 'Yes, the Citadel.'

Niaz said, 'Good. It is a splendid hotel. You and Mister Joe have a nice meal and then you sleep.'

He made a pillow with his hands and laid his head on it, just in case I didn't get the idea. He guided us out via the front office. The fat woman had gone. Niaz clutched my hand and shook it. It would be nice to report that his grip was slithery and slimy. It was a good firm honest-to-God handshake. It had no place here.

We made it back out to the car. Varun was bouncing up and down with excitement. He said, 'You got your story, Mister Max?'

I nodded. I didn't feel like talking to anyone.

'And you got your photos, Mister Frank?'

Frankie said, 'I did. And I pinched this one too.' He pulled out the group shot of the boys taken by Niaz. Varun was horrified. 'You stole the photo? That is very bad.'

'That's nothing,' said Frankie, reaching into his jacket. 'I nicked our whisky back and all.'

It was a subdued little trio that sat around table thirteen in the MacDuff hotel. Frankie was fretting over what to do with his snaps – whether to have them processed here or air-freight the film back to London or just go back with the roll in his camera bag. Varun was waiting to be arrested for aiding and abetting a pair of international thieves and con men. I was trying to wash away the taste of the day and working out how the whole thing – the murders, the child abuse – fitted together. The answers took their time in coming. But after a few hours of largely silent contemplation I thought I had it worked out. It went like this:

Claudine was not party to the deal. She had found out about it. Her mother had told me there was a big scandal – 'bigger than money' – about to break in the WorldCare Foundation. That's why she was topped. Shirley had gone a little too far down the same track. That's why she got a rope round her neck. The killer/killers feared she'd passed the stuff on to me, hence the attempt to cook me. Hence the letter bomb – a warning to keep what I had to myself.

Sir James Tomlin was not a paedophile. He'd made just one visit here. But he seemed to be behind the whole deal. Why? To cater for the whims of his deviant mates. And why should he do that? For money, most likely. His ex-wife, the one down in Virginia Water, had told me Tomlin would never have any money worries; his chums would always bail him out. The Kandy racket gave him powerful leverage with his City playmates, and a way of making all sorts of influential friends. People like the foul Lewis Trefoyle. Plus, according to Lal, Tomlin's son and heir, Michael, was a perv.

So what did I have as a story? Not a lot. I could not sit down and go through that tape again, not then – the awfulness of things was still in the quick of my mind. But I could dispassionately review the show so far. Any right-thinking member of society will agree that the Tomlins and all their ilk should be exposed to the world and then consigned to sew mailbags for life in E-wing max-security Durham. Those who are more right-thinking than most might prefer them to be hung, drawn and quartered. It is sad but true that newspaper lawyers are not right-thinking members of society. They would far, far rather let a mass murderer wander the streets than land the paper with a penny in libel damages. I imagined how Royce, our monocular lawyer, would react to my story.

*Who is your source?*

An eleven-year-old orphan, locked away in Sri Lanka.

*Do you have his sworn affidavit?*

No, but I've got him on tape.

*Inadmissible. Does he know what an affidavit is?*

Sure, Royce. The boys in the orphanage talk of nothing else.

*Do you have a secondary source?*

Yes. A six-year-old boy.

*And he is too young—*

—To know what an affidavit is. I know.

*Did you see at the orphanage any of the people whom you have named?*

No. But the creep who runs the place said they visited. Frankie heard him too.

*Would the manager testify in court?*

Yes. Against us. He'd say I made it all up.

*Did you speak to anyone else who has seen the men named at the orphanage?*

No.

*Do you have any photographs confirming that Tomlin or anyone else has visited the boys?*

No. Photographs are banned.

*Do you have any evidence that they are engaging in similar acts against children within the United Kingdom?*

Nary a whit.

*What is our defence if they issue a writ for libel?*

That it's true: that we're exposing it because it is in the public interest.

*How do we justify in a British court that an alleged incident in Sri Lanka allegedly involving Sri Lankan children is within the British public interest?*

I don't know, Royce. You're the lawyer.

*Do you have any forensic evidence that the children have in fact been abused?*

No.

*So our entire case rests upon the wholly unsubstantiated word of an eleven-year-old child?*

And the six-year-old.

*Shut the door on your way out.*

Even if I got the story nailed down, there was still a slight problem. To give it maximum bite, we would have to use big pix of Lal and the other boy, Ajit, staring dead-eyed at you out of the paper. The bigger the pix the better. We would also identify the boys by name, just to convince our sceptical readers we hadn't made the whole thing up. Sometimes they think that, you know.

So we would be identifying very clearly the child victims of a sex ring. If the boys involved were from Tunbridge Wells, our editor would end up in chokey, sharing the bedpan with Frankie and me, and the paper would be fined millions. Judges get very prickly about newspapers naming minors in cases like these. But because our boys were Sri Lankan, and they were abused there, we could stick their names, their faces, their fingerprints, their sock sizes in the paper and nobody could say boo. All right, our paper isn't exactly a soaraway seller in Sri Lanka, so you might think no one locally would ever link the boys. Up to a point. The story itself would be too big to ignore, therefore all the Sri Lankan press would leap on it. They'd contact our syndication people and buy Frankie's pix and my copy. End result: everyone in the entire island would know the boys' names and could point them out in the street. I could argue that this would be the responsibility of local editors, so don't blame me, guv. But when you come down to it, the boys' public exposure would be courtesy of that well known pair of social workers, Max and Frankie. And knowing all that, I would still name them.

We wiped out the Glenfiddich and went to bed. There was a fresh bowl of mangoes and papayas in my room. There was a minibar cram full of cheap drink. The coverlet of my bed was turned down and crisp clean sheets beckoned. Tomorrow I would wake to honeyed sunshine. I looked on all this and wished like hell I was somewhere else.

The sun was shooting shards of brilliance off the lake as we breakfasted. We discussed tactics. We'd already got the dirty stuff. Now we needed the ordinary foot-in-the-door pix and quotes from Samarsinghe and Niaz.

We hit the gift shop first. I strode right up to the sales counter. Behind me Frankie was going zip-a-dee-do-dah with all the cameras he possessed. It was good to see him back in his monkey suit.

You could tell that the beauteous Malini wanted me to drop dead on the spot, but the customer is always right, so she had to grit her teeth and ask how she could help me.

I said we'd been to the orphanage, and no doubt her boss might like to know it was a front for a child sex ring. Drag him hither, I commanded. Malini gave me an odd look. It said that she had ordered the jury out to have a re-think on the question of my guilt.

She fetched Samarsinghe. Gone was the big-hearted shopkeeper of yesterday. In his place was a spitting, eye-rolling nutter. 'Out! Out! Out!' he yelled, pointing helpfully to the door. I stayed In! In! In!

I said, 'Mister Samarsinghe, are you aware that your English friends are using children as young as six for sex? That money from this centre is used to supply the victims? That—'

I didn't get much further because he grabbed up a walking cane (price 150 rupees) and began thumping me around the head. Frankie had retired to a safe distance and was popping away. You could hear him go zzzip-zzzip-zzzip, then Samarsinghe's whack! then zzzip-zzzip-zzzip, and so on. I was glad Samarsinghe wasn't fitted with a motordrive. I backed all the way out with these two lunatics running amok around me. In the background I could see Malini's anxious eyes. I like to think she was worried about me. Samarsinghe followed me out onto the steps, still whacking like billy-oh. There was better light out here for Frankie so I obligingly stood there, letting Samarsinghe beat the living Bejasus out of me. I kept on firing off questions, like: 'Do you rape the boys?' and 'How many have you murdered?' and 'How much do you charge for your own sons?' – questions framed to make him go berserk, thereby providing us with tastier pix. He responded with whacks! and a string of cuss words you just could not print in a decent newspaper. The *Guardian*, yes, but not a God-fearing tabloid. None of what he said was particularly enlightening but it didn't worry me. I'd just verbal Samarsinghe and get him to say some shocking things when I was writing up the story. After all, I had a witness. He didn't. Frankie was taking his time over the snaps. I had the uncalled for suspicion he might be enjoying the spectacle. Our noble driver, Varun, threatened to come to my rescue but Frankie waved him out of shot. I'd had enough. I grabbed the stick from Samarsinghe and said, 'If you hit me one more time, I'll rip your lungs out.' That gave him pause. It also gave us enough time to bundle into the Datsun and scoot off. I was bloodied but unbowed. Frankie was cock-a-hoop, whatever that means.

He said, 'I got some great smudges.'

I said, 'I got some great bruises.'

Varun said, 'I break that man's back, yes?'

No. I tried to explain the tabloid hack's code of ethics. It was a bit like trying to explain the jokes in Kafka.

Three miles down the road we rumbled up outside the Perelawaya Children's Refuge and the whole jolly game started again. Frankie skimmed off half a dozen exteriors. He got a terrific shot of a couple of cowed boys looking out the window. He had switched his attentions to the smaller bungalow before Niaz steamed up. And steamed was the word. His language was much the same as Samarsinghe's, only without the clean bits. If my mother had been there she would have boxed his ears for the things he said about her.

I had a hidden agenda in coming back to the orphanage – to pretend that the boys had told me nothing. It was my feeble strategy for trying to protect the children we had seen. I let Frankie get his grainy snaps and then I pinned Niaz against the wall. I said, 'Why are the boys here too frightened to talk to me?'

He said something nasty so I banged his head off the wall. It made a pleasant boom.

I said, 'Why did the two boys refuse to tell us who comes here?'

Niaz said he was going to have us arrested. I tested his head again. It still boomed.

I said, 'I already know who visits – Leon Knapp gave me their names. But why won't the boys talk?'

Niaz was torn between the desire to spit in my eyes and to keep his head off the concrete. His head won. He went mutinously quiet.

I said, 'How did one boy die?'

He wasn't saying. I shook him around a bit more. Frankie thoughtfully offered to help but I said he might get his hands dirty. Varun wanted to floss his teeth with the car jack. I was sorely tempted.

In the end I let Niaz go. But before we left, I grabbed his grubby little ear and told it, 'Those boys were scared stiff, they're too frightened even to help themselves. But I'm going to help them. And if I find you've as much as slapped their wrist when I'm gone, I'll break your bloody neck.'

'We'll tear your head off,' Frankie contributed.

'We will kill you,' Varun said, clashing his teeth together.

We drove off in the general direction of beer. Behind us Niaz gulped and felt his bumps.

*

The raven-haired receptionist at the MacDuff was a girl of many talents. She spoke English to the English, French to the Frenchish, Japanese to the rich. If there'd been any Americans around, doubtless she would have spoken broken English too. She saw me loping across the lobby and sang out, 'Good afternoon, Mister Chard. You had a caller a few minutes ago.'

'Who?'

She said, 'I'm afraid the gentleman would not leave his name.'

Note the use of the conditional tense.

I said, 'Was there any message?'

'No. He just wished to know if you were staying here.'

Frankie and I looked at each other. Varun looked at the bar. Frankie said, 'You know what this means?'

I knew. Frankie said it anyway. 'It means they've tracked us down here. We'd better move it.'

We left Varun watering in the bar while we packed. Sri Lanka is a place of beauty with beauties all over the place, but we wanted to be far gone from it. Just say, for instance, that Niaz made up some totally Mickey Mouse story about me threatening to kill him and ran screaming to the cops. You're never quite sure how the Old Bill will behave in foreign lands. Are they addled and raddled with corruption? Are they the type likely to throw two honest journos in the slammer? Would they believe the word of some local sleazebag instead of two upright gents from Her Majesty's Press?

The best answer I could come up with was yes, they damn well would. This, I'm sure, is grossly unfair to the Sri Lankan constabulary, but having been banged up by their brothers in Denmark, Nigeria, Sweden and Kenya inter alia, I tend to lean on the paranoid side. Therefore I packed with haste. We still had three days on the island before KLM sent in a 747 to get us out. If we had to hang around in Sri Lanka for the next seventy-two hours, at least we could hang around somewhere less risky. Mount Lavinia beckoned.

# Chapter Fourteen

There aren't many roads out of Kandy. That made it easier for them.

We tootled off southerly and westerly, banging along at fifty miles an hour. It doesn't sound much, but with buffaloes, goats and escaped mental patients on bikes lurking behind every corner, it felt like a hell-for-leather burn-up. En route Varun embarked on a long family saga, involving uncles in Trincomalee, aunts in Saudi, brothers in poverty, etc. Catherine Cookson could have knocked out a dozen block-busters from his ramblings. I have a very low tolerance threshold to stories about other people's families; my own are bad enough. So I looked at the scenery. It was mostly green with here and there a pretty hamlet, just to keep your eyes on the job. The overall effect was one of pastoral tranquillity. My eyelids drooped.

We were five miles out of Kandy when the bandits struck. I woke to find Varun leaning on the brake.

'Wotsit?' I said.

What it was, was a couple of Sri Lankan young-sters, each about ten foot tall. For a nanosecond I thought it must have been something I'd drunk, then

I realised they were on stilts. They wobbled about in the middle of the road, blocking our progress.

I asked Varun what the blankety-blank they were doing. He was grinning. He said, 'It's okay, Mister Max. It's a local custom. In the south we have fishermen on poles and they get money from the tourists for taking their photographs. Here the children do it on stilts.'

'What? We're supposed to give them money for pissing about in the middle of the road?' I was cross. These ten-year-old Dick Turpins had just wrecked a perfectly pleasant memory of Rosie misbehaving herself. I told Varun to tell them to sling their hooks. He gave a ripe chuckle and did nothing of the sort.

He said, 'Admit it, Mister Max. You have been caught in the children's net. Let Mister Frankie take their photo, you give the children a few rupees and we go on. Everybody happy.'

I wasn't. I didn't see why I should pay for Frankie's holiday snaps. I was grumbling along these lines until it occurred to me that the pic might come in handy when I eventually got round to writing my travel feature. It would take up space and cut down the amount of junk I'd have to write. Plus the stilt highwayboys gave me just the right sort of daft anecdote for the intro. I pushed Frankie out with instructions to smudge. I had to give him the money before he would get out. Varun and I puffed on our Bensons while Frankie laboured under the tropical sun. The children wobbled all over the shop. They weren't very good at it. We watched Frankie fiddle with his f stops and shutter speeds. He was all hot and moist. It was good fun watching him work. He didn't think much of it. He wasn't smiling. Nor were the boys. Not even a tiny grin.

*They weren't smiling.*

I sat forward and stared through the windscreen grime. Christ! I'd seen these faces, these unsmiling eyes before. Only last night these dead eyes had stared out at us from the orphanage playroom.

I shrieked, 'Run, Frankie! Run!'

He ran. He didn't know what was up, but he ran. He's been in far too many hairy places before to hang about. I thumped Varun on the shoulder. 'Get us out of here! Move it!'

The next bit took forever. Varun turned his bewildered gaze towards me in slo-mo. I remember him saying, 'What's wrong, Mister Frankie? Why are we going?'

I thumped him again. 'Go! Damn you! Go!'

Frankie was back in the car. The rear door was hanging open. He screamed, 'Back! Back! Back!' He was in the middle of the second Back! when they opened up. You just heard the bangs as the bullets socked into the Datsun. Varun's mouth was opening and closing without words.

I screamed, 'For Christ's sake, Varun! Panic!'

The two kids were still in front of us. He smacked the gearstick into reverse and kicked the accelerator. The engine roared and the tyres screeched like a bunch of stabbed sopranos. We rocketed back accompanied by the pong of burning rubber and the cracks of bullets. Frankie slammed the door and ducked down behind his camera gear in the back seat.

I was in the front passenger well, arms around my head. Our idiot driver was sitting up, one arm casually thrown across the top of my seat and looking back down the road to make sure we didn't hit any goats. I yelled at him, 'Get down!'

In the back Frankie said, 'Oh God! Oh God!'

I poked my head up. 'Have you been hit?'

'No.'

At which point the windscreen shattered and I had safety glass all over me like dandruff. Varun was still sitting up, spitting out glass. I'll say this for him. He could drive a hell of a lot faster going back than going forward. The bullets kept coming but whoever was firing them wasn't Annie Oakley. They were zinging past a yard or so abeam. Varun yelled, 'Don't hit my car!'

That did it for Frankie and me. We just started rolling about with laughter. It was the sheer surrealism of it all. The Datsun slewed round a right hand bend, nearly impaling us on an advancing truck, but we were out of the line of fire. Varun took his hoof off the accelerator. That stopped our roars. 'Keep going!' I bellowed.

'Faster!' shouted Frankie.

We must have done the best part of a mile before we let him ease up. Varun said, 'We'll call the Army.'

'Eh?'

'Tamil Tigers,' he explained.

I said, 'Since when have the Tamil Tigers been hiring local orphans to stage ambushes?'

Frankie said, 'We call an emergency underwear shop.'

That's one of the things that endears him to me. He can joke after nearly copping a bullet in his aperture setting. We wanted to inspect just how close we had come to a three-paragraph obit, but I wasn't happy hanging around. For all I knew, the gunslingers had a Maserati Bora parked up a banana tree and were about to give chase. I told Varun to forget Colombo and take to the hills. He interpreted this literally. He strongly recommended Nuwara Eliya where terraces of tea bushes perch on the high-rise countryside. He found himself a track and off we bumped, the sweet sunkissed air blasting through where the windscreen used to live. We examined the car's interior. The bullet which knocked the screen out had exited through the roof, indicating to a trained crime hack that the marksman was either a dwarf or he was firing from the ground. The exit hole was on the righthand rear passenger side, a spot normally occupied by Frankie's head. If I'd been sitting up, I'd have caught it somewhere around the left ear. Frankie whipped out the Olympus and started popping. He said, 'How many do you think there were?'

Varun said, 'Dozens.'

I said, 'We're talking about snipers, not bullets. I say there was at least one.'

Frankie said, 'I reckon two. One either side. We'll see when we get out.'

We stopped half an hour down the track. Judging by the holes in both sides, there'd been two hot shots. Or one with a gun that fired in stereo. The driver's mirror was gone. There were four deep gouges down the left wing. We'd lost both lights and half the number plate. They missed the tyres.

Frankie said, 'Looks like semi-automatic fire.' Monkeys like saying things like this. It makes them sound almost smart. I thought we'd been hit with hand guns, and not very macho ones at that. Otherwise the shots that peppered the wing would have continued on their wicked way and turned me into a tea bag.

Varun didn't care whether it was a bazooka or a water pistol. He wailed, 'Who will pay for my car?'

'We will,' said Frankie, meaning me.

That made Varun happy again. He smiled. 'No worries. Now I take you somewhere safe.'

I was proud of our little gofer. Most drivers in this situation would throw a fit or join the enemy. Not our Varun. He'd literally saved our lives and all he wanted in return was a new windscreen and a bit of bodywork. I felt a wave of reckless affection sweep over me. 'Varun,' I instructed, 'take us somewhere I can buy you a very tall, very special bottle of arrak. You deserve a drink.'

Mind you, I felt I deserved a few too.

We overnighted in the foothills of Nuwara. We had to stop early because the tropical night was coming down like thunder and we were minus lights. Also, Varun was less sober than the back road demanded. There was a hotel, a rickety old thing, knocked up in the days when they built the Empire. Varun stowed the air-conditioned Datsun out the back and we checked in using German names. I was Michael Schmeichel, Frankie Helmut Becker. We paid up front so the manager would not demand to see our passports. I said to him, 'Ver ist der bar?' And he answered in ripe German. Fortunately he also pointed to it. Many years ago the bar had been decorated in cream, possibly even white. Now it was yellow with nicotine and dead things. The central fan didn't work. The beer was warm. Somebody had murdered all the sofas and stuffing spilled out of the stab wounds. But we weren't bitching. We sat around a table mounted on an elephant's foot and pondered our past, present and immediate future. We all agreed that Samarsinghe and his dacoits had tried to do us in. Presumably they'd hoped we'd both get out of the car so they could pick us off at leisure. We diverged on what we thought they might do next. Frankie had them creeping through our windows at deep dead of night with oriental daggers chomped between their teeth. I guessed they would run for cover, fearing we had called in Plod and the British High Commission. But I also suspected there was more mischief lurking in the undergrowth. Varun went along with that one. He cheerfully asserted they would get Frankie and me at Colombo airport on our way home. There was logic behind this. Right now, Samarsinghe & Co were probably unaware of our hideout and we could stay hidden until it was time to fly away. But the only way out was via Colombo's Katunayake airport. The villains could easily bribe somebody there to keep them supplied with passenger flight manifests. They might even know already that we were scheduled to depart at noon on Friday. I rubbed a worried brow and ordered more drink.

There were other ways off the island, Varun informed. We could sneak down to Galle and catch a boat to the Maldives and fly home from there. Frankie liked the sound of that one. I didn't. It would take too long. But at least it offered the prospect of getting home alive. Frankie might have won the argument but for Varun remarking, 'Of course, the Maldives are Moslem.'

'So?' I said.

'So they do not have alcohol.'

So that knocked the Maldives off the map. We were back to Colombo airport and the prospect of an untimely end. We ordered more drink. I invited Varun to use all his skill and judgement and pick the spot where we would be most likely to fall bleeding. Without hesitation he chose the main hall. I recalled my first impressions of a rave party for half of Asia with people stampeding this way and that and back again. No one would notice a couple of hired killers mingling with the mob. Varun warmed to his theme. They could get us in the toilets, in the crowded cafe, in the press around the money changers.

'In the duty free shop?' Frankie asked.

Varun said that was unlikely and why bother asking anyway because we'd be murdered long before we got within sniffing distance of the tax free liquor counter.

I was intrigued. Why should we be safe there? Varun laughed at my ignorance. Because the killers would have to go through security, he explained.

They'd be frisked for guns, knives, what-have-you. And once you got into the departure lounge, there wasn't the same heaving mass of humanity.

I brooded. Frankie brooded. Varun hummed a mournful air. We could always ring the bells, I mused. A single call to the office would get them jumping on the Foreign Office. They'd get us protective custody. If I wanted, they'd send in a pack of minders to cover our backs. They'd lay on a private plane, if we needed. And they'd want to know what the bloody hell was going on. And I didn't want to tell them. Not until I had the whole shebang written up and tied with a bow.

Frankie was thinking aloud. He said, 'Is there an airport here?'

Indeed there was, said Varun. But that wasn't much use. It flew you to Galle, Trinco, Batticaloa and other sundry spots. All within the island.

'Yes,' pursued Frankie. 'And Colombo?'

And Colombo. I suddenly saw what was stirring in the candlelit corners of Frankie's brain. It was an idea of rare beauty.

I said, 'And in Colombo we can get an airside transfer to the KLM flight without having to check in.'

We'd lost Varun along the way. I let Frankie explain. 'We check in at Nuwara Eliya and tell them we're catching the Schipol flight out of Colombo. They transfer us to KLM at Colombo. We're already through security. We just wait around in the departure lounge until it's time to go.'

I said, 'And meanwhile the baddies are waiting for us to check in on the main concourse.'

A slow slice of a smile split Varun's face. 'That is very clever, Mister Frankie,' he said. 'I knew Mister Max was clever but I see you are just as smart.'

Mister Frankie, the smart ass, was so tickled he bought us all a drink.

We stayed put in Nuwara Eliya. I spent all of the next day drinking the local tea and writing up my notes. I didn't bother turning them into: *A child sex storm last night rocked the Government and big business* . . . That would come later. I got myself a wad of hotel note-paper, sepia with years of storage, and wrote everything out in a legible longhand. This wasn't an insurance policy. It was a last will and testament. If they were going to get me I was damn sure I'd get them. I wrote the whole yarn, right back to Claudine's mum predicting shock horror scandal in the World-Care Foundation, right up to our present plight. When I was done I read it in one solid sitting, checking for grammar and spelling bloomers. The last thing I wanted was some down table sub standing by my grave muttering, 'The bugger couldn't spell his name: we just made him look good.'

I did a proper job of it. I didn't even invent a single quote. This was the St James Version. But by the time I finished I felt about as happy as a sandboy facing a tidal wave. That was down to the tapes. It was grim work sitting there in that dusty room listening to the thin voice of Lal, describing without emotion the orphan boys' hideous life. Afterwards I yearned for company. But Frankie was hunting around for somewhere to develop his film and Varun had gone to check flights out of Nuwara Eliya. I wandered down to reception and got the directions for a shop with a photocopier. I ran off four copies and moved on to the next stop, a shop selling stamps and big envelopes. I posted one copy to Rosie, another to my sister in Yeovil. I thought about it for at least five minutes, then I addressed a third to Mr Ross Gavney, 27 Magpie Court. I thought about it some more and tore up that envelope. I wrote on the first page of each: 'By the time you receive this, I should be back in Blighty. If not, please forward these notes to Suptd. Ben Ashbee', with the relevant address. I still had two copies. I wanted to post them from some other place, just in case the local post office caught fire. I also had my original notes next to my heart.

Varun got back around six. I yipped a warm 'Hello!' because I was drinking alone in the gloom-laden bar and was beginning to view suicide in a fonder light. He was just as tickled to see me. He hadn't had a drink all day. But it had been worth it. He had two tickets for Friday's early bird flight into Colombo. I'd given him a whole heap of money. I didn't press him for the change. Frankie limped in dripping perspiration and joined the party. He had processed one roll and run off a string of contact prints. He must have used the Olympus because they were in focus. They mostly showed Ajit, the six-year-old, with a single shot of Lal. They were absolute knock-outs. Frankie said, 'I've got both on other films, but I'm posting these back now, just in case things get iffy.'

He wanted Varun to wire them out of AP in Colombo but I argued him out of it, pointing out that our Pic Desk would go spare if they knew he was in Sri Lanka and hadn't told them. Also, I didn't want AP nosing round my story.

Anyway, we had our escape mapped out, our tickets bought, my notes written and his smudges in our hands. It was time to enjoy ourselves.

We enjoyed ourselves for two solid days. I woke on the morning of the third to a sky as pink as Blackpool rock and to the chitter of grey monkeys armed with loud hailers. The room rocked when I walked. I tiptoed downstairs so as not to wake my hangover and forced myself to down a couple of hoppers – pancakes as thin as a butterfly's wing, with a fried egg plonked in the middle. Frankie had already gorged himself and was in hearty form. Snappers are too thick to get hangovers.

Varun stumbled around the place collecting our luggage. I was pleased to see his eyes had turned red in the night. We had a twenty minute drive to the airport. I thought at first it was a cricket pitch, until Varun pointed out a windsock, limp in the breezeless air. We checked in. We were the only passengers. Peering out of the terminal I could see why. Our plane was a 17th century single-decker bus with a rough approximation of a wing clapped on top. Somebody yelled out something in Sinhalese and Varun said, 'Your flight is ready.'

We said our farewells. It was a strangely subdued moment. Varun had been a good old mate through all the fun and games, getting shot at and getting ossified just like us. We shook each other warmly by the hand and swore undying friendship. Varun was still a shade subdued. Ooops. I'd forgotten to pay him. I hauled out my now slender wallet and did some mental arithmetic. Forty quid a day over five days was, what, two hundred. What the hell. Let's make it fifty a day, I doled the notes out in his hand. He counted them again. He said, 'For hire car there is also ten pounds a day insurance.'

I gazed into his crimson eyeballs. I said, 'Don't try your five-card trick on me, Varun.'

He laughed. 'Just keeping in practice, that is all.'

I planned to sleep all the way to Colombo but the pilot had a better idea. He saw the trip as one long fun-filled roller coaster ride, zooming up the crest of every thermal and plummeting like a shot parrot down the other side. Frankie loved it.

Colombo was wide awake and kicking up a stink when we juddered to a halt. In the front seat Baron von Richtofen got on the wireless and summoned up a mini minibus which ferried us over to international. There were too many people around in the departure lounge for us to feel comfortable. We sat there back-to-back, seeing a suicide bomber, a crazed knifeman in every passing Sri Lankan. We had about fifty pence left in rupees so there was nothing to do but sit there and imagine things. By the time they called our flight Frankie was Grade A Broadmoor material. We didn't speak until KLM 481 was a mile above Sri Lanka and we could smell the drinks trolley.

London arrived next day. A big grey island of concrete, blotched with parks and unexplained holes. It looked beautiful. As our dashing pilot, Captain van Transit, aimed for Heathrow, I made a momentous decision.'

I said, 'Frankie, I want you to live with me.'

He was horrified. Maybe not as horrified as me, but still shaken. I explained my thinking. Before Sri Lanka, I'd been the villains' only hate figure. But once Frankie started clicking in Kandy he became a target too. They had it in for both of us. We still had a chunk of scribbling and snapping to do, so why didn't Frankie share my hideaway until it was safe to stagger the streets again?

Frankie thought of the free food and drink in my bunker and he saw it made sense. 'Okay,' he said.

Five minutes after we got back to the Barbican I saw it wasn't okay. Our relationship made David and Goliath look the closest of mates.

'Clear that mess off the table,' I snarled, indicating half a ton of cameras.

'What mess?'

'That mess.'

'Where am I supposed to put them?' asked Frankie peevishly.

'I don't know. Under a bed. In a cupboard. Out of the way.'

My brother's flat was built for a bachelor, a tidy, clean, unencumbered bachelor.

'There's no room under the bed. He's got books and things there,' Frankie complained after a brief exploration.

'Try the wardrobe.'

In the end we pulled the settee away from the wall

and stuck everything there. We moved on to the next phase of the war. I said, 'Right, let's get the ground rules clear from the start. I sleep on the bed, you can kip on the floor.'

'Why should you get the bed?'

I said, 'Because it's my flat.'

He said, 'No it's not. It's your brother's.'

I said, 'Oh for God's sake, Frankie. Do you think my brother would want you in his bed?'

He saw the logic in this but he was still moody. I said, 'Okay, that's settled. Now meals. I do the cooking, you do the washing up.'

Frankie railed, 'Why should you get the easy bit?'

I thought of the endless minutes slaving over a hot microwave. I said, 'Because it's my flat.'

He said, 'And I'm your guest. Do you usually ask your guests to do the dishes?'

'Yes.'

Frankie muttered and went off to pour himself an outrageous whisky. I pretended not to notice. We haggled on about who should tidy the lounge, who did the shopping, who had the TV remote control. I let him have the buttons and he brightened up. The next battle caught me unawares. He picked up the phone and began picking out a number.

I said, 'Who are you calling?' I wasn't being nosy or anything. Just interested.

He said, 'A girl.'

I said, 'I'd better ring Rosie too.'

Frankie said, 'Yes, great. We can have them both round for a party tonight.'

Something went 'Uh-Oh' in my head. I said cautiously, 'Who is she?'

'Who? Mine? Just a girl I know.'

'Who?'

'Tara-lynn.'

Tara-lynn! May all the saints preserve us. Tara-lynn Throw-up-in-the-back-of-the-taxi Beavis. I said, 'You can't have her here. She'll wreck the place.'

Frankie said bitterly, 'I get it. It's okay for you to have Rosie round but I can't invite my girl. Why not?'

'Because, Frankie, the last time I saw Tara-lynn she was pouring a pint over some bloke's head because she thought he was somebody else; because she is the only person in recorded history to be barred from Hampton's; because she dances on tables after a small vodka.'

His eyes misted over with happy memories. He said, 'Yes, she does.'

'Well I don't want her dancing on any tables around here,' I said.

Frankie was scandalised. 'She wouldn't do a thing like that. She's changed now.'

I wondered if that meant she had started wearing knickers but I didn't say anything. I suppose I realised it was unfair to keep Frankie and the object of his sweaty passions parted. But I made him swear he'd pay for the damage and he'd kick her out as soon as she got boisterous.

There followed a happy hour of peace while we waded through the whisky and planned our next steps in the Tomlin affair. I'd already done a bit of thinking. I knew neither Tomlin nor his son would cough up.

Nor would Lewis Trefoyle. These days you need nothing less than a fork-lift truck to prise a sleazy politician out of office. Martin Crowley would break my neck if I asked him the time of day. Proudhoe Veizey would run bleating to his lawyers. Gus Clernthorpe would have us horsewhipped. And then there was Leon Knapp.

He was frightened and he was friendless. They'd blackballed him from the Kandy club so he might also be feeling hard done by. All that plus the verbal evidence from Sri Lanka. And even his own mother would have to admit Leon is not of the great thinkers of the day. If we leaned on him hard enough who knows what he might divulge. I outlined the master plan to Frankie and I think he caught enough of it to know what I had in mind. He was all set to go collect his motor and get snapping. I said this wasn't too clever. If the traffic plods stopped us they were liable to get alcohol poisoning from his breath. So he watched *Emmerdale* while I rang around to say honey, I'm home.

At least Rosie sounded pleased about it. She wanted to come round right there and then. I told her I had Frankie as an unpaying guest. She didn't want to come anywhere near the place. It took all my skills as a trained negotiator to make her change her mind. If I'd said anything about Tara-lynn's scheduled visit, she'd have left town.

Next, the office. I called Angela Whipple. She was busy, but not too busy to drop in a cheap crack. She said, 'While you were off sunning yourself, Jed

Kennedy picked up a nice little exclusive on the Tournier murder.'

Angie must have been under the cosh. It's not her style to snipe, especially about anything Kennedy might have written. He's a freelance who is better known as Cape Kennedy because of all the fliers he puts up. A flier is a news story which is the sole invention of the reporter. It has the merit of sounding as if it might be true. It has the demerit of being utter balls. I don't mind that. What I object to is being told to follow up a flier. It is useless to point out to a news editor that the whole thing is rubbish. What matters to a news editor is that it got a good show in the *People*, the *Mail* or wherever. It looked good. And that's all that counts.

I got Angie to put me through to Dinesh, a down table hack who owes me a favour and a tenner. He called up Kennedy's story from the library and read it out with many a chuckle.

*Murder squad detectives probing the killing of beautiful business tycoon Claudine Tournier say the name of her killer could be in her little black book.*

That's 25 words in the intro. Do they not have any subs over there? I read on:

*The curvaceous 34-year-old was found shot dead last month and her body tossed into the Thames in London.*

I don't think Cape Kennedy has quite caught the gist of things. Her body was not tossed into the Thames after they found it. Even the Old Bill draw the line at that. Cape burbled on:

*Suspicion first pointed at an underworld hitman, known to be operating from a penthouse flat in Mayfair.*

*But 'tecs grilling her jet set friends now believe*

*Claudine, the wife of financier Sir James Tomlin, was leading a secret double life.*

*A senior officer said, 'She was a passionate woman with a string of devoted male admirers.*

*'We want to interview them all and we're going through her little black book. But many of them are married and we are meeting a wall of silence.'*

I said, 'Balls, balls, balls.'

Dinesh said cheerfully, 'It gets worse.'

*A close confidante of the dead woman who would not give her name said last night, 'Claudine had a list of lovers. She told me she couldn't resist young men with tight bottoms.*

*'It was an obsession for her. But she said she was frightened of one of them. She would not tell me who he was.*

*'I warned her to stay away but she couldn't help herself. It was a fatal attraction.'*

*The woman friend broke down in tears as she added, 'I'm sure she was killed by her jealous boyfriend when she tried to ditch him.'*

*Sir James Tomlin was too shaken to comment on the revelations last night but a City source said, 'This has come as a dreadful blow to him.*

*'He believed she was happy with him. He has been shocked to discover she was conducting affairs when he was out of town on high-pressure business trips . . .'*

'Enough!' I told Dinesh. 'If you read any more I'll be sick.'

Now let us examine Cape Kennedy's world-beating exclusive. Its whole inspiration, I knew, came from iffy hints that I had stuck in my original copy the night of the murder. His story appeared in Monday's paper and he doesn't work Sundays. Therefore it was knocked up on Friday as a Sunday-for-Monday. We often do this. If there's not a lot in the diary for Sunday, the weekend news editor gets the hacks to write up all sorts of tosh on Friday. He has it in the bag. Come Sunday, he sends it to the subs, and they have half Monday's first edition sewn up before a single reporter has tapped a key. This is why Monday's tabloids always carry half-baked surveys – Do Girls Make Passes at Men Who Wear Glasses?/ Britain's Favourite Fantasy Harem/How to Squander A Million In A Day.

Getting back to the subject: whenever you see terms like 'senior officer' in a story, allow yourself a chuckle and turn to the horoscopes. You'll find them more factual. There is no such animal as the senior officer. He is on a par with the 'Buckingham Palace insider', the 'Cabinet colleague' and the unicorn. So, when you take the mythical animals' quotes out of Jed Kennedy's stuff you see it's nonsense with a capital S.

I rang the famous flier anyway for he is a mate.

'How goes it with the unemployed?' he asked impertinently.

I said, 'I was thinking of writing a great work of fiction and then I read your story.'

'Which one?' The man has no shame.

I said, 'The one about Claudine Tournier's little black book.'

He laughed. 'Great show, wasn't it? Anyway, it was nearly true.'

I said, 'Which word was that? I must have missed it.'

Kennedy said, 'No, seriously. Some guy called us last week. Wouldn't leave his name. A casual took the call. The bloke just asked us if we knew Claudine was putting it about. Our man asked who was she putting it about with. The bloke just said married men. Nothing else. End of story.'

I said, 'What do the murder squad say about it?'

'Don't know. Didn't ask.'

On such rock solid foundations many a page lead is built.

# Chapter Fifteen

The girls came round that night. I feared we might have a cat fight on our hands. Frankie hoped we would. But everyone was on their best behaviour, by our standards anyway. Rosie engorged me with hugs and kisses and I didn't do much to dissuade her. She was tickled with her souvenirs of Sri Lanka. She was even more taken with my pith helmet. I rather liked it too. But I am a generous soul. I said, 'You have it.' More demonstrations of extreme affection. I wished I'd bought a dozen of the things.

Tara-lynn battered on the door with enough Chinese takeaways to feed Beijing. She was seven tenths sober, so she didn't eff and blind and, for all I know, she was wearing knickers. The four of us tucked into the grub and the laughter came easy.

Much later, in the refuge of Dominic's bedroom, Rosie got serious. She said, 'What next?'

'Next? I unbutton your blouse with my teeth. You've read the script.'

She pushed me away. She said, 'You know what I mean. So far you've been nearly murdered twice. If you get up their nose again they might make it third time lucky.'

I didn't want to talk about it. It was a news story. It was my province and she didn't know how things worked there. Hacks don't talk about their trade except to other hacks. We're not alone in this anti-social behaviour. Many feel the same. For instance, I can't imagine a brain surgeon coming home and saying to his wife: 'I've got a tricky ippydippyochtomy on tomorrow. What should I do?' Mind you, if he was married to Rosie, she'd probably tell him.

I said the Claudine Tournier story was mine, all mine. I wasn't going to walk away from it. The whole thing was set to blow to bits and I wanted to be there to watch it. Rosie threw a wobbly. She said, 'You're being irresponsible. Leave it to the police. You think a big story with your name on it is the most important thing in the world.'

I do think this, because I know it to be true. She went into a mile-long catalogue of my sins. I got home late. I drank too much. I never phoned her. I kept bad company. I frittered my money on riotous living. Until then I was unaware there was anything else you could do with money. And I never turned up when promised. And, and, and . . .

And I tried to jolly her out of it. Oh, and that was another thing: I patronised her all the time. I said, 'Has Tomlin hired you to monster me to death?'

Rosie went into a sulk. She knows I can't stand that. I surrendered. 'All right, all right. First thing tomorrow I go to Ben Ashbee and ask for protection. And I won't do any more snooping around.'

'Promise?'

'Promise.'

'Cross your heart and hope to die?'

'Cross my heart and hope to die a horrible death.'

Rosie looked me searchingly in the eyes. They were candid and unclouded by lies or trickery. She believed me.

But how was she to know I'd my fingers crossed behind my back.

Tara-lynn was first up. She'd polished off the last of the milk and skedaddled before either Frankie or I awoke. I left Rosie still in the arms of slumber and penned a note: 'Gone to give myself up. Call you later. Gallons of love.'

I didn't want to hang around in case she felt like escorting me to the cops, so Frankie and I slipped off to a greasy spoon and dined like kings. We got a taxi up to Muswell Hill, collected his office car and pointed it due west. I used the mobile en route to get the office to trace Leon Knapp's address. It was a house called Chantelle in the village of Barden, just the far side of Newbury. I remembered Chantelle was the name of a hit record for Leon in the days when young girls used to burst through reinforced concrete to kiss his jowls. I had a song in my heart too. It was a June morning of the type we used to make before we went European. Old England looked in pretty good nick as it flicked past us at 90mph on the M4. Even Frankie was moved to poetry: 'Nice, innit?'

And so we wended our blithesome way, in careless ignorance of the havoc we were about to wreak.

The house which called itself Chantelle looked as

if it had just been nicked from Acacia Avenue, Alicante. There was a spanking brilliance to the white stucco, set off by sun-baked red tiles and mysterious shadows in the cloisters. This is something else I never understand. Why do English people with wall-to-wall money build themselves houses which belong somewhere else? Take a trip along the upper reaches of the Thames and you are surrounded by Mexican haciendas and Disneyland castles. They don't half look daft in the English rain.

We parked the motor outside Maison Chantelle and gave it our scrutiny. A Japanese four-wheel-drive job tethered by the porch jarred with the Spanish motif. The Knapp mansion displayed a freshly nibbled acre of lawn and a bunch of bushes that looked as if they went to church twice on Sundays. A creeper of some sort had begun inching up the wall. Chantelle was spelled out in wrought iron at our end of the driveway and again on the wall of the house for the benefit of absent-minded postmen. The front door was woody and gnarled and black, as if it had narrowly survived the Spanish Inquisition. There wasn't a doorbell, just a chunk of pig iron serving as a knocker. I gave it a blatter and stood back. Frankie was silent but I could hear him thinking: 'This must have cost a packet.'

We waited ages until the mediaeval door sprung open to reveal a mediaeval figure in a red and white striped towelling robe.

'Yus?' said the figure. Knapp himself. This was the first time I'd ever seen him up close. I never knew he wore a rug. He'd just come from the shower so the hair over his ears was clinging wet. The rug was dull and dry.

I said, 'Good morning, Leon. I am Max Chard, and this is my photographer, Mister Frankie Frost.'

Frankie's Canon went click in my ear and the door went bang in my face.

I said, 'Hello, door.'

The door was the strong and silent type. I talked to it anyway. I said, 'Sorry to bother you door, we really want to see your master. You see, we've just come from Kandy.'

No response. I said, 'And everyone at the Perelawaya Children's Refuge sends Leon their greetings. They miss him. They send you their fondest wishes too, door.'

Nothing. I continued, 'Yes, and Lal and Ajit told me all sorts of things. But I suppose if you're not going to open up, you'll just have to read all about them in the paper.'

I left that one simmering quietly for a full minute. Still not a murmur.

I sighed. 'It's sad, door. Jimmy and Martin and the boys are pinning everything on Leon. They say he's the only one involved. Dearie me, the things they say he got up to . . . but I suppose if you're not going to let me in, I'll just have to take their word for it.'

The door opened its letterbox. 'It's lies. I'll sue you for every penny if you print a word.'

I said, 'Oh no you won't. Sir James Tomlin has given me twenty-four carat evidence. He's told me how Leon went to a bona fide orphanage and abused the boys. How he took snaps of them. How he has banned Leon from ever visiting the children again.'

The letterbox gulped. It said, 'Jimmy said that?'

'Indeed he did. And Martin Crowley and Lewis Trefoyle. And all the rest. If Leon sues my paper, we'll subpoena every one of them to testify against him.'

The letterbox flapped wordlessly for a moment, then it said, 'What do you want?'

I said, 'It's what Leon wants that counts. He needs damage limitation in spades. I am his only hope. Turn me away door, and your boss is stuffed.'

The letterbox threatened to call its lawyer.

I said, 'Do that. While you're at it, call the Sri Lankan High Commissioner, the Foreign Office and Detective Superintendent Benjamin Ashbee.'

'The police?' squeaked the letterbox.

I said, 'Not yet. But if you don't open up, you leave me with no alternative but to hand my dossier to Scotland Yard.'

The door gave me a black look and opened. Leon was a shade older, paler and uglier than when last seen.

He said, 'I'll talk to you. But no pictures.'

I cordially lied that we wouldn't take any snaps and we were in. The hallway was a chequerboard of black and cream tiles. A couple of shady nooks played home to darkly Spanish guitars. It was a dead ringer for Old Seville, though old Sevillians were most likely averse to stapling platinum discs to the walls. Leon, barefoot, padded down the hall and right out into a Spanish back garden, encrusted with a swimming pool. The pool was in the shape of a record, or maybe it was just round. He perched on the edge of a sun lounger, his eyes swivelling from Frankie to me. He didn't know whom to watch. I dropped into one of those swinging chair things and lit a cigarette. I said, 'They've hung you out to dry, Leon.'

'What?' One hand massaging one knee.

I said, 'You're the scapegoat.'

He said, 'I don't know what you're talking about.'

I furrowed my brow at him. 'Oh, come on, Leon. I've got Trefoyle – a Government minister – rubbishing you. Imagine how that will look if you sue us. Want to hear what he says?'

Knapp nodded dumbly. Both hands massaging both knees.

I ruffled through the back pages of my notebook and imagined Trefoyle's orotund English. I said, 'Here it is. Trefoyle says, "The orphanage has the highest criteria for the care and welfare of its young inmates. Its staff are of course aware that many have been traumatised by their previous experiences through the civil conflict. The director's primary objective is to ensure that these traumas are not exacerbated, that indeed they are mitigated by the work of the centre. Mister Niaz was most concerned when some of his charges began manifesting symptoms of distress. Naturally he called upon the expertise of a qualified child psychologist who inferred from the children's statements that they had been molested in a sexual manner. Mister Niaz instituted a most rigorous inquiry and informed the trustees of the WorldCare Foundation of his concern. The children were subject to diligent medical examinations and further counselling. These established that the children had in fact been abused. Each child so molested cited Mister Leon Knapp, a Foundation trustee, as the perpetrator. Mister Niaz obtained conclusive evidence of this when Mister Knapp was apprehended taking photographs of the boys whilst engaging in obscene and unnatural practices . . ." '

Leon had started to emit a strange whuffling sound. I said, 'Tough stuff, wouldn't you say? Do you want to hear Martin Crowley on the same subject?'

He didn't say no, so I flipped to another page. I read: 'I know Leon Knapp through my work on the Foundation. He always struck me as an oddball, a bit too full of his own ego. You know the type, he was famous for fifteen minutes once and he never learned to cope with the real world. The Foundation just used him as a minor celebrity. It was good for fund-raising. None of us had the faintest idea he was a pervert. If I could get my hands on him, I'd . . .'

'A minor celebrity?' Leon was hurt. Too hurt to notice Frankie squeezing off shots.

I said, 'They've screwed you to the wall. You'll never be anybody's king again.' This was a below-the-belt reference to one of his mawkish ballads which went: 'I wanna be your king, and you be my queen forever, Ooooh yeaah.'

It was in the mid-seventies out there by the pool but Knapp was hugging himself for comfort. A more civilised man might have taken pity on the wretch. I enjoy blood sports.

I said, 'The other trustees are holding a meet this weekend to which you're not invited. They will vote to kick you out. Then they'll go public. That's the story we're going to run all over page one, with the boys' pix and quotes across the centre spread on Monday. Unless you have a better idea.'

A pin prick of light shone briefly in his muddied brown eyes. 'What sort of idea?'

I said, 'You tell me all about the others' involvement and I'll play down your naughtiness. Call it plea bargaining.'

He gave a nervous laugh. He said, 'I call it blackmail.'

I said, 'Blackmail is an ugly word. Call it a dirty great threat.'

He said, 'You want me to talk about people like Tomlin? You want me to incriminate myself? You must be nuts. No deal.'

I stood up, closed my notebook and stuck it in my pocket. I said, 'Come on, Frankie. The man doesn't want to listen.'

I turned and began to walk away. I got five and a half steps before he tried another laugh. It was more of a jeer but it was ragged around the edges. He said, 'You're making it all up. I've done nothing. You can't print anything.'

I turned around slowly. I put on what I hoped was a thin cruel smile. I said, 'Pick up your paper on Monday and this is what you'll read: "Seventies rock idol Leon Knapp was last night branded an evil sex monster who preys on helpless orphans." Stop. New par. "The has-been singer exploits boys as young as six to gratify his depraved lust." Stop. New par.'

I'm not sure which bit got to him. I think it was

that crack about the has-been singer. At any rate, he buckled up and started feeling sorry for himself. I stood patiently waiting. Frankie banged off a whole roll. We let him bleat away to himself. I carried on with my imaginary news story: 'Bachelor Knapp broke down and wept when confronted with his shameful secret . . .'

He wiped a runny nose on the towelling robe. He said, 'Don't say any more. What do you want?'

I returned to the swing chair. I said, 'First of all I'd like a large gin and tonic while I think up a way to get you out of this mess.'

He actually looked grateful. He scuttled off, returning with ice bucket, bottle of Gordons, the lot. I took my time pouring the drink. You have to watch it with the tonic. I settled back and said, 'Right, Leon. First of all you should know I'm not all that interested in a tacky little sex scandal halfway across the world.'

I'm one hell of a liar. A flicker of relief chased across his eyes. I said, 'I'm a chief crime correspondent, which means I'm picky about the sort of stories that deserve my talents. This isn't one of them. Who cares what happens to a couple of Third World kids?'

More unconfined joy from the child molester. I said, 'What interests me is big stuff – drug barons, Mister Big gangsters, brutal killers, that sort of thing. Which is why I'm giving you a bad time.'

He said, 'I'm not with you . . .'

I was patient. I said, 'Claudine Tournier got herself murdered last month. So did a girl called Shirley

Ham. I'm betting it's because they found out about Kandy and—'

'—It wasn't me!'

I said, 'No. You had the perfect alibi. You were off in Sri Lanka abusing children. So who did it?'

He gripped the edge of his chair and leaned forward. 'You're not going to involve me?'

I said I wasn't. The fibs you have to tell in this job. His thin lips spread in a half smile. He said, 'I haven't a clue.'

I said, 'That's it, Leon. You've blown the deal.' And I stood up again. It took all the warmth of his lovable personality and an earnest promise to tell the truth before I consented to have another gin. Knapp's was a sordid and trite story. Once upon a time in old Amsterdam there was a club catering for paedophiles. It was there he first met the likes of Michael Tomlin and Gus Clernthorpe. They formed themselves into a seedy group, calling themselves the Young Boys Network. Knapp recruited his chum, Proudhoe Veizey. Tomlin added Trefoyle and Crowley. A couple of blue chip City types joined the fraternity. Happy times were had by all until the Dutch Old Bill took an interest. The Network tried Denmark but that was risky too. Then Claudine Tournier embarked on the WorldCare Foundation, with husband Sir James Tomlin and stepson Michael looking after the business side of things. Michael went to Sri Lanka to set up the Kandy project and found child sex on tap. Then Sir James took an interest.

He knew all about Michael's little peccadilloes. He also knew the Network numbered various influential types. He wasn't interested in paedophilia. But he was most anxious to have the City men and Trefoyle as business allies. He set up boys for them, they set up deals for him. It was his idea to launch the orphanage. This way the Network could run their own show without fear of leaks. He had the members made Foundation trustees, which gave them perfect cover for sex jaunts. They could even claim their travel expenses against tax. The local Law thought they were do-gooders and smiled on them. What could go wrong?

What went wrong was Claudine. She began asking questions about why Kandy was such a popular spot. Then, back in Britain, Michael nearly got done for indecently assaulting a schoolboy. Claudine made the connection. She blew up and tackled Sir James, threatening all sorts of mischief. She was hellbent on exposing his pals, thereby derailing his gravy train. He was less than enthusiastic about the idea.

Therefore Sir James had his wife murdered? Knapp thought that was it. And Shirley Ham? I had to explain to him who the late Shirl was. Yes, Tomlin probably topped her too. There was something that didn't fit, I said. Why was Tomlin so anxious that 'Kandy must be stopped' after Claudine's death. That was easy, said Knapp. The Network imposed a blanket ban on visits to the orphanage as soon as Claudine sussed what was really going on. Tomlin was frightened she might have private investigators turning it over. The whole operation went into cold storage until the trustees felt it was safe again.

But Leon broke the ban. And he took pix, which

was absolutely taboo. The boys told Niaz, he told Mike – Michael Tomlin – and he got Crowley to visit Knapp, offering to string him up unless he handed over the prints and the negs. Knapp handed them over.

And who was the merry matchman who nearly incinerated me? Knapp didn't know. Crowley most likely. Knapp was never privy to the Network's innermost council. Why did they ever admit him to their company anyway? The answer was the little plastic bags of cocaine he provided for Michael Tomlin. And there you have the whole story. Knapp sat back.

I said, 'Would you testify to all this in court?'

His eyes went slideabout. I produced my tape. I squawked it back a couple of revs and let him hear the sound of his own voice. He looked disappointed with me. I said, 'You'll testify?'

He said yes in a very small voice.

He didn't wave goodbye as we booted off home. But then we didn't wave to him either. When last seen he was a little red and striped thing standing alone in the cloisters.

I saw the light on the road to Hammersmith. I was sifting through my notes to take my mind off Frankie's driving. I was puzzling over one line of fractured shorthand when all of a sudden it hit me. KERPOW! I said, 'Jesus!' Frankie didn't blink. It's probably something all his passengers say.

I sat there savouring the moment. I said, 'I know who the killer is.'

'Oh yes? Who?'

'Michael Tomlin.'

Frankie said, 'How do you know it was him?'

I explained. The line of notes I'd been decoding read: 'He was a friend of Mike's.' I at first deciphered it as 'a friend of Max'. It's easily done – the shorthand outline for Mike's and Max are the same. The names are very similar. They can easily be confused in conversation. On the telephone for instance. A distant doorbell chimed in my brain. And that's when an idea walked in and turned the light on.

Frankie said, 'What are you raving about?'

I told him of the night Shirley was killed. Her dad had told me she'd gone to see Mike, and I, egotistical dimwit that I am, told him no, no, no – she'd gone to see me, Max. And while we were arguing about it, Mike Tomlin was wrapping a rope around her neck and slinging her in the Thames.

Frankie said, 'It might have been a different Mike.'

I said, 'Yeah. And maybe it was a different Adolf Hitler.'

Royce, our lawyer, listened to the tape and threw a fit. 'No corroboration. You've used menace. Knapp will withdraw everything he said. We'd be wide open to libel writs from every single one of them.'

I said, 'Apart from that, how do you like the story?'

He hated it. Newspaper lawyers hate anything true. They wander around muttering, 'The greater the truth, the greater the libel.' They also hate bald statements of fact. Here is an ideal intro in their world: 'An alleged man, in premises purporting to be a law court, was said to have been found guilty by person or persons unknown of driving under the influence of drink or drugs to such an extent as to impair his driving, as laid down under Section 37 of the Road Transport Act.' Riveting stuff, isn't it?

I saw I was getting nowhere with Royce so I roped in Angela Whipple and we cornered the Editor gazing out the window and scratching his backside. He looked allegedly guilty.

I went through the story at a gentle amble, for it was after lunch and his faculties were not at their sharpest. When I had done, he chewed his lip for half a minute. He said, 'Write what you've got and I'll have a look at it.' This was him saying, 'I haven't understood a word you said. I'll read your story when I sober up.'

I returned to my desk and hammered it out. Eighteen hundred words, which is an awful lot for a tabloid. I was checking it for spelling when I smelt something disgusting on the left flank.

Belker said, 'In my office. Now!'

It was a brief yet sunny conversation. He accused me of disobeying him by going to Kandy. I said it was my R&R leave and I was unaware certain countries were banned. He charged me with high treason for not telling the office what I was up to. I said that as a loyal hack I had forgone my hols to provide the paper with an exclusive. He stumped up and down, glaring at the ceiling and firing accusations over his shoulder. I let him. I have a theory: The Chard Theory of Relative Sobriety. You always hear people saying things like: 'You've got to forgive Charlie for throwing up in your bidet – he was drunk', or, 'I wouldn't have stuck the corkscrew in your shoulder if I'd been sober.' But this is wrong. In my experience, people are generally a whole lot more civilised when they're rat-arsed. Therefore, what we should say is: 'You can't blame Belker for running amok. He hasn't had a drink all day.'

I find that if you apply my theory to life, you are more tolerant of others' misbehaviour. So it was with Belker. I smiled sorrowfully at him. It didn't help. He booted me out of his office. And then he went off to do his damnedest to spike my story.

Between him and the scaredy-pants lawyer, they did a good job of it. All references to the Tomlin clique were excised. I ended up with this:

*Wrinkly rocker Leon Knapp last night confessed he uses orphan boys to gratify his evil sex lust.*

*And he claimed a sinister paedophile ring murdered cuisine queen Claudine Tournier.*

*She was gunned down and her body thrown in the Thames after she stumbled on their sordid secret.*

*The perverts – who style themselves the Young Boys' Network – include a senior politician and top tycoons.*

*They abuse helpless children as young as six – rewarding them with cheap plastic toys or gaudy crayons. And Seventies' star Knapp says the ring also ordered the murder of secretary Shirley Ham when she learned of their depraved activities.*

*Knapp broke down and confessed to his role after we confronted him with evidence of systematic child sex abuse.*

*He stressed he played no part in the double murder, but admitted he was a frequent visitor to the phoney orphanage where the boys are caged.*

*We tracked down the Network's activities to a refuge for war waifs in Sri Lanka.*

*But when our chief crime correspondent Max Chard and ace lensman Frank Frost tried to see the boys, they were ambushed and shot at by hired gunmen working for the Network.*

There was much more in like vein, with paragraphs beginning with And, For and But. Words like vile, seedy and sinister littered the copy like currants in a cake. I believe the posher schools tend to frown on tabloidese. It ain't good English, they sneer. Well maybe they should get Marcel Proust to write up the story of the call girl, the curate and the carrot. That would shut them up.

My story was set for Saturday's splash, with the Kandy pix and interviews on the centre spread. But some berk in West Lothian murdered his ex-wife because she won custody of their stupid white rabbit. Also, sports desk bagged the spread for a Wimbledon preview. My stuff was rejigged for a single column on page one, with the rest scrunched up at the back of the book. Then they had an even better idea. Why not hold it as a Sunday-for-Monday? That meant they'd slot it away in the twilight zone between the woman's pages and the bingo. The Chard Theory of Relative Sobriety failed me. I was fit to be tied. But then I was relatively sober myself.

I lassoed Frankie and we plunged into The Stone dive bar. We set off on a kamikaze drinking mission, pausing only to badmouth Belker, the Editor, the lawyer, and anyone else we could think of. Coming up eight, I had a window of sobriety. I remembered I'd better tell Ben Ashbee the score before the story hit the paper. I left Frankie congealing on a stool while I cabbed it to the nick. Big Ben said hello, and he'd nothing new to tell me, so would I kindly go and clutter up somewhere else. I said all right then, he could read all about it on Monday morning, right after he'd got his bollocking from the Commissioner. Ben invited me to sit.

It took an hour to tell, and a civilian clerk with nice legs wrote down every word of it. Ben listened to my brilliant theory about the Mike/Max conundrum and didn't laugh. D.I. Harry Pennycuik came in halfway through and started making smart remarks. Ben told him to rustle up some tea and that got rid of him. When I'd finished, Big Ben did a strange thing. He smiled. It rocked me. Then he said, 'Thanks, Max.' That knocked me off my chair.

Ben said, 'You've given me the excuse I needed.'

'What for?'

He said, 'To turn that lot over. They've been as tight as a duck's arse. Nobody's said a thing. Of course, you haven't got anything on the murders. On the basis of what you say, I can't even pull them in for questioning about the murders.'

Something here was passing me by. I said, 'So why are you so happy?'

Ben cleared his throat and said, 'Because I have reasonable suspicion that Michael Tomlin might be involved in the peddling of sex tours, in contravention of—'

'I know,' I said testily. 'But how does that help your murder inquiry?'

Big Ben smiled again. 'Because I have reasonable suspicion that pornographic literature or material might be—'

I caught on. 'A search warrant!'

'Several search warrants,' said Ben. 'And we'll look under every speck of dust.'

I said, 'When?'

Ben said, 'As soon as I get a sworn statement from Leon Knapp.'

He ordered the clerk to rush off and type him a transcript. He said he needed it right away. I didn't like the way things were going. I could see my story going out the window. I said, 'Are you seeing Knapp tonight?'

'Yes.' He reached for the phone.

I said, 'Ben, you owe me a favour. Don't lift Knapp, Tomlin or anyone until after my story's in Monday's paper.'

He said, 'Why not?'

I said, 'Because the Yard's press bureau will tell everyone you've got him and it will be in all the Sundays. Our lawyer will spike my story, saying it's sub judice.'

Ben looked uncertain. I said, 'Think of it. People read on Sunday that Tomlin has been lifted for running a child sex ring. Then on Monday they read my stuff that Claudine Tournier was murdered by a child sex ring. They'll say, "Just fancy that – it was her stepson what done it." I'd cop the lot for libel, contempt of court, the works.'

Ben's hand floated above the phone but he didn't pick it up. He said, 'Don't you ever tell a soul I did this: I'm giving you until Monday morning, after your paper is on the streets.'

I said, 'And then a dawn swoop?'

Ben said, 'And then we get the bugger out of bed.'

I rolled off into the night a happier man. I now had just the push I needed to force the Editor to give my story a decent show. News stories have a very limited shelf life because news executives have very limited intelligence. What happens is they read your raw copy one day and they say great, terrific stuff, let's run with it. But for one reason or another it doesn't make the paper – usually because advertising department have suddenly sold another three pages. So next day you put the story up again. The execs dimly remember having read it before. They say: 'It's old. It's already been done.' And no matter how sensational the story, they spike it. Until my interview with Ben, I feared my Kandy exposé was doomed to such a fate. They also had one insurmountable objection to it: they hadn't thought up the idea themselves, and that rankled.

But now I could go back to the Editor, tell him the Old Bill were nicking Mike Tomlin as a result of our exclusive, and he'd have to run the story. Then, after the jury found Tomlin guilty of something or other, we could run a big backgrounder on how our fearless investigation put him behind bars. The Editor would get to write one of his celebrated leaders on Why The Press Must Not Be Muzzled (Except When It Might Do The Tories A Mischief).

I tooled up back at the Barbican sometime in the early hours to find Rosie in residence. Asleep. There followed a brief but pathetic attempt to get her to make wild, abandoned love. She told me to go asleep: that she'd love me in the morning. Though how you can preplan wild, abandoned love is beyond me.

When the first faint fingertips of noon propped my eyes open, I felt more like a wild, abandoned funeral. I'm getting too old for this drinking business. I turned on Radio Four and listened to the heads. All foreign, apart from the traditional Friday night council house blaze in Jockland. Rosie was out. Her note told me that. I cranked up the coffee maker and leafed listlessly through the rivals. They offered standard Saturday morning fare – too many Royals, too many telly stars in love split mysteries. I thought what things would have been like if we'd run my story. All across Britain people would be going 'Strike a light!', 'Flaming 'eck!' and 'Och Aye the Noo!' Instead we offered them the stupid rabbit story under the head: 'LOOK BACK IN ANGORA – Hubby blasts ex in bunny battle.' No wonder the Press gets a bad name.

Rosie returned full of bounce. She'd nicked her sister's little blue Metro and was all set to take me for a whirl. I needed an outing, said Rosie, a qualified doctor in her spare time. Now, where should we go? I suggested Hampton's. She prescribed somewhere further afield. I said let's stop at Hampton's for a livener. Only for one, she said. Only for one. I agreed, hoping she might fall under the spell of Hampton's ageless ambience.

There were a few hacks from the Sundays leaning

on the bar for support. We swopped the usual vile slanders on our absent colleagues and ran through the current repertoire of jokes. I saw Rosie looking at her watch. She was on Buxton mineral water, so I suppose she wasn't enjoying herself as much as the rest of us. I waited until she slipped out to the loo and I ordered in another round. They charged £1.50 for the water. I know bars where you can get a decent pint for that. I was paying for her spendthrift ways when Gerry, the barman/owner, said, 'Did you meet your friend?'

I said, 'What friend?'

Gerry helped himself to a fistful of stale peanuts. He said, 'The bloke who was in here this morning.'

I pointed out that (a) I had many friends, and (b) I had not been in the dump in the morning. Therefore I didn't know who the hell he was talking about. He didn't know either. The man wasn't a hack. Gerry thought he was casually dressed, but he couldn't be sure. Was the man green, purple, orange, black, white? He hadn't asked him. Did Mr Mystery leave a message? Just said he'd catch me later. If Gerry had been the deep throat in Watergate, Nixon would still be president. I congratulated him on his observation skills, he said no problem, and off he rolled to rook another customer.

Rosie dragged me screaming and tearful out into the sunshine and tucked me into the passenger seat. She stuck Mozart or something like that on the tape and off we went to mix it with the weekend drivers. I fell asleep. When I awoke there was green all around me. Green trees, green fields, green hedges. I felt car sick. I said, 'Where are we?'

Rosie had no idea. Somewhere in Sussex, she guessed. Wasn't it glorious? It wasn't, but I didn't want to shatter her illusions.

She found us a country pub with roses fighting each other outside the door and a sign saying Bar Meals Served All Day. That meant they served drink all day. Inside it was one of those cosy welcoming inns so dear to our hearts. Everywhere you looked there were signs saying No Credit, No Denims, No Singing, No Dogs, No Dancing On Tables Without Your Drawers On. They hadn't got around to banning drink yet.

Rosie said, 'When I am a rich and famous designer, I'll buy a cottage in the country and keep chickens.' She had rationed herself to a weakish glass of white wine so she wasn't thinking straight.

I said, 'Will you come and visit me at weekends?'

She chirruped, 'No. You can have a summer house in the garden where you can sit and write famous books. In the evenings, we'll stroll down to the village pub and listen to the local gossip.'

I cocked an ear to the present local gossip. They were talking about double-glazing and grain subsidies. I told Rosie, 'I'll come to your cottage when I die. You can use my ashes to fertilise your roses.'

We drove back north along lanes that dipped and dived by rivers and pig farms. Rosie crooned soothing pastoral music. By the time we got back to London she had mellowed enough to unchain me for another bite at Hampton's. She went off to see a mate, promising to collect me later, for she was staying the night at the Barbican.

My mysterious friend had been in again but Gerry still hadn't bothered to ask his name. I wondered if it was a minion from the Law, seeking my assistance in solving the rest of the country's crime. Then I forgot all about it as I caroused with the Wildebeest and a herd of hacks from the *People.* It was five minutes off kicking out time when Gerry sang out, 'Car for Mister Chard. Max, your driver awaits without.'

I made my farewells and picked up a few receipts for my exes. It had been a night well spent. We set off for the Barbican by way of Battersea; an unusual route. But it allowed Rosie to pick up her toothbrush and sundries. She tossed them in the back and we headed back across the city along dark and drear back streets, following one of her mystic short cuts. We were tootling along merrily when she said with exasperation, 'For God's sake, pass.'

'What?'

She said, 'Not you. It's that silver car behind. It's stuck on my bumper.'

I craned round the headrest for a peek. The silver car was a top of the range BMW. I believe one should be considerate to fellow motorists, no matter how stinking rich they are. I said, 'Pull over and let him through.'

Rosie slowed to twenty. So did the Beemer. I said, 'Pull in to the side. He's frightened of scratching his new toy. Or maybe it's a woman driver.'

Rosie trundled up by the kerb. So did the Beemer. I sat up and had another look. The BMW had a tinted screen so you couldn't see anything inside. Also, it had lamps like Eddystone Lighthouse. I said, 'He might just be lonely.'

My chauffeuse said, 'Maybe he's looking for somewhere. Should we stop?'

I said, 'Where are we anyway?'

She said, 'I'm not sure.'

I said, 'Oh that's okay then. For a minute I thought we were lost.'

Rosie slapped the Metro down a gear and pumped the accelerator. We shot off like a nervous greyhound. The G force nearly knocked my head off. She said, 'I don't like it. I'm going to find somewhere less lonely.'

It was a good idea and it might have worked if the Beemer had behaved itself. Instead, it swung out behind us, accelerated and roared past, coming to a shrieking halt half way down the deserted street. Its front doors flew open simultaneously and two men stepped out.

Rosie started braking. I shouted, 'Don't stop, Rosie. Go!'

For I had noticed something she hadn't. The BMW's numberplate. It was MT something. As in Michael Tomlin something. Rosie found her right foot again and we scraped past, causing the driver to jump out of the way. I saw Tomlin's startled angry face flicker in our lights.

Rosie said, 'What's going on? Do you know him?'

Yes, I said. The bloke whose little toe she'd just pulped was Tomlin junior.

'The one you think murdered Claudine Tournier?'

'And Shirley Ham. That one.'

She said, 'Oh God, what does he want?'

I thought about it. I didn't feel he was looking for directions to the nearest doner kebab. I said, 'Don't talk. Just drive like the wind.'

I twisted round again. Tomlin and partner were back in their car and in hot pursuit. Rosie took the words out of my mouth. 'Oh shit!'

I was trying to think fast and not having much success. I said, 'Listen, Rosie. You've got nothing to do with me. You're a minicab driver for London and City. Okay? You're just driving me home. I'll get out right here and you scoot off. Find the nearest phone and ring nine-nine-nine.'

She said, 'No. I'm staying with you.'

'No. Drop me quick.'

'No.'

The Beemer was back licking our bumper. I said, 'Stick to this road. There's lights up ahead.'

Rosie promptly hurtled left into the darkest street in Christendom. Tomlin overshot. I heard the roar of his engine as he whizzed back and had another go at the corner.

The Metro's headlamps picked up empty buildings and sightless windows stretching all the way down the street to a brick wall. A brick wall ten feet high, straddling the roadway like the rock of ages. We didn't get close enough to inspect the graffiti. Rosie clipped a passing lamppost instead and we slewed round, coming to an untidy halt in the path of the pursuing Beemer. 'Double shit,' said Rosie.

We sat in our dented Metro watching the enemy. They pulled up ten or so yards away. Tomlin killed the lights and stepped out. He was in no hurry.

'Remember you're a minicab driver,' I told Rosie.

'No I'm not.'

'Please.'

She said, 'That's the last time I pick you up from Hampton's.'

'You may, alas, be right.'

Tomlin's pal had got out too. He stood leaning against the BMW and looking our way. We couldn't see his face, but I knew he wasn't the Good Samaritan. Tomlin arrived at the driver's side. He said, 'Good evening, Miss Bannister.'

So bang went my plan to pretend Rosie was a cabbie. He had both his hands in his pockets. He sounded chummy and relaxed. He strolled round to my side, stopping to admire the crumpled wing en route. He said, 'Had a bit of a bash, have we?'

I said, 'Just a pint of shandy, offisher.'

He thought that was funny. He smiled anyway. He leaned down to my level and said, 'Might I have a word with you, Max – in private?'

I unfurled myself and stepped out. I leaned through the window and whispered to Rosie. Get the engine started. There's just enough room for you to zip past his car and get away.'

She looked as if she hadn't heard me. I turned to face Tomlin. He was still sporting his used car salesman smile. He said, 'Let's talk by my car.'

I followed him like the faithful little puppy dog I am. I didn't speak. I was too busy negotiating with the Almighty his terms for letting us out of there alive. They were pretty steep. We reached the BMW and I saw Tomlin's passenger. It was Martin Crowley, well known thug of this parish. He smiled with the warmth of the big bad wolf. The Almighty's terms shot up.

Tomlin looked upon my parchment face and trembling limbs and somehow guessed my unease. He found it amusing. He said, 'Don't look so frightened – we just want to talk to you.'

As long as he did the talking. My lips weren't up to it. I looked back over my shoulder and saw Rosie frozen in the Metro. Tomlin pulled a paw from his pocket and made an urbane gesture. He said, 'I apologise if all this seems a shade melodramatic. I'm afraid Miss Bannister drove off from her flat before we could talk to you.'

So they'd been watching Rosie's place. I said through locked teeth, 'How did you get her address?'

Tomlin thought that was hilarious too. He said, 'Elementary, my dear Watson. When someone attacked you in your flat your paper carried a couple of stories about you. In one you were pictured with your girlfriend. The paper named her as Rosie Bannister. Did you know, that's how she lists herself in the phone book. Rosie Bannister. Martin tried to contact you at Hampton's today. When you didn't show there, we tried your girlfriend's flat. Simple, really.'

I tugged this about. If they were set on doing me a mischief, Crowley wouldn't have shown his face in Hampton's. What were they up to then?

Tomlin kindly explained. His voice was still as sweet as Muscadet. He said, 'We believe you have been to Kandy and we believe you might be contemplating writing a story for your paper.'

I said the thought had occurred. Tomlin pretended I hadn't said that. He said, 'Naturally, we are very concerned. Our work in Kandy has been blameless and if you were to put a slur on it, you might cause irreparable harm to the WorldCare Foundation. And, by implication, you might harm the reputations of the individual trustees.'

He gave me a moment to swallow this drivel. He said, 'Of course, we would be obliged to issue writs for defamation. Your newspaper would be faced with massive damages. Your own reputation as a respected journalist would also suffer.'

I said, 'You're saying I've got it wrong?'

Tomlin took his time. He said, 'The facts are these. One trustee, and we believe you may already have interviewed him, is alone responsible for an abuse of the trust we placed in him. We have subsequently dealt with him. He is no longer connected to the Foundation. His offences took place in a foreign country where Britain is unable to prosecute a case against him. We assure you that had these incidents taken place within the United Kingdom, we would have reported the matter to the police.'

I glanced back towards Rosie who showed all the animation of a robot in a Volvo ad.

Tomlin was still enthralled by the sound of his own voice. He said, 'We acknowledge you have gone to considerable efforts in your pursuit of this false story. We are prepared to make substantial recompense, providing you agree not to publish the story.'

I said, 'How substantial?'

He said, 'One hundred thousand pounds.'

He said it just like that. No emphasis. No rolling eyeballs. I leaned against the Beemer and counted up the noughts. There were five of them.

Martin Crowley chipped in from across the bonnet, 'It's a lot of money for what was it your newspaper called it – a few smacks with a wheel brace.'

Tomlin jumped in hastily: 'Not that we were party to that. I give you my word we were not involved. The sum I have mentioned is for your time and your discretion.'

I said, 'Discretion is my middle name.'

Tomlin said, 'Please don't misunderstand us. This is not what one might call hush money. We are simply anxious that the work of the Foundation is not jeopardised by baseless allegations.'

I peered up and down our dead-end street. This was the street that time forgot. Not even a scavenging mongrel, far less a busload of bobbies. I said, 'What happens if I say no?'

Crowley laughed. Tomlin didn't. He said, 'As I mentioned, we would be forced to seek legal redress against you, your editor and your newspaper.'

I said, 'And that's it?'

Tomlin seemed perplexed. 'I don't quite gather—'

I said, 'If I say no, do I end up in St Katharine's Dock with a bullet through the frontal lobe?'

The very idea caused him intense distress. 'Good heavens, no. I take it you are referring to the murder of my stepmother. I swear I had nothing to do with that.'

Tomlin had nothing to do with an awful lot of

things. I acted as if I was thinking the deal over. Tabloid journalists have one hidden weakness. Everyone thinks we're capable of anything dastardly. True, we're capable of anything in getting a story. But we're hopelessly incapable of forgetting a story.

I said, 'When would I get the money?'

He smiled again. 'That depends on you. Might I suggest you provide us first of all with your notebooks and photographs, then perhaps—'

I didn't hear what came next because Rosie suddenly woke up and started hooting the horn. It brayed through the street's black canyon, bouncing off the walls. I saw Crowley detach himself from the BMW's left wing and start running towards her, I jumped in front of him and he knocked me flat on my backside. He was fast. The horn stopped blaring before I picked myself up. There followed a slap like a thunderclap. I screamed, 'Rosie!' and legged it towards her. I needn't have worried. Martin Crowley was standing well back from the Metro and rubbing his jaw.

'Leave her alone, you bastard!' I yelled in a brief blaze of bravery.

Crowley turned. He was not particularly tall, but he had the sort of build you see in Staffordshire bull terriers and Panzer tanks. He said, 'If the bitch hits me again I'll drop her.'

Fortunately Rosie stayed put in the driver's seat, otherwise I would have been forced to tear his head off. We stood there glaring at each other until Tomlin steamed up and rescued him. He said, 'Let's be calm, Martin. There's a deal on the table and I would like to know how Max feels about it.'

I said, 'Max likes it.'

He beamed. 'Good, good. Perhaps you can let us have the material tomorrow?'

I was getting braver by the second. I pointed at Crowley. 'Just as long as he isn't around. Chain him up somewhere.'

Crowley squared off his eyebrows at me. Tomlin said, 'It's cool. Martin needn't be there.'

I said, 'Where's there?'

He gave me an address in Primrose Hill. I scribbled it on the back of my chequebook, along with his phone number. My writing was a touch fraught. Tomlin said, 'Fine. Everything's settled. I look forward to seeing you then, say around eleven?'

I said, 'When do I get the hundred grand?'

Tomlin was soothing. 'Let's say we'll give you part tomorrow, as an act of good faith.'

'How much?' I demanded in my craven mercenary way.

'Let's say twenty-five per cent.'

'Let's say fifty per cent.'

He rippled a laugh. 'All right. You win. Perhaps you should have been a businessman instead of a journalist.'

And he should have been a human being. I hammed it up, whingeing on about when he would hand over the rest. He said when he was satisfied I'd kept to my side of the bargain. He stuck out his hand and, so help me, I shook it cordially. So everyone was happy. Apart from Rosie and Crowley. Tomlin ambled back to the BMW. Crowley hung around looking thoughtfully at the Metro for a moment.

'Nice little car,' he said. And he stepped back and gave it the most savage kick right in the headlamp.

Then he looked at Rosie and he said in exactly the same tone, 'Nice little girlfriend.'

We trembled in our socks. He sneered a last bleak smile and rejoined Tomlin. We watched wordlessly as they reversed out of our street and were gone. I said, 'Jesus!'

Rosie began to cry.

# Chapter Sixteen

She wanted me to go for the money. We were back in the flat and she'd dried her cheeks. Her eyes were still a bit snappy and she talked too fast, so I poured out a quadruple whisky and stuck it in her hand. She flopped herself over me on the sofa. It might have been an ordinary night except we don't ordinarily sit around talking about a stray one hundred thousand pounds. She said, 'That's twice what you make in a year. Grab it.'

She didn't really want the money. She just wanted me to let go of the story. That way we might be able to drive around London again without being shot, set alight, menaced or otherwise inconvenienced. I let her ramble on because she had to talk it out. I said yes and no at all the appropriate points but all the time I was thinking about what I did next. I was on what we weavers of words call the horns of a sodding huge dilemma. If I went to the Law and told them the score, they'd haul in Tomlin and Crowley, charge them with general nastiness, and lock them up. This had the advantage of stopping them from killing Rosie or me. It had the disadvantage of spiking my exclusive. Once the two loons were on a charge I couldn't write an unkind word about them. I was rather fond of my story. And what a great story it was turning out to be – Honest Crime Hack Offered Massive Bung To Stay Schtum About Child Sex Ring. Even the lawyer couldn't kill that. So I ruled out calling Plod.

I examined the other horn of the dilemma. It indicated that Rosie and I would end up with tags on our toes unless I surrendered the notes and negatives to Tomlin. Which again meant spiking my story. So that was out too.

I cast around for an alternative. I came up with it about three in the morning, with Rosie snoring in my ear. I put her to bed, set the alarm for seven, brushed my teeth and said my prayers.

Anyone who is not in the hack trade has already hit on a simple alternative: take the money and live. But I wouldn't be a hack if I did that. If this sounds very high-falutin' and sick making, I'm sorry. But it's true. Hacks willingly risk their lives just for the sake of a story. Sometimes they lose. Dozens of journos have been killed in what we used to call Yugoslavia. And why? For the sake of the story and the by-line, that's why. The victims weren't on danger money or a special bonus. Some newspapers were so mean they wouldn't even buy flak jackets for their boys. And when a hack gets home he is greeted by the likes of Belker, bollocking him for his expenses. Yet wander into any newspaper office and ask the assembled drunks would they like to go to Beirut/Sarajevo/Rwanda. You'd get trampled to death in the rush. It has nothing to do with courage. I suppose in the end it's all down to vanity. Reporters lucky enough to run for their lives through Sarajevo's Sniper's Alley are the envy of their mates. Yet what do they have to show for it? – a couple of picture by-lines and a story or two. That's the prize. And what a glorious prize it is.

The alarm buzzed like a bee with a stammer, waking me from a dream in which I was patiently explaining to Big Ben Ashbee how I knew that Martin Crowley was the git who incinerated all my worldly goods.

I shot up like a Saturn Five. I did know that. I knew for absolute stone cold certain that Crowley was the mad matchman. But how did I know? I sat there lacing together the torn shreds of my dream. And then it came to me. In our dead-end street meet, he'd said the hundred grand was not bad money for 'a few smacks with a wheel brace'.

Okay, so he might have read my story about the fire. But I remember I'd made a mistake when I was dictating copy that night from the hospital. I'd said the attacker bashed me with a car jack. Only the Law, my shins, and the man in black knew it was a wheel brace.

Something inside me said, 'Okay, so now you know Crowley is the villain, you must ring the Old Bill forthwith.' But I ignored it, recognising it as just a piece of brainwashing by Rosie.

I arose, brewed myself a coffee that would kill a horse and set to work. I found a virgin notebook, dug out the Sri Lankan original and began copying it. I scrawled off a few righthand pages in blue Biro, then a single one in red, a couple in black, back to blue, and so on. I altered the slope of the characters so that some looked scribbled, others leisurely. I jotted down fictitious phone numbers and names on facing pages. Hotel Demerara 216–333. Kandy Hire Cars 217–001. That sort of thing. I didn't write anything about the boy victims, Lal and Ajit. When I'd finished the notebook looked almost convincing. I sploshed coffee into a saucer and dipped the back cover in it. I got a bottle of Bud from the fridge and sprinkled it on the occasional page. Then a dash of whisky mixed with cigarette ash. I found a couple of 50 rupee notes and gummed them in towards the back with a mix of sugary coffee. Now it looked so much like the original notebook I had difficulty telling them apart. My strategy to keep Rosie and me and the story alive was progressing apace.

Next I phoned the Editor. It was nine thirty-three on a hazy Sunday morning. I know that because he asked me what time it was. He did not like being disturbed. He wanted to know why a menial such as I dared rouse him from his scratcher. I said I urgently needed his help. He didn't seem to want to help. I changed the angle. I said, 'Michael Tomlin and Martin Crowley have offered me one hundred thousand pounds if I don't let you see my story. Or they'll kill me for free.'

That shook him. He likes to think he's the only one around here with the right to kill me.

I added, 'If you run the story, they'll also kill my girlfriend.' All right, maybe I was pushing it a bit, but I had to keep him on the hook.

He said, 'Have you rung the police?'

I said no, and I explained why not – that my story

would collapse as soon as Tomlin was charged. The Editor was impressed. He said, 'We'll kill the story.'

I said another no. I'd like the story to run, the bigger the better. What gives Tomlin the right to censor our paper? 'You're the Editor.'

That one got all the way home. The Editor said, 'Right. Let's have every word of it – the threats, the child sex, the murders. We'll splash it and throw out the centre spread. Forget the lawyer. We'll take our chances. No one tells me what I can or cannot put in my paper.'

At the nice end of the phone I hopped around like a gleeful chimpanzee. Something occurred belatedly to the Editor. He said, 'Of course, my first concern is for you, and indeed, your girlfriend. We'd better move you somewhere Tomlin wouldn't suspect. Just for tonight anyway. You're sure he'll be arrested in the morning?'

As sure as bones. He'll be clapped in irons five minutes after my story breaks, I promised. And the police will play football with any bail application.

The Editor thought Rosie and I should go to ground in a quiet hotel outside London. I said what a clever idea, but where could we go? The Editor had the very place in mind: Standingbrooke Hall Hotel, a leafy mile or so from Tring, Herts. Very expensive, very exclusive, very discreet. He knows this because every six months the office hires out the entire west wing of Standingbrooke and invites the execs to what are laughingly called Think Tanks. Anyways, he ordered me to book ourselves a modest suite there and hide from the forces of darkness. This gleeful chimpanzee was half way up the wall by now.

The Editor told me to get there pronto. I said I had one more teensy weensy bit to do. I wanted to see Tomlin and reassure him I was still in his pocket. That might get me a few more good quotes. The Editor was awed by my quiet heroism in visiting the lair of the evil monster. Actually I was too. He didn't offer me half of his kingdom and his daughter's hand in marriage, which is just as well, for she's got a bum the size of Russia. But he did say: 'Good man', and, it was a great story. Congratulations. I blushed and said it was all thanks to his editorial leadership and he went away believing that.

So phase two of the master plan was up and away. On now to thc tricky part. I shaved, showered and encased myself in the best suit on the premises. The green and yellow striped tie was not quite up to the occasion. I inspected myself in the mirror. I looked more serious than usual. Sober was the word. It was all wrong. I wanted to look greedy and gullible. But big brother didn't have anything filed in that section. I settled for a green polo shirt, blue sports jacket, grey trousers and brown Oxfords. By God, it was hideous, even for a Sunday. I wanted to fit myself up with the tape and hidden mike, but I suspected Tomlin might be on the lookout for tricks. I packed a spare notebook out of habit and blew a cheerio kiss to a sleeping Rosie. I went out, letting the door close with the softest of clicks.

London's entire black cab population was off somewhere eating bacon sarnies and I ended up having to call a minicab on the mobile. By one of those weird coincidences which Life puts into our humdrum day, the driver turned out to be Sri Lankan. He told me where I should have gone for cheap silk shirts, jewellery, glasses. I wrote it all down – it gave me authentic detail if I ever got round to writing that travel feature.

We purred up outside Mike Tomlin's gaff, a three-storey Georgian model with a garden the size of a beer mat. As I rattled the knocker, a solitary shaft of sunlight pierced the haze and landed on my head. A happy omen, I decided.

The door flew open as if he'd been waiting behind it. 'You came,' he declared with that ready perception that demonstrates the value of a good public school education.

'I came,' I agreed.

Tomlin ushered me indoors. He was togged out in a faded rugby shirt, worn jeans and scuffed trainers. He looked a lot better dressed than me.

I went straight for it. 'I haven't got the negatives yet. My snapper is up in Blackpool on the Sunday school sex lessons story.'

His face went down.

I said, 'But I have my notebooks. And the photographer should be back by Tuesday, so I'll get the pix then.'

His face went up again. He said, 'Just a moment.'

He walked off, leaving me to admire the red flock wallpaper of the hallway. It looked like he'd nicked it from a Chinese takeaway. He returned with Crowley snapping at his heels.

I feigned dismay. It was easy. I said, 'You promised me he wouldn't be here.'

Tomlin gave a smile that meant anything you wanted it to mean. He said, 'Just a precaution, Max. He'll be gone in a moment.'

Crowley stepped forth and produced a bug detector. He ran it up and down my outraged limbs. Nothing blooped or bleeped. But he was a cautious man, our Martin. Next he frisked me in a most intimate manner. He found my cigarettes. I had to show him they were ordinary Bensons. I even offered him one. He examined my lighter, my pens, my notebook. I half expected him to produce a sniffer dog out of his hip pocket. But that was it. He stepped back, nodded okay to Tomlin, and muscled off to the back of the house.

Tomlin led me into the lounge, another fine example of Chow Mein neo-Gothic, and invited me to make myself at home. I opted for centre seat on a sofa sprawled along the door wall. He played the genial host, offering me first a sherry and then a decent drink.

I swigged hard and said, 'You got the money?'

'First the notebook.'

I handed it over. Tomlin found himself a seat by the window and started reading. Half the stuff was in shorthand so he needed me to decipher it. I explained the basic symbols of Mr Pitman's shorthand system and after a while Tomlin was making inspired guesses at whole words. I told him he was very clever and he thought so too.

I said, 'There's nothing much in the pix – just a

few shots of the orphanage sign, a head and shoulders of Samarsinghe. Things like that. The real stuff is there, in the notes. But I'll have to give the photographer half the money to keep him quiet.'

Tomlin tapped the notebook against even white teeth, smelt the stench of assorted beverages, and thought better of it. He didn't make any move towards a safe or even a wallet. I said, 'You promised me half today.'

Tomlin laughed. Not a proper laugh. More the plastic sympathy chuckle of an insurance salesman telling you that you should have read the small print first. He said, 'You'll recall our deal was for the notes and the photographs. I have only the notes, or what you claim are the notes.'

I dripped out a craven smile. 'Yes, but you can see that's everything I've got. I'm honouring the deal. You should stick to your side of it.'

He didn't think so. He reckoned pay day came when the whole package was handed over. I got stroppy and said, okay, give me back my notes until I can deliver the pix too. Tomlin said quietly, 'I don't think Martin would agree to that, do you?'

I let my face play about at being narked, shocked, wounded, insulted. It enjoyed itself. I said, 'You mean I don't see a penny until you have the snaps?'

Tomlin said that was about the size of it. This would never do. I'd come here for money and I wasn't going away until I had filled my fevered little fist with fivers. I had a sulk.

He said, 'Don't worry, Max. You'll get the money. You say your photographer will be back by Tuesday?'

'At the latest.'

He said, 'Well then, you just have to wait until Tuesday and you'll get the money.'

I said, 'I won't.' It was a flat statement, without an ounce of defiance.

His eyebrows did a few press ups. 'You won't?'

I fiddled with my loose change. 'I mean I can't.'

'Why not?' Ah, this was more like the Michael Tomlin we have come to know and hate. A whisper of menace there.

'I mean I can't.' I elaborated, looking deadpan. 'Frankie – that's my monkey – won't hand over his smudges unless I bring something to the party.'

'What?'

I translated. Tomlin caught the gist. He said, 'You're saying you'll have to show him some money first?'

I nodded, speechless with admiration at his raging intellect. Now it was his turn to act furtive and mercenary. He said, 'How much will it take to convince him?'

I waved an extravagant arm. 'Ten thousand, anyway. We each spent about five grand on the trip – the office wasn't paying.'

Tomlin found his mock chuckle. 'I am not paying serious money until I have everything in my hands. However, I appreciate your situation. Let's say a goodwill payment of one hundred pounds each might help.'

Yelps of horror from the settee. He pushed it up a couple of notches. An encore of outrage. I was getting good at this. Tomlin got up, wandered around and looked at himself in the mirror above a black marble fireplace. I whinged away amid the cushions. At last he reached a decision. I could tell that because of the masterful way he breathed out his nose. He said, 'I'm still not satisfied that you are telling the truth. I am not satisfied that these are your notes in their entirety. I still need to be convinced. However, I am prepared to pay you one thousand pounds as a gesture in good faith. That's all.'

I licked my lips and said, oh all right then, give me the money. He reached for his pocket and fished out a wad of £50 notes. He counted them. They added up to £1,000. Exactly. So that's what he estimated paying out all along. But he'd made a big enough song and dance about it. He hesitated before stuffing them in my outstretched fingers. He said, 'I trust you will honour your end.'

He didn't say otherwise I'll knock your block off, but my telepathic powers picked up the message. He handed over the notes. I counted them again. Twice. I whined, 'I just hope this is enough to convince my photographer.'

Tomlin suddenly remembered he had a pressing engagement, so would I kindly hop it. He didn't shake my hand on the way out and I thought that was nice of him.

I called the Barbican from the mini cab and ordered up Blue Mountain coffee, eggs benedict, freshly squeezed papaya juice and a bowl of Rice Crispies. Rosie said she'd lost the map to the kitchen, and anyway, what was I doing, and, and, and. She was still pelting questions down the phone when I opened the door and said hello. I made the coffee because I had a mystery guest on the way. He turned out to be Dec somebody or other, a freelance monkey. In the meantime, I turfed Rosie's things off the bedside table and, wearing a pair of blue kitchen gloves so as not to mess up Tomlin's fingerprints, replaced them with his £1,000. It looked a pretty show. Dec confined himself to saying, 'Cor!' because he thought there was a lady present. He banged off a few flash shots inside, then on the balcony, where I was obliged to look grimly into camera whilst holding five hundred smackers in each blue-gloved hand. The notes didn't look much, but at least they were real, with Tomlin's whorls all over them. What lawyers call evidence.

Dec clattered off and I got down to rewriting my original copy. It would have been a lot easier if the Editor hadn't kept ringing me up to ask daft questions. Here is one of his more inspired: What, he asked, do the deviants eat when they're in Sri Lanka? I said curry. He said aaah, as if a great light had shone upon him. I tapped the story up on the laptop. Marcel Proust might have made a better job of it, but there you go. I hammered out the first few pars:

> Pin-striped perverts yesterday offered me a £100,000 bribe to hush up a squalid child sex ring.
>
> They vowed to murder me – and my girlfriend – if I refused their sleazy slush money.
>
> But today I name the top tycoons who use children as young as six in their barbaric orgies.

And I can reveal that:

* Provocative millionairess Claudine Tournier was ruthlessly gunned down when she stumbled on their secret.

* Wrinkly rocker Leon Knapp preys on helpless orphans for kinky sex.

* A squeaky clean politician is among the sinister group of paedophiles who style themselves The Young Boys Network.

I wasn't bothered about libels. The night lawyer could weed them out. He gets paid a lot more than me and I didn't want to deprive him of job satisfaction.

After I'd knocked it out – 2,500 words top whack – and sent the copy through the modem there was a long, long silence from the office. This often happens but you still get nervous about it. You picture teams of trouser-wetting lawyers tearing the stuff to pieces. What's really happening is they're sticking 'alleged' between all the interesting bits. Yes, theirs is a dirty job.

While I waited and fretted, Rosie did the sensible thing and packed us a pair of overnight bags. For once I had more clothes than her. She was skipping about the flat singing something from Beethoven or Tchaikovsky. It worried me. Only last night, awash with tears, she had begged me to drop the story and hide under the bed. Why this new-found chipperness? I wrapped her fondly around the waist and she said not until we get to the hideaway hotel. I explained that I just wanted to know what prompted her sunshine. After all, hadn't I ignored her heartfelt cry and written a story that endangered her life?

She said, and she smiled a loving smile when she said it. 'Oh, I always knew you'd write the story anyway. I was only telling you how I felt.'

Wasn't that nice? I swung her towards me to say something soppy and the phone rang just in time. The Editor with a verbal herogram. Great, terrific, super. Makes you sit up. Sells papers. Now, flee to the hidey hole, Chard, and get cracking on a follow-up. Oh, and love to Ruby.

I told Ruby who didn't like being thus called.

We grabbed our bags and the dented Metro and jogged up the A1 towards where they've stuck Tring. Every now and then I looked over my shoulder to check we were not towing a silver BMW. But we were as lacking in tails as a Manx cat. We were trickling along a country byway when Standingbrooke House Hotel jumped out of the hedges at us. It's a big, creamy white chunk of a place, half hidden by porticoes, battlements and assorted extravagances. Our rumpled Metro looked as if it belonged at the tradesmen's entrance, but the retainers who rushed to open the doors didn't say a word about it. Nor did the receptionist blink her violet lashes when I announced, 'I'm Oki Mboya of the Anglo-Nigerian Oil Corporation. You have my reservation.'

She tossed a welcome smile at Rosie. 'And you must be Mister Ndoke Emogu.'

Rosie affirmed that she was. I always use the Mboya alias when I'm hiding out in a hotel. That way if the opposition runs a check on the guest list they never think O. Mboya might be their old chum Max. They're looking for Smith or Brown or Jones.

We were ushered to a suite twice the size of Dominic's flat. A silver-haired porter with the demeanour of Our Man in Washington suggested we might like a drink to recover from our travels and we heard the clank of the Dom Perignon bucket before Rosie kicked a shoe off. We parked ourselves on the balcony and admired the back garden.

'We should do this more often,' said Rosie, appraising the scenery through a champagne flute.

At three hundred quid a night that wasn't the smartest idea she ever had, but I said yes, and ordered up another bottle. I felt it was the done thing. The hours glided past but not so as you'd notice. We tried out the circular bath tub, playing footsie under five fathoms, to the clink of crystal. I could see why the Editor held his Think Tanks here. It gave you all sorts of ideas.

Coming up dinner time I gave Ben Ashbee a ring. He was at home, staking up his beans, he said, which I thought was a euphemism for all sorts of high jinks. But he didn't appear to mind being disturbed.

I made sure he hadn't done anything silly, like feel Michael Tomlin's collar before my story appeared. He said no, but come the dawn, he'd have Tomlin as planned. I said, 'While you're at it, you'd better pinch Martin Crowley too.'

Ben prefers to make his own decisions. He grouched, 'And why should I do that?'

I told him of the hundred grand and the threat to

Rosie and me, laying it on with a shovel. Ben whistled, nearly breaking my eardrum. He was all set for lifting the pair of them right there and then. I had to remind him of his promise to hold back. I also swore I'd be a nice tame little prosecution witness for him. That reminded him. Last night they'd binged on Lonesome Leon's bell. He talked them half to death without the stimulus of rubber truncheons. They had a signed statement in the bag – enough to justify a search warrant at half a dozen homes. Add my complaint about the death threats – I'd gone a bit over the top there – and the Old Bill had just cause to make a nuisance of itself.

So much for the good news. The bad news was that Leon hadn't the faintest idea who popped Claudine and Shirley. I said never mind, the search warrant might turn up something. But Ben went back to his beans in melancholy.

In Suite 20, Rosie was making merry with the complimentary perfumes and powders. They even had stuff to spray on your armpits, though it was hard to imagine the usual denizens of Suite 20 having body odours. Maybe that was just for our Think Tank weekends.

A distant dinner gong rang in our tummies and we descended to dine. We were hardly dressed for the occasion. At least I wasn't. Rosie elected to wear a red silk shirt as an outrageously short frock which took the other guests' eyes off the Jocasta Innes green and silver decor. The maitre d' said 'Good evening' to Rosie's legs and propped her in a chair where he could keep a good eye on them. I don't think he noticed me.

The room was full of big beefy pillars so that each table found itself in an alcove, like a candlelit clearing in the forest. Behind each pillar there lurked wandering bands of waiters. One staggered up with a menu the size of Encyclopedia Britannica: another came burdened down with the burgundy-jacketed wine list. Everything cost a bomb. You knew that because they'd left the prices out.

It was probably sometime around when I was dithering whether to guzzle the Sancerre or the Meursault that Leon Knapp prised open his front door and stepped into the night. He didn't bother closing the door behind him. He walked down the portico and round the corner to the aircraft hangar which served as his garage. He used the gizmo on his key ring to raise the door. He went inside and turned on the light. This time he shut the door.

A waiter hove to off my left shoulder, brandishing what purported to be Celeriac Remoulade and I took his word for it. Rosie was already in possession of a pink soup. We hoisted our glasses and offered each other elaborate toasts.

And while we laughed, Leon was sitting in his sky blue Porsche with both courtesy lights on and a notepad on his lap. He began to write.

The Standingbrooke House chefs do not believe in stuffing their guests to the gills. Two forkfuls, and the celeriac was but a pleasant memory. A fresh covey of waiters whipped away the plates, and the wine wizard made another guest appearance. A Chateau de Malle arrived suffering from hypothermia. On came my crevettes. Rosie laid waste to a baby brill in black butter.

Leon kept writing. He had a lot to say and not much time to say it.

We cold-shouldered the game course and pushed on to the entrée. Roast lamb in the manner of Shrewsbury for me, fillet of beef teriyaki for her. She'd forgotten she was a vegetarian. A bottle of Aloxe-Corton helped ease the pain.

Leon finished his letter. He put it in an envelope, sealed it and propped it on the dashboard. He turned on the ignition. He was crying.

We breezed onwards through the desserts and cheese and vintage port, our conversation becoming jollier by the moment. The waiters suspected we were newly-wed. By God, how they hated me. We whistled up the coffee and Rosie stuck her nose in a goldfish bowl of brandy. I settled on a noble scotch. Our innocent glee bounced off the pillars and sang in our ears.

In the garage Leon stopped coughing. His head slumped forward on the steering wheel. That's the way they would find him, crumpled up with his wig uncombed.

Rosie and I made it back to Suite 20, pursued by a wagonload of tinkling bottles. She fiddled with the stereo while I gave Night Desk a call. Vic took it. He sounded as if he was having a rotten night. I told him about our evening, just to make things worse. Green venomous envy seeped down the phone. I made him tell me all about our first edition. I had the splash and a double-column WOB by-line. A WOB is when they print your name in white on black to make it look important. He read out the first half dozen pars. It was more or less as written. I had the centre spread too, with pic bylines for both Frankie and me, Vic said. Now would I piss off and leave him to news edit. I said I was so moved by his sweet nature that I would bring him a souvenir shower cap so his baldy head wouldn't get wet if he ever thought of having a shower. He banged the phone down.

Rosie poured me a bumper whisky and joined me on the chair. Dire Straits hummed out of the stereo. I had a great story in the paper, a lovely woman in my arms, music in my ears and the scent of Speyside in my nostrils. What more could a man want? Rosie thought of something.

# Chapter Seventeen

A dawn as light as a kitten's purr was tickling the trees on Primrose Hill when they rat-tat-tat-tatted on Michael Tomlin's door. He was a heavy sleeper. They tattooed again with greater gusto. A window shot up. 'Whaddyawant?' he yelled.

They told him who they were, just in case he hadn't noticed the flashing lights and the funny uniforms. He asked them if they knew what time it was. They did. It was five-thirty. He grumbled awhile but he let them in. When he saw the search warrant he screamed blue murder. They gave him five minutes to dress, under the watchful eye of a D.C. with a nasty suspicious mind. Then they squeezed him in the back of the car between two Plods and off they drove.

I learned of all this several hours later while Rosie and I breakfasted in bed without our clothes on. I'd phoned Ben Ashbee to check that Tomlin was definitely in the nick. Oh yes, he said, but did I want the bad news or the bad news? I said I'd have the bad news first.

Ben said, 'Leon Knapp topped himself last night.'

I said, 'That's bad news?'

It was rotten news, said Ben. Leon was to be his

star witness if they found any child porn stashed in Tomlin's drum. Now their only hope was that his statement would be treated like a deathbed confession and admitted as evidence.

I said, 'Is it definitely an own goal? Tomlin didn't lace his cocaine with rat poison or anything?'

Ben said, 'No. Straightforward suicide. Shut himself in the garage and turned on the motor.'

I said, 'Any famous last words?'

Ben said, 'About twenty pages of them. You'll be pleased to hear he blamed press harassment and mentions you. He didn't say anything about the two murders.'

I said, 'What's the other bad news?'

They'd lost Crowley. He'd got away, largely thanks to them kicking in the door of the flat beneath his and scaring the drawers off a respectable old lady of Italian extraction. 'Who-a are-a you-a?' she cried, to which one of their number replied, 'Old Bill.' She said, 'Old-a Bill-a live-a uppa-da-stair-a.' By the time they'd sorted it all out, Crowley had taken to his toes.

I said, 'Ben, this is terrible news,' realising that Rosie and I would have to spend another night incarcerated in Standingbrooke Hall.

He promised to send a sympathetic plain clothes bloke to take our statement about the death threats. I told him to wait until I'd had my sauna and Rosie her facial. He said it should be the other way around.

I called the Editor. He still loved me. I said the police had warned me Crowley was on the loose and hunting for me. The Editor said oh dear, stay there until they catch him. I said whatever he thought best.

He reported that everyone was raving about my story. I don't think he'd canvassed Crowley's opinion. But I made all the right noises and praised him again for his campaigning leadership.

Rosie skipped off in the afternoon and looted a boutique or two while I cobbled together a follow up to the tune of:

*Shamed rock star Leon Knapp killed himself yesterday, hours after he was branded a pervert.*

*His body was found in the fume-filled garage of his £1m Berkshire mansion.*

*His dead hand was still clutching a pathetic note telling how he chose to die rather than face the scandal over his life as a child molester.*

*Seventies teenybopper favourite Knapp was exposed by us as a ruthless paedophile who preyed on helpless orphans.*

*He was a leading member of a sinister group of deviants, calling themselves the Young Boys Network.*

*In a dawn swoop yesterday detectives investigating the sex ring arrested Knapp's pal, City whizz kid Mike Tomlin.*

*And they are seeking round-the-world yachtsman Martin Crowley. All three are trustees of the WorldCare Foundation, which Knapp admitted was used as a cover for child sex orgies.*

*Both Tomlin and Crowley had offered me a £100,000 bribe to stop me exposing the scandal.*

*Last month Foundation boss Claudine Tournier – Tomlin's stepmother – was mysteriously slain.*

*Bachelor Tomlin was arrested at his palatial London townhouse . . .*

And so forth. I knew the Law wouldn't charge Tomlin until Tuesday morning so I could still get away with having a pop at him. I let the copy run to about 30 pars, leaving it up to the agencies and showbiz to fill in the backgrounder on Knapp. I looked at my watch. It was high time for high tea.

I had a lot of faith in our bobbies. I was banking on them failing to catch Crowley for at least six months, during which Rosie and I could continue to whoop it up at Standingbrooke Hall.

Therefore it came as a nasty surprise when on Thursday morning Big Ben rang to say they'd found him. This was not exactly true. He found them. And they'd tried to lose him again. Armed with his brief, Crowley had turned himself in at Whetstone nick, where the desk woodentop assured him nobody wanted him. In the end he had to go out to a phone box and ring Ben Ashbee who in turn called the nick and told them that if Crowley reappeared they'd better hold on to him. He did and they did.

But Ben had even bigger news to impart. In the process of turning over Mike Tomlin's gaff they came across a navy blazer with strands of stuff on the lapels. The forensic boys wheeled out their magnifying glass and discovered (a) fragments of the rope of the type used to throttle Shirley Ham, and (b) several dirty fair hairs of the type worn by Shirley Ham. They'd got him.

So far he hadn't coughed to murdering either her or his stepmother, but they expected him to stick his hands up any day now. They left Lewis Trefoyle alone because that's what you do with government ministers. Besides, they knew we were out to get him, and we are a thousand times worse than anything the Old Bailey can sling at you.

They charged Tomlin with Shirley's murder after Crowley grassed on him. They grabbed Gus Clernthorpe and he promptly fingered Crowley as the man with the matchbox. But they didn't charge him with that yet. They just hit them all for criminal conspiracy. They pulled in Proudhoe Veizey who cast himself in the role of supergrass. He came up with a motive for Claudine's killing. Two motives in fact. Yes, she had rumbled the orphanage racket and was threatening to blow it, along with every deviant on the Foundation's board. Veizey also revealed that Claudine was a girl with a libido which needed taking out for exercise every now and then. She was particularly partial to married men. And the hubbies, it seemed, were happy to oblige. Sir James Tomlin was well aware of his wife's horizontal hobbies, but he didn't care; he was twice as bad. So the betting was still that Claudine was murdered, probably by her loving stepson, to hush her up.

The office took me off the story because it was all wrapped up and anyway, as a prosecution witness in the threats case, the Law warned me to stay out of it. I was bored. Rosie had gone home to mum for a week's counselling. I returned to the Barbican, a squalid slum after Suite 20, and tuned in to *Neighbours* again. But it was no good. I'd lost the thread.

There were occasional moments to enliven the

dull days. The Sri Lankan press attaché invited me out for a lively lunch and told me what a great man I was. Out in Kandy they'd grabbed Samarsinghe, his mate Niaz, and a handful of other undesirables. They moved the boys to a pukka orphanage and were teaching them how to smile. And all because of my story.

It sent many a ripple around Fleet Street. The *Sunday Times* dep. ed. took me out for drinkies and dangled a job before me, but I said no, I preferred working for a newspaper. End of drink.

# Chapter Eighteen

I began spending too much time and money stopping Hampton's from going broke. They were rowdy nights to be sure but I suppose I was still on a come down from the big story. I remembered Wellington's quote after duffing up Napoleon at Waterloo: Nothing is half so desolate as a battle lost, except a battle won. Something like that. Well that's the way I felt.

The Law eventually got around to charging Martin Crowley with attempting to set me alight. I got my picture in the paper again, but no by-line.

That night my bleep went when I was in the middle of telling a joke to Hampton's regulars. I rang Vic. He said Ross Gavney had phoned to pass on congrats and ask if we might meet sometime.

I thought about it for at least half a bottle. Even then I wasn't sure how I felt. The way I remembered it, my mate Ross had failed me in my hour of need. He had known something about the people who were out to get me, yet he'd refused to tell. Not the behaviour of your average tried and trusted ally. In just ten minutes he had shredded a friendship built on years. He knew he was doing it, but he still said tough luck, Max, you're on your own. And I'd said piss off and I never did like your rotten whisky anyway. So whatever way you looked at it, the old friends act was out the window. Why then should Ross start acting chummy again, knowing damn well he had broken Clause One, Para One of the Mates Charter? I didn't have an answer to that. And why now?

In the end I rang Magpie Court. I suppose it was more out of curiosity than anything. Ross picked it up on the third briiinnng. I said, 'Hello Ross.'

'Max!'

I took it he was glad I called. He said, 'I've phoned your office several times, but you're never in.'

I said, 'I'm always out.'

He laughed. I didn't.

There was a gap. He said, 'I've read your stuff on Tomlin – it's a fantastic story.'

I said, 'No, it's not fantastic. It's real. There's a difference.'

He started off trying to laugh but changed his mind. He said, 'We have unfinished business. At least I have. I owe you an explanation.'

I said, 'If you feel bad about something, you'd better work it out yourself. It's your problem.'

He said, 'I said I owe you an explanation, not an apology. There's a difference.'

I didn't feel like picking that one up. Ross said, 'It's your call, Max. We can get together and talk or we can hang up.'

I said, 'You mean you'll talk now they've locked Tomlin up? And Crowley? That's big of you.'

Ross said evenly, 'Yes, I'll talk, now they've got them.'

I laughed. I couldn't help myself. I said, 'Christ, Ross, you've got some weird ideas about friendship.'

He said, 'Do I take it that means we get together or we hang up?'

Hanging up seemed a good idea but my curiosity argued against it. He didn't regret keeping me in the dark. The way he saw it, he'd done it for a reason. A good reason. And he still felt that he was right. So what was the reason?

In the end I said okay. That I'd meet him.

Ross asked, 'Where? Here?'

I'd already made my mind up. I said, 'The Port O' Call.'

He said, 'Where's that?'

I said, 'It's the place where you first didn't tell me what you knew.'

The laugh didn't even have a smile on its face. He said, 'You have an over-developed sense of irony.'

I said, 'I know. I'll get rust one of these days.'

The taxi dropped me outside the Tower Hotel and I trickled around to St Katharine's Dock. I was in no particular hurry. There were spots of rain in the wind and a wall of smoky cloud was pushing across the river from Southwark. People walking by had their collars up and heads down. When I got to the dockside I had a look at the water, from force of habit. All you could see were boats and buoys.

It was a Wednesday evening and the Port O' Call was three-quarters empty. Ross had a table in the far corner where he could see the door. On the table was a bottle of red with a full glass for him and an empty one waiting for me. There was not much left in the bottle.

I sat down and lit myself a cigarette.

He said, 'Drink?'

I nodded. He poured it half way up, the way they do in restaurants. I sipped and smoked. I had nothing useful to say so I left it to him. He made a big play of lighting his cigar and checking the smoke was coming from the right end before he spoke. Ross said, 'First of all, Max, that was an ace job you did on the Claudine Tournier story, though I'm sure your fellow journalists have already told you so.'

I said, 'They have. But don't let it bother you.'

He turned on a chuckle. He said, 'I see. You want to give me a bad time.'

I had another sip. The wine tasted of cigarette. Ross said, 'What I did – what I did in not telling you the little I knew – I did out of honour.'

That deserved a crooked smile. I said, 'I always knew you were an honourable man. Brutus was an honourable man.'

He shrugged. 'Okay. Let's be dramatic about it. What do you know about honour? No, not honour – loyalty?'

My eyes said I knew a whole heap more than him. He put his glass down so that it made a loud clack. I leaned back and fluted smoke at a fibreglass anchor. I wondered what Rosie was doing tonight, and what was she wearing, how were her eyes.

Ross said, 'I'll talk about loyalty then. You have a loyalty to your paper, a loyalty to Rosie, a loyalty to your family, your friends. But most of all you have a loyalty to your paper.'

Close enough. I didn't interrupt.

He said, 'You fix your own priorities on loyalty. Everybody has to. You demanded total loyalty from me – not for yourself, but for your bloody newspaper. Jesus Christ, Max, you're more loyal to the paper than you are to yourself. You don't even see that. And I can't understand it.'

I said, 'Let me make it easy for you. I'm faithful to my story. I don't give a toss which paper carries it.'

He sorted this out while I flagged for another bottle. I filled my glass. He could look after himself.

'Okay,' he said, 'this isn't getting through. Let's go back to the night you reckoned I was keeping something from you. I admit it. I was.'

I drawled, 'Well, ain't that a surprise, folks?'

He ignored it. 'You wanted to know about Claudine Tournier. Let me tell you about her. She was a vicious, destructive, cold-hearted bitch, and she should have been drowned at birth.'

I said, 'Doesn't mean she was a bad person.'

He said, 'If you had known her you would have felt the same. Her marriage to Jim Tomlin was a sham, just to give her the social cachet and access to the money tree. His connections, his money got Claudine's Cuisine up and running. She needed him. She also knew a damn sight more about his stooges on the Foundation than you guessed. Remember, some of them funded her at the start.'

I said, 'So why would she expose them?'

Ross ground out a laugh. 'She would never have

done that. She just wanted to ruin Mike Tomlin. She tried to seduce him, you know. She didn't know he was a paedophile.'

I said, 'I want to get this right. Wicked stepmother is told to eff off by perverted stepson whereupon she vows to expose his sordid sex life whereupon he shoots her brains out?'

His mouth was still down at the corners but he managed a sort of smile. 'That's it.'

I watched Ross pour himself a glass. His hand didn't shake. His gaze didn't waver.

I said, 'So why are you still lying?'

He looked up with wide candid eyes. 'Lying?'

'Telling porkies. Being economical with the truth. That sort of lying.'

His face said he didn't understand. He said, 'I swear to you, it's all true.'

I said, 'No, Ross. It may be true, but it isn't all.'

He pushed his glass round and round and round on the table. Then he did it again anti-clockwise. I watched him through the smoke. He was arguing with himself. I don't know which side won.

He said, 'We're back at the beginning. We're talking about loyalties again.'

I said, 'I'm too tired for the game. If you want to tell me the full bit, go ahead. If you don't, then don't bother lying about it. We could both be somewhere else and liking it.'

He started doodling with the glass again. I looked around. The barmaid snapped a bright overbite at me. Yes, I could easily be somewhere else.

Ross opened up with a question. 'What would you

do to get a story? No, I don't mean that. I mean what would you *not* do?'

He thought he had the answer so I let him tell me. He said, 'I think there's nothing you wouldn't do, Max. I think if Rosie came in here now and said she'd been gang-banged by Cliff Richard and the Archbishop of Canterbury, you'd be on the phone to the paper before you even dried her tears.'

I smiled thinly. 'It's a great story,' I said.

He said, 'Yes, it is a great story. You'd get your name all over it. That's what I was trying to talk about. Your loyalty to the paper gets in the way of everything else. The story is all that counts.'

I said, 'And that's why you still won't tell me how you knew Claudine.'

'What?' He was wary.

I said it again slowly. He'd heard me all right the first time. He was just sorting out how to answer. He looked around first, as if to check for eavesdroppers. Then he leaned forward and his voice was as soft as prayer. He said, 'I met Claudine Tournier just before Christmas.'

He stopped and took a sip. Then he had a breath. He said, 'It was a charity do at the Mansion House and she was with a friend of mine, David. Lots of guests had celebrity partners because it was that sort of affair, but I was surprised to see David with Claudine Tournier. He has a real honey of a wife who usually goes everywhere with him.

'At one point in the evening I asked David about Babs. That's his wife. He winked at me. That's when I knew he was up to something with Tournier. I thought he was crazy. Though Claudine was a very sexy piece of business. I've got to say that.'

My glass was empty but I did not refill it. I was as still as last night's beer.

Ross said, 'I guessed right away that she was trouble. There was something hard about her, despite all the pouting and French accent. But I thought maybe it was a one night stand so I didn't say anything.'

He sipped again. 'Then just after the New Year, David told me he was in love with her. It was idiotic. He and Babs were the dream team. They have a young daughter and he dotes on her too. I told him to stop playing silly buggers but he was too far gone.'

Ross brooded on some memory. His face was set and sombre. He said, 'We'd planned a foursome ski trip – him and Babs, Chloe and me. I rented out a chalet in Champery for early February. David joined us the second week. With Claudine Tournier. He was like a sixteen-year-old in love for the first time. She loved every minute of it. She got her kicks out of making him obey her every whim. That really gave her a buzz. If she wanted a drink, she said go fetch, and he did. If she wanted to go shopping in Evian instead of skiing, that's what he wanted too.'

Ross leaned closer. He said, 'It was pathetic. It might even have been comic. But there was a real tragedy behind it. By this time Babs knew the score and she was devastated, totally shattered. She overdosed on barbiturates and they got her just in time. Babs was in a private psychiatric unit when we got back. He didn't go to see her. She farmed their daughter out to her mum. I don't think David even picked up the phone to ask how they were.'

I said, 'Does this story go somewhere?'

Ross gave me a look as bleak as winter. 'Oh yes, it goes somewhere. It goes to the end of March. That's when Claudine Tournier got tired of David and told him to find himself another girlfriend. For she'd just got herself a new boyfriend. He was a lot like David. Younger than her, wealthy, amusing. And married. I think that was an important plus. Claudine Tournier was a serial marriage wrecker.'

I said, 'So David jumped off Beachy Head?'

Ross said, 'He felt that way. And then he felt something different. He was angry and bitter and hurt. Claudine Tournier wrecked his life and he wanted her to know how it felt. He'd lost his home, his wife, his daughter. And she'd enjoyed watching him lose it all.'

I said, 'Cut to the bit where they fish her out of the dock.'

He gave a sliver of a smile. 'Yes. That night they found her. As soon as I saw her I thought: "Christ! David has killed her".'

I said, 'Which is why you didn't tell me?'

He nodded. 'Max, I know you. It was a story, a great story of sex, betrayal, murder. You couldn't have resisted it. You wouldn't care what Claudine Tournier had done to him. You would have splashed David all over the paper. That's why I kept quiet.'

I topped up both glasses and lit a cigarette. There were things coming back to me, little things, like a home-made silencer and the empty look on a certain man's face. I studied Ross. The tension lines around his mouth had eased. He thought he had finished. He had hardly started.

I said carefully, 'You showed remarkable loyalty to your friend David. What is his real name, by the way?'

He shook his head. 'No way. You might still turn him over.'

I said, 'You asked him if he'd killed her?'

'Yes. He denied it. But I wasn't certain.'

I said, 'And you doubted him all the way until the Old Bill lifted Mike Tomlin for the killing?'

Almost a nod.

I said, 'So you think it's safe to talk to me now they've got their hands on the alleged murderer?'

He didn't nod this time. He looked at me and you could see a dark question in his eyes. He said, 'The alleged murderer?'

I flicked ash off my cuff. I said, 'Yes, alleged. You know the quaint tradition of these isles: a man is innocent unless the jury says he's not. That goes for all of us, even Mike Tomlin, child molester and part-time murderer.'

Ross said, 'I don't know what you're saying, Max.'

I said, 'Mike Tomlin has coughed to just about every crime since somebody nicked an apple in the Garden of Eden. He says he abused little children, that he aided and abetted his cronies in doing likewise, that he's implicated in the attempted murder of one Max Chard, plus he was party to sending him an explosive love letter. He's banged to rights for the murder of Shirley Ham. They've got him screwed. He's going down for life. Maybe longer.'

My old mate was watching me, hardly breathing. I

canted my glass against the light. I said, 'But here's the strange thing, Ross. Never once, not even for a split second, has he ever admitted to topping Claudine.'

Ross said in a grey voice, 'But they've charged him . . .'

I said, 'Yes. They got carried away. But by the time he does his turn at the Bailey, they'll have dropped it, on the nitpicking grounds that he didn't do it.'

Ross echoed, 'He didn't do it?'

I said, 'So you see, you should have waited before you contacted me again.'

He didn't say anything but I knew what he was thinking. I gave him ten seconds and then I said, 'But I know why you rang me today. And today was the first time you rang.'

He said, 'No. I called you sev—'

I cut the lie in half. 'No, Ross. Today was the first time. And today was special because the papers told you Martin Crowley had been charged with attempting to murder me.'

He had his mouth open, still in the middle of his broken sentence. I said, 'And all along you thought it was your dear friend David who had tried to burn me alive.'

He shook his head slowly from side to side. The wine was acid on my tongue. I said, 'It wasn't David. It was Crowley. Isn't that funny, Ross?'

He didn't laugh.

I said, 'But you were right about Claudine – David murdered her. That's funny too.'

He slid his eyes away from me. He had nothing

more to say. I watched him and I waited. I waited until all the world was silent. I waited until he lifted his eyes once more.

I said, 'By the way, how's your lodger?'

'What?'

I said, 'Your brother. Euan. You know the bloke. He's the one who nearly took my eye out with a home-made gun. He's the bloke who's having to shack up with you because his old lady threw him out. He's the one who looks like an advert for Mogadon. The man who lost his wife and twin sons – two kids by the way, not a daughter – all for a rumple in the duvet with his French mistress. The man who put a bullet through her head. Bang!'

His face was gaunt and old and unhappy. When he finally spoke his voice was edged with entreaty. He said, 'Max, leave it. Please leave it.'

I said, 'I can't. You said it yourself. It's a great story of sex, betrayal, murder. I don't walk away from that. I even have the backgrounder – Brother Tells of Besotted City Whizz Kid's Fatal Attraction.'

I pulled back my sleeve and showed him the little black mike under my watch strap and the wire snaking up my arm. I said, 'I've got it all here.'

He gabbled for words. 'Jesus, Max, he's my brother. You can't do this to him. To me. Believe me, Claudine deserved it. She took his whole life away. Let him go.'

I sat there with the tape still running. He said, 'He's paid for it. He's still paying. What is Euan for you anyway? He's just another story, another by-line. But he's my brother. I mean, where do you stop, Max?

Would you turn over Rosie's family? Would you tear your own brother apart for a story?'

All of a sudden I felt very tired and lifeless. I stood up. I looked down at my old friend. One of us was a stranger.

He said it again. 'Where do you stop?'

I said, 'I don't know, Ross. Honest to God, I don't know.'

# Chapter One

It snowed in the night and the place where they found her body was now all white and winter wonderlandish. You could have stuck the scene on a Christmas card. It would have looked even better if Plod hadn't plonked a great yellow tent over her mortal remains. Also, there were dirty-grey patches of slush where the uniforms had parked their hooves.

So far we knew nearly nothing. They'd roped off the area and were keeping us at bay until they got a press officer out of bed to say no comment.

But the betting was that under the big top lay the corpse of one Joni Poelma, last seen, as they say, leaving a disco in Dulwich. Until then none of us knew that Dulwich had a disco. That was a week ago. Since then there had been the usual hullabaloo – TV appeals, posters, back checks on miles of video tape, the full bit. But Joni Poelma had stubbornly refused to reappear.

In the meantime nobody else was reported missing in Dulwich, therefore our lightning brains deduced that Joni had finally turned up.

It is not my usual practice to hang around in the snow waiting for the Old Bill to identify a missing

Dutch au pair. But February had been a thinnish month for news, and we'd run two splashes and three page leads on the story so far. Plus, in a surfeit of red biddy, our deranged Editor had stuck up a five-grand reward for information leading to Joni's whereabouts. He'd forgotten the proviso that we wanted her alive.

Unless he managed to worm his way out of it my bet was that the loot would go to the geezer with the frostbitten poodle nattering away to the Law on their side of the cordon tapes. We were perched on what in sunnier seasons you would call a grassy knoll so we had a ringside seat to all the action, not that there was any action to write home about. Below us the park fell away sharply before rolling into a little dip and finally running out of steam against a row of Victorian railings. The ironwork had a fine tracery of snow. Very chichi. It looked like it belonged in Dulwich.

Centre stage in all of this was the big yellow tent. We had nothing else to look at so we watched it. Every now and then the walls rippled as some Herbert inside biffed his head against them. They were either looking for clues or playing Twister.

The air was brittle and you could hear the forensic boys panting away in there. Nobody was saying anything. Outside the tent was the lumpish shape of Chief Inspector Tom Skelly in a red and white ski jacket. He and the tent clashed. He was standing by the bloke with the dog but they weren't talking. The dog was playing dumb too. Skelly had got all he wanted from the bodyfinder and pooch. He was just making sure we got nowhere near the man. Every now and then Skelly pitched us a baleful look.

I suppose if I was him I would have felt likewise. If we hadn't all made such a fuss about the vanishing Joni Poelma, a mere Detective Inspector would be chilling his toes out there in the park while Skelly sat in the station canteen, scoffing bacon sarnies and having the *Mirror* cartoons explained to him.

We weren't feeling too happy either. Everybody was out of fags so we just puffed out white plumes of air and pretended we were smoking. It was still too early for the pubs. Anyway, we had to hang around in the outlandish hope that Skelly or the press liaison officer might say something interesting. We shuffled our feet and looked bored. It wasn't hard.

Down below, a new character trekked into shot. A low moan of dismay escaped us. 'Oddjob!'

He heard it but he acted as if he didn't. Bob Jobley is a Scotland Yard press liaison officer. He is not a copper. He is a civilian only minus the brains for that task. Liaison officers know nothing, except what few crumbs the detective in charge bothers to tell them. Oddjob always knows less than nothing, hence our dismay.

Skelly somehow restrained himself from clasping Oddjob to his bosom and telling him all. They had maybe twenty seconds of chit-chat, then the liaison officer turned to face us. This was our signal to slalom downhill and pick his brains.

'Morning, Oddjob,' I greeted him.

He has no pride. 'Morning, Max.'

An agency hack fired the first question: 'Is it Joni Poelma?'

Oddjob simultaneously shrugged, strangled a

yawn, squeezed up his eyes and shook his head. The man's a polymath.

'It's not Joni?'

We got a repeat performance.

I said, 'Is that on the record?'

Over his shoulder I could see the great pink ham of Skelly's face. He was grinning. The only time Plods like him smirk at us like that is when they have something to smirk about, such as finally tripping over Joni Poelma's body. Or having somebody else doing the tripping over bit for them.

You could see that Skelly had no intention of telling us anything. That's why he was happy. You could also see that they'd found Joni. If it was some other stiff he'd be back down the nick scratching his chilblains by now.

Oddjob said: 'It is a body.' Thereby dispelling any suspicions that the tent might be harbouring Scotland Yard's camping club.

'Male or female?' This from someone behind me.

'It's too early to say,' lied Oddjob.

We ignored that. 'How was she murdered?'

Oddjob waved his mittens about. That meant our guess was as good as his. Better.

'Has she been here long?'

Oddjob said, 'That has yet to be established.'

After that there was a snowball fight of questions. I refrained from taking part and let the kids enjoy themselves. Anyway, I'm a minimalist. I find the less you know about a story the easier it is to write. For starters, you don't find awkward facts getting in the way. Nor do you get useless chunks of information cluttering up the narrative. I mean, right now a local radio hackette was asking Oddjob the name of the dog of the geezer who'd found Joni Poelma. Do the Great British Public really want to know what the dog was called? Indeed not. But just for the record, its name was Jack.

The alleged press briefing wound down to the point where even the bloke from the local weekly had run out of questions. Oddjob promised to meet us all at Dulwich nick around oneish when he should have yet more red-hot news for us. We grunted and shambled off as the pubs had opened. I looked back over my shoulder. Oddjob was standing at the cordon with his mitts sticking out, a forlorn figure that nobody wanted to talk to.

In the nearest bar I was on my second Gordon's and halfway through a slanderous story about my News Editor when my bleeper went off. It told me that the very same News Editor wanted me to ring her URGENTLY. I finished the story, listened to someone else's lies, ordered in a new round, and gave her a bell.

'Lo, Angie,' I said. 'You're missing me?'

She wasn't in the mood for banter. 'Yes, I bloody well am. I'm just about to go into conference and I need a schedule line on Joni Poelma. Is it her?'

'Yup.'

She said, 'Scotland Yard have confirmed it?'

'Nope.'

'But you're sure it's her?'

'Yup.'

She said, 'So what's the schedule line?'

I said, '*Gazette* Reader Finds Murdered Joni.'

Angela's a stickler for facts. 'Does he read our paper?'

I said, 'Probably not, but by the time I get to him, even his dog will be a lifelong reader.'

She said, 'OK, that'll do for conference. But before you slope off to the bar, I've got a job for you.'

I didn't like the sound of that. I said warily, 'Oh?'

Angie went all breezy which meant it was a crummy job. She said, 'I want you to go and see the Cardigans and set up an exclusive interview for features.'

'Who's doing the interview?'

She said, 'Beverley Nephews. She'll be down—'

Beverley Nephews! Otherwise known in the trade as Beverley Hills, for two very good reasons. I hauled my mind back to what Angie was saying. '. . . so we need you to stick your foot in the door and keep everybody else away from the Cardigans until Beverley gets there. OK?'

The Cardigans were the couple who until last week employed Joni to ride shotgun for their children. I remembered that he was big in chemicals and they played happy families in something marginally smaller than Buck House.

Angela said, 'They might need some convincing so we'll go for a buy up.'

And what nutter thought that one up? I just said, 'How much?'

'You can go up to a thousand.'

I said, 'Angie, the Cardigans spend that on dental

floss. They probably help the Sultan of Brunei when he's a bit strapped for readies.'

She sighed. 'All right, go to two thou, but no more.'

I holstered my mobile and returned to the bar. There are times when this game is just too silly for its own good.

Meriel, a hackette from the *Mail*, was thinking along the same lines. 'You'll never guess what News Desk have asked me to do,' she said.

I had a very good idea of precisely what but I listened politely.

She said, 'They've asked me to try and buy up the Cardigans.'

I chortled merrily. I said, 'Don't they read the papers? Wedge Cardigan uses fivers for wallpaper. How much are you offering them?'

Meriel stuck her nose in a glass of house white and said, 'Twenty.'

'Twenty thousand?'

She nodded. Now this was serious. The Cardigans might just bite on that. I put on my gravest face. I said, 'I don't think that's a very wise idea.' There was a strange undercurrent in my voice.

She darted me a curious look from under her Shetland pony fringe. 'What do you mean?'

I took a mouthful of gin and lit a Benson's before I bothered to answer. I simply repeated, 'It's not a wise idea.' This time my tones were so laden with sinister nuances that I sounded as if I was talking in slo-mo.

Meriel's fringe eyed me intently. 'Why?'

I took another swig and had a shufti around to

make sure no one was eavesdropping. I said, 'Because the police are going to lift Wedge Cardigan.'

The fringe swished hither and thither. 'What!'

I said, 'Keep your voice down. I've just had a tip from a detective mate. Don't tell anyone else.'

Meriel squeaked, 'They think he did it?'

'Sssh. Yes, he's in the frame, so you'd better forget trying to buy him up. Wait for the one o'clock briefing. They'll probably announce it then. But don't do anything in the meantime.'

The fringe trembled with a pitiful gratitude. She said: 'Thanks, Max. I owe you one.'

Those of you of a more squeamish disposition, that is to say who are not reporters, might regard this as a scumbag trick on my part. But look at it my way: the *Mail* has great buckets of cash to sling at any passing story. We don't. Yet my News Desk requires, no, *demands*, that I deliver the story, regardless of the *Mail*'s megabucks. If I fail, then I am seen to be a lesser hack than Meriel Fringe-face, and that would never do. Therefore I had to use an evil ruse. Besides, it's more fun playing dirty.

I licked my glass clean and said I had to hotfoot it back to the office. Meriel squeezed my arm and gave me a conspiratorial goodbye wink. I winked right back.

JOHN BURNS

## Snap

Macmillan £16.99

When millionaire's au pair Joni Poelma goes missing after leaving a late-night club Max Chard's newspaper puts out a reward for information. Unfortunately they forget to mention that they want her found alive. And now Joni has turned up – very dead – in a snow-covered park in Dulwich.

In pursuit of the inside story, Max offers Gabriella Cardigan, Joni's employer, two grand for the lowdown. But the gorgeous Gabriella has a better idea: she offers Chard two grand instead.

*Snap.*

The deal is he takes Gabriella's son Jason, a would-be journalist, under his wing. Much to Max's surprise, Jason proves rather useful, for he has more than a passing knowledge of drugs. And the story is that Joni was killed because of her predilection for strange substances.

*Snap.*

But was she? Chard and his motor-mouth, motor-drive photographer, Frankie, go banging on doors and making nuisances of themselves. And that's when Max gets the bigger picture.

*Snap.*